Slee

Evan Baldock

SRL Publishing Ltd

SRL Publishing Ltd
Office 47396, PO Box 6945
London
W1A 6US

First published worldwide by SRL Publishing in 2021

1 3 5 7 9 10 8 6 4 2
ISBN: 978-1-83827982-0

A CIP catalogue record for this book is available from the British Library.

Yet again my editor, Gail Williams, has worked wonders and turned my ramblings into something suitable to be forwarded to publishers, thank you so much.

To Luke and Josh, my heroes

1

Kabul, Afghanistan
Wednesday 26th June 2024, 8.55am

Louise Kenton walked swiftly from the Kabul Star Hotel and turned right onto Sulh Road, adjusting her hijab as she went. The Kabul Star was inside the Green Zone of the city, a heavily fortified section of Kabul, where journalists, diplomats, politicians, and aid workers were offered some semblance of safety.

She was running late for work with 'New Beginnings,' a multi-national aid organisation operating in central Kabul. Their task was to encourage people to sign up for training as agricultural workers, mechanics, construction workers, and teachers. It was one of several aid organisations involved in the continuing efforts to rebuild Afghanistan's shattered society, twenty-three years after the brutal five-year reign of the Taliban was brought to an end.

The Taliban had been driven from the city in October 2001 by the United Islamic Front ground forces, backed by US Special Forces and air support, but a quarter of a century later they were still operational and capable of carrying out effective raids on the city. This fact hadn't deterred Louise when she was offered the chance of employment as an aid worker; she was aware of raids the Taliban had carried out away from the green zone, but personally she had enjoyed a trouble-free year.

Louise's interest in the Religion of Islam had its roots long before arriving in Afghanistan, but during her time in Kabul she'd also become fascinated by its history and the devotion of its followers. She had loved her year in Kabul, making several friends among her work colleagues and even a few of the locals.

The sky was cloudless, the temperature a very warm 25 Celsius and it was set to be another scorcher. Louise was feeling rather pleased with life as she reached the large roundabout at the outer limit of the green zone. She showed her pass and avoided eye contact with the Afghan Army guards manning the concrete and steel barriers, erected to prevent attacks by suicide bombers in vehicles. This was not out of rudeness, but in order to comply with local religious sensibilities.

Glancing up at the clear blue sky, she set off towards the temporary recruitment offices where she worked in a small, scruffy building on one side of Haji Yaqob Square, only a few hundred metres away.

Four minutes after leaving the green zone, as she hurried past the Majid Shopping Mall, there was a bright flash of light, accompanied by a deafening explosion, an explosion so loud it caused crippling pain in her ears. The subsequent blast and shockwave followed a millisecond later, throwing her to the ground. She was showered with debris, as chunks of wood, brick, and glass rained down on her body. Choking clouds of dust filled the air and for a short while there was silence, a deafening, smothering silence that lasted for several seconds, before being slowly replaced by muffled shouts, screams, and a loud ringing in her ears. Louise knew at once that a bomb had been detonated somewhere between where she now lay on the ground, and the offices where she worked.

Raising herself to her hands and knees, she became aware of chaos erupting all around her. Three Afghan Army soldiers were running towards her from the green zone, guns raised, shouting instructions she couldn't comprehend. Then, somewhere among the noise and confusion, she heard a shouted command in English.

'Get down! Stay down!'

Louise dropped instinctively to the ground. She lay terrified on the dusty road, her breathing ragged, panic rising inside her. The temptation to ignore the order to get down and stay down but instead to stand up and run for her life, was almost overpowering.

Hearing a growing chorus of screams and shouting to her left, she looked away from the oncoming Afghan soldiers and turned her head back in the direction of the explosion. As the dust slowly cleared, she could see that the seat of the blast was a ten-metre-wide crater, about fifty metres away, in a small market on the edge of the park.

Mutilated bodies and the tangled remains of market stalls littered the ground, market stalls that seconds earlier had been proudly displaying their fruit and vegetables. Louise was struggling to make sense of the terrible scene playing out before her; she couldn't understand why nobody was stopping to help the victims. Instead of helping, people were leaping and jumping over the injured lying on the ground, begging for help. Everyone seemed to be running, some towards Haji Yaqob Square, and others into the park.

That's when she saw them. Four men wearing scruffy and ill-fitting Afghan Army uniforms came jogging out of a side street opposite the park, each one carrying a rifle. Louise watched, horrified, as they fired into the crowd attempting to flee their pursuit. She stared in disbelief as men, women and children were brought down by bullets fired into their backs, while the men carrying out the shooting shouted, 'Allahu Akbar!' - 'God is Greatest.'

Dressing in Afghan Army uniforms had been a popular method used by terrorists for mounting attacks in Kabul over the years, and Louise was only too aware from her knowledge of past attacks how ruthlessly indiscriminate they could be.

At that moment, two of the terrorists turned down the street towards her while the other two crossed the road in the direction of the market and park, continuing their pursuit of the terrified crowd. She heard bullets fizzing like fireworks over her head in both directions, a sound that bizarrely reminded her of her childhood.

She now had two terrorists thirty metres to her left and three men whom she recognised as real Afghan Army soldiers the same distance to her right. Then Louise froze, as one of the terrorists trained his rifle on her and fired. Immediately, she felt a searing pain across her right shoulder blade and screamed in agony. Burying her head beneath folded arms, Louise braced herself for the next impact, which would in all probability kill her.

The dizzying cacophony of sound grew louder and louder: guns being fired; the fizz of bullets carving their way through the air; the pings and dull thuds as they connected with metal, glass, concrete, mud, tarmac, and sometimes human flesh; the screaming and wailing as the horror unfolded, together with the shouting of combatants on both sides. The sounds merged and rose to a deafening crescendo.

But, for some reason, the second bullet didn't materialise. The pain in her shoulder blade was excruciating but she steeled herself against it and braved another glance towards the terrorists. The man who'd fired at her had been hit, presumably by one of the soldiers from the green zone. He was lying on his back, rifle in his right hand. His face was turned towards Louise, eyes wide open but undoubtedly dead.

The other terrorist heading her way was crouching behind a low wall, firing at the Afghan Army soldiers. Louise turned her head to look in their direction and noticed that one of them was also lying on the ground face down; she had no idea if he was dead or alive. The other two were finding cover, one behind a vehicle, the other behind the corner of a building, training their fire on the man behind the low wall, keeping him pinned down.

Out of nowhere, four men in US Army fatigues appeared and unleashed a brief hail of machine-gun fire. The terrorist crouching behind the wall was hit twice in the head and disappeared from view, presumably dead.

Louise knew there were still US Special Forces active in Kabul. Despite assurances from their president that they would all be home by 2020, many had remained, chiefly for the purpose of training the Afghan Army. She had seen small patrols of them fleetingly, on two separate occasions many months before, but had never actually witnessed their fearsome capabilities.

The two remaining terrorists had crossed Sulh Road and were standing on the edge of the market. They had been firing into the civilians fleeing into the park but were now training their fire at the US Marines.

One of the US soldiers ran out into the road and lay flat on the ground next to Louise, shielding her from the terrorists' fire. As he propped himself up on his elbows, she saw the word 'Marines' on his shoulders and above the pocket on his chest, as well as a name badge on his chest: 'Sanders.' He shouted something she didn't understand in a language she assumed was Dari, the most common language in Kabul.

'I'm English!' she shouted back.

'For fuck's sake, English? What the fuck are you doing here?'

Louise opened her mouth to reply but he cut her off with a wave of his hand.

'Stay low and follow me to the corner of that building.' He indicated a smart new-looking red brick office block on the same side of the road as the park. 'My buddies will provide us with covering fire.'

He spoke into his radio. 'Tango-Charlie units, Tango-Charlie units, from Tango-Charlie 4-7, covering fire on my command. Let those fucking ragheads have it! Copy?'

Louise didn't hear the replies as the Marine was wearing an earpiece and no sound came from his radio. Her shock at his use of the phrase 'rag-heads' was tempered by gratitude that he was saving her life.

He fixed her with a piercing gaze and shouted, 'Remember, stay low!' then spoke into his radio. 'In three, two, one, COVER!'

A hail of machine-gun fire was provided by his colleagues, making the two remaining terrorists take cover as best they could.

Dragging Louise to her feet and supporting her under an armpit, he helped her swiftly to the building line and safety. The intense pain from her shoulder blade when she was lifted had been countered by a massive dose of adrenalin. She was experiencing a mixture of fear and excitement; she had never been so frightened, yet so exhilarated in her life.

Once they had reached the building and taken cover behind its corner, Louise breathed heavily several times to control the excruciating pain in her shoulder blade, before managing to say breathlessly, 'Thank you so much, you've saved my life.'

He looked at her for the briefest of moments then checked on his colleagues. His next words were preceded by a sigh of weariness and exasperation.

'This country is a fucking shit tip lady. It's full of sand monkeys who hate white people, especially from decent countries like ours. Take my advice. Never trust any of them and get yourself back to England, back to somewhere safe, back to civilised people.'

With that he turned, shouted a command to his colleagues and they moved off as a group, staying close to the building line for cover, exchanging intermittent fire with the terrorists as they went.

Suddenly, the two remaining terrorists ran from the market area, breaking cover and heading straight towards the US Marines screaming, 'Allahu Akbar!' again and again, while firing wildly at them. The immediate response was another burst of machine gun fire and they both dropped to the ground, dead.

Louise had heard of this happening on terrorist raids before. They were deliberately martyring themselves in the belief that they would be welcomed in paradise, where they would be rewarded.

The area was soon swarming with Afghan Army personnel, but the Marines had disappeared as quickly and mysteriously as they'd come. Louise would never see them again.

Reaching round to feel her shoulder blade, she experienced a nauseating wave of pain and felt dampness; when she looked at her hand, it was covered in blood. People clearly now felt confident enough to move towards the victims and were slowly appearing from hiding places inside buildings and alleyways. It seemed that some degree of normality was gradually returning to Sulh Road.

Gingerly, she stepped out into the street and started walking painfully through the debris back towards the green zone. Her ears were still ringing and shock was beginning to kick in; she was queasy and shivering uncontrollably.

Suddenly a familiar voice made itself heard above the others, coming from the direction of the square.

'Lulu! Lulu!'

Louise's boyfriend, Haasim, a fellow aid worker with New Beginnings, pushed swiftly through the crowds and on reaching her, gently took her in his arms. Although contact between an unmarried man and woman in public was strictly forbidden and would normally be frowned upon, these were unusual circumstances and as Louise was clearly badly injured, Haasim was prepared to deal with the emergency, certain that he wouldn't be offending anyone.

2

Louise and Haasim weren't in love, but she liked him a lot, and whenever they could they sneaked into one another's hotel rooms. When she'd first arrived, they soon discovered that they shared similar political views, in particular their opposition to the involvement of western powers in Afghanistan. It was this realisation that initially brought them together.

Haasim was a handsome twenty-five-year-old, tall and slim, with short black hair and a neatly trimmed short beard. He could probably have had his pick of women, so Louise was flattered when he seemed to single her out. Initially he said it was her piercing blue eyes and bubbly personality that had drawn him to her. He hadn't even seen her long, wavy blonde hair at that point, because she complied with local traditions for women to keep their heads covered, but once the relationship became intimate, every moment they were alone together he would ask Louise to remove her hijab and let her hair down.

However, what Louise didn't realise was that Haasim's interest in her was far from innocent. In the early days of their relationship, it had quickly become apparent that he was far more radical in his views than she was. This was hardly surprising because, unknown to

Louise, he had been placed into the aid programme by a terrorist group called Harb Alsheueb, with the specific task of identifying females who could be persuaded to join their group. Her physical attractions were merely a bonus.

As the affair blossomed, they had talked more and more about politics, Islam, and the relationship between western governments and Muslim countries. Over a few weeks, Haasim had employed every emotional and rhetorical trick in the book, gradually and subtly distorting Louise's picture of the world, gently drawing her towards the group's radical viewpoint.

Before she had realised what was happening to her, she increasingly accepted his views, feeling privileged to have such a wonderful guide. In fact, she wanted to learn more, much more, which was great news for Haasim and more importantly for Harb Alsheueb. On learning of Louise's enthusiasm, the group's hierarchy had swiftly issued Haasim with further instructions.

As a result, he'd begun taking Louise to the group's secret meetings, although in reality they were meetings in name only. Their actual purpose was to gather together people who had been identified as susceptible to indoctrination and Louise was a prime target. Over time, they were taken to camps where they would be gradually inculcated with the ideals and methods of Harb Alsheueb. Louise loved being accepted as part of the group and had begun to look forward to these training sessions.

For reasons she couldn't quite understand, she enjoyed mixing in clandestine circles, getting quite a thrill from secretly meeting other like-minded people. Haasim would collect her in his car and they would drive to a small village just outside the city, where about thirty people gathered together in a disused warehouse. Louise was often paired with a more experienced woman, someone to help ensure she complied with Islamic traditions and help her to learn which prayers she would be required to learn by heart and then recite.

Louise worked hard at learning the prayers, which were recited in Arabic, and more importantly learning their meanings. Although she had been in Afghanistan for a year, she hadn't learned much of the language, other than the very basics and how to politely greet and say goodbye to people. This now seemed a terrible oversight and she was eager to make amends.

During the first month of training, recruits were bombarded with videos of Muslims suffering in their own countries, mainly as a result of western intervention in their nation's internal affairs. Instructors conveniently omitted to mention that western governments were often responding to terrorist attacks on their own cities and towns, or that the government of the Muslim country in question had begged for help from the west to depose a despotic leader. Such balanced considerations were swept aside in the drive to indoctrinate followers in the group's hard-line beliefs. Louise was dragged along with the herd mentality cleverly cultivated by her trainers and her own views soon became increasingly radical.

The walls of the warehouse were covered with paintings depicting paradise, showing beautiful countryside or scenic valleys and streams flowing with milk instead of water. Instructors would regale trainees with stories of how operatives who had died on active duty had appeared to them in dreams, always claiming that they were blissfully happy in paradise.

A standard day's training would include memorising prayers from the Quran, which she would then be made to chant over and over, sometimes for an hour or more. She was constantly reminded of the social injustice they were fighting against, a message that was reinforced by projected images, while an instructor made subtle comments about each one, ensuring that her anger and indignation slowly built up. There were anti-Muslim statements made over the years by famous people or politicians from around the world, while an instructor pointed at the statements over her shoulder, reinforcing how shocking they were, and how the speakers should be punished.

She was also persuaded to attend 'Islamic classes', delivering an extremely slanted history of how poorly their people had been treated throughout the ages, intended to slowly build a siege mentality among the trainees. Instructors insisted that she carry out at least an hour of physical training each time she attended, and throughout each work-out an instructor would scream hate filled rhetoric about the west into her face. Above all, she was constantly reminded that committing violence for a justifiable cause is not wrong or immoral, but the right thing to do.

Slowly but surely, Louise had been drawn in and was fascinated by everything about this false view of Islam. More importantly, she completely believed in the instructions she'd received during her training; the process had been carried out so subtly over several months that she could no longer distinguish between education and brainwashing.

Louise became more and more incensed with the attitude of western governments. She was angered by the behaviour of their military forces operating in Islamic countries and she hated the disregard of suffering endured by the Afghan people, not just by military forces, but by the UK public and the western media. Over time she had become utterly convinced that using violence to achieve the group's goals was entirely acceptable; she would do whatever the organisation required of her. Her faith in Allah and her loyalty to Harb Alsheueb were more important than anything, or anyone, including her family and friends.

In short, Harb Alsheueb had successfully radicalised Louise, the only white westerner at the sessions, and therefore a particularly valuable convert to their cause.

After several months of indoctrination, Louise had been judged ready to receive training in anti-interrogation techniques, which would be invaluable should she be arrested. To combat every type of interrogation, she had been instructed to spend all her time in captivity praying to Allah, who would eventually relieve her suffering.

The first test had been sensory deprivation. She had been locked in a tiny, soundproofed room on the outskirts of the village in total darkness, unable to hear or see anything, with no means of knowing how much time had passed or even whether it was day or night. There was no toilet and she had to relieve herself in a corner of the room, which she had initially found disgusting. Louise was left there from Saturday morning through to Sunday afternoon, with no food or water. When she was released, her instructors had been impressed to find that the experience hadn't broken her and that she still wanted to be involved in operations.

Of all the anti-interrogation techniques Louise endured, by far the worst had been hooding and waterboarding. This involved being tied down to a bench with her head slightly above the level of her waist, her feet raised, making her whole body into a long 'v' shape. A tight cloth hood was pulled over her face, and interrogators shouted questions repeatedly at her.

Louise had been warned that the experience would feel like drowning, but she'd been assured that no western government would actually kill her during this type of interrogation. The way to resist their questions was to put every ounce of her faith in Allah and remember that not answering the interrogators' questions would please him.

As water was poured onto the hood over her nose and mouth for up to thirty or forty seconds, Louise had felt like she couldn't breathe; the sensation of panic was overwhelming. The water would be stopped, and the hood pulled away from her airways for just enough time to take half a dozen breaths, during which the question was screamed at her again. If she failed to answer, the process would restart. This continued for twenty minutes and each time the terrible sensation of drowning was the same; the terror and panic didn't ease with repetition; they were just as extreme each time.

When the hood was eventually removed for good, she was gasping for breath, her head splitting, she angrily pushed away the women who untied her, before collapsing to the floor. She hadn't broken down under interrogation, she'd prayed in her head the whole way through the ordeal and hadn't answered any questions; her instructors were delighted, they were certain they'd unearthed a gem.

During her spare time, she followed the group's instruction to read the Quran every day and attempted to commit the more important passages to memory. She'd prayed five times a day, sometimes when she was with the other women at training sessions, sometimes on her own inside her hotel room. Under no circumstances was she permitted to pray with men.

She didn't realise it at the time, but the brainwashing had changed her personality out of all recognition. The beliefs she'd held throughout her life and the morals she'd always lived by, were not her beliefs and morals any more. Harb Alsheueb had given her a whole new set, and over the following years they would alter the course of her life.

She'd been taught that Islam was at war with the west, in most cases not a military war but a social war, and just like in any other war there was bound to be collateral damage. People would suffer because of her actions but that was a consequence she had to accept. The knowledge that she would one day be required to do something to harm or even kill another person had initially worried her greatly. But over the months, her training had done its job; she would gladly do whatever Harb Alsheueb wanted.

3

Louise's upbringing had been conventional: raised by middle class Christian parents, who also happened to be active Labour Party members and supporters. Political discussion was the norm in their household and one topic of conversation had always been the involvement of western democracies in the internal affairs of sovereign countries, particularly ones with different cultural and religious identities. They had been very much against the US led coalition's invasion and subsequent occupation of Afghanistan in 2001.

Louise hadn't even been born in 2001, but from listening to her parents and their friends, she knew the history of the conflict and grew up having no doubt where her sympathies lay. Thanks to Haasim and her training, her support for the Muslim cause in Afghanistan would later become fully established, but her disgust at the way Muslims were perceived in the UK started much earlier - at school.

Louise had attended a mixed grammar school in Tunbridge Wells, seventeen miles from her home in Fletching. During her time there, she had been appalled by the casual racism endured by the few Muslim children at the school. The vast majority of pupils treated Muslims exactly the same as everyone else but there were enough ignorant students to make life unpleasant for some of them. Muslims were subjected to varying levels of verbal abuse, being called tea-towel wearers, flip-flops, sometimes even terrorists. Their classmates passed it off as 'banter', but Louise saw it as abuse nonetheless, abuse that she couldn't understand and wasn't prepared to stand idly by and do nothing about.

At the age of fifteen, she befriended then became the girlfriend of, a sixteen-year-old Muslim boy named Mustafa. Over the weeks and months of their relationship, she had to endure many jokes and sarcastic comments from classmates. The final straw was when three of her closest friends joined in the 'jokes', prompting a furious reaction from Louise; she was desperately sad when her fiends gradually became more distant but she wasn't prepared to give up her relationship with Mustafa just to appease them.

On top of their problems at school, the religious differences between her family and Mustafa's meant they had to keep the relationship hidden from both sets of parents. Mustafa was a devout Muslim, praying five times a day and regularly attending the local mosque. As a Christian who had never experienced Islam close up, Louise was fascinated by the faith and devotion he showed and his unshakable certainty that Islam was the one true faith.

He enjoyed explaining to Louise that Allah was the word Muslims sometimes used for God and that Christians, Jews, and Muslims all shared the same God. Islam, he explained, was a peaceful religion, that there was no room in Islam for people who supported violence to achieve their aims, and to reinforce this message he would regularly read passages to her from the Quran.

Over time she began to feel that Islam made more sense to her than Christianity; she knew it was the religion she would choose for herself. She also knew that this would create a huge problem, because wavering from the path of Christianity and transferring her faith to Islam would devastate her parents, who still attended church every Sunday. They would be distraught to discover their daughter had become a Muslim convert.

After eight months, wanting to spend more time focussing on her forthcoming exams, Louise had broken up with Mustafa. However, it was an amicable separation and they remained friends throughout their time at school. The relationship had left her drawn more powerfully to Islam than to her parents' faith; she had been given her own copy of the Quran by Mustafa and would secretly pray in her bedroom whenever possible.

Louise continued to be a diligent and hard-working student, obtaining three A* grades in her A-Levels, and securing a place at Cambridge University. She had always longed for a career in politics. An idealist, she hoped one day to make the world a better place, a more tolerant place, and she was prepared to work hard to achieve that goal.

In one respect, Louise *had* followed in her parents' footsteps. Whilst still at school, she had become a Labour Party activist and continued with her support throughout her years at university, where she became a member of a Labour Party Action Group. Through this, she met several other Muslims and would meet frequently to pray with women in the group, after which they would sometimes read the Quran together. She loved how peaceful, welcoming, and friendly they were; there was none of the bitchy in-fighting she'd often witnessed between members of the mainly elderly congregation at her parents' church.

After leaving Cambridge with a first in Human, Social and Political Studies, Louise applied for a position in Afghanistan with New Beginnings. By joining them on a one-year contract, she was hoping to immerse herself in the culture and learn as much as she could about the people and the Islamic religion. Above all, she wanted to prove to the people of Afghanistan that not all westerners were the same; she wanted to show that some of them truly cared.

4

Kabul, Afghanistan
Wednesday 26th June 2024, 9.23am

Haasim held her close, unconcerned that her blood was soaking into his shirt.

'God be praised, you're okay!'

She was just happy to be alive. 'Oh, Haas, I thought I was going to die.'

The tears she had been suppressing now flowed freely. She suddenly pushed back and stared intently at him.

'Did our brothers carry out that attack?'

He knew why she was asking. 'Yes.'

Louise stared blankly. Haasim could see she needed reassurance.

'Lulu, the authorities need to be made aware how far we're prepared to go to achieve our goals. Remember, there can be no room for weakness or sentimentality until true Muslims are running this country and every other Muslim country.'

'But why carry out attacks in your own country?'

'By carrying out attacks like this, we are letting our government, who sided with the invaders, know that we want them out. The only reason they are in government is because they bowed down to the Americans and the British. That was how they were able to drive our brothers and sisters into the mountains.'

'I do understand that I need to be strong but it was hard to witness innocent Muslim women and children being killed right in front of my eyes.'

Louise was now shaking. Haasim held her tightly by the elbows.

'If those killed were true believers, they will now be in paradise with Allah. Don't pity them, they are the lucky ones.'

Something inside was telling her he was right, however horrendous it had appeared to her at first sight. As the full meaning and brutal impact of his words began to sink in, she began to realise that if she were ordered to carry out a violent operation, she would probably do it. Obeying Harb Alsheueb's wishes and gaining Allah's blessing was all that really mattered. Louise was moving towards a whole new world, a world where she too might be required to kill or maim in the name of Islam.

Haasim continued to stare into Louise's eyes.

'The brave brothers who carried out this operation will have attained paradise. May the blessings of God be upon them.'

She forced a smile then winced with pain. Haasim was suddenly reminded that she was suffering a huge amount of discomfort and guided her gently towards the security of the green zone.

'Now, stop talking and let's get you some treatment.'

An hour later, Louise's wounds had been treated by a medical orderly in the hotel, where a temporary casualty centre had been established. Her wound was caused by the bullet grazing skin and flesh above her right shoulder blade as she lay on the ground. She would be left with a nasty scar and although the wound was painful, requiring twelve stitches, there was no serious injury.

Sadly, it would leave her unfit for work for several weeks as movement of her right arm was constrained by a sling to prevent the wound being continually re-opened as she flexed her shoulder. Louise realised this would almost certainly mean her work with New Beginnings coming to a premature end.

Back in her hotel room, Haasim sat at her bedside.

'How are you feeling? Is there anything I can do to make you more comfortable?'

She smiled and shook her head. 'No, I don't need anything thanks. I'm horribly uncomfortable and the stitches feel really tight but all in all I suppose I should count myself lucky.'

'That's putting it mildly. You were very lucky indeed,' he smiled, 'but with an injury like that, New Beginnings will have to let you return home. They won't keep you here if you can't work.'

She looked down at her hands which fidgeted restlessly. After a few seconds she slowly nodded her head and looked up.

'You're right, I'll have to go home, but I'd rather stay in Afghanistan. I love it here. Kabul feels like home now.'

She unlocked her hands and ran her fingernails gently through the hairs on Haasim's forearm. She was thinking back to the months of intensive training, a determined look forming on her face.

'Going to the meetings has taught me so much. I know I've got to return home, but I still want to be involved. I want to help the cause however I can.'

Haasim raised his eyebrows and leaned forward.

'There's something I think you should consider, Lulu.'

'What?'

Although no-one could hear them, he lowered his

voice to a whisper.

'This could be an opportunity! You could be of great assistance to Harb Alsheueb in the UK. We have people there who support our views. I could put you in touch with one, if you'd like?'

Louise sat up eagerly then grimaced with pain.

'I'd like that very much. I'd be thousands of miles away, but I'd still be of use to the cause.'

A serious expression spread across his face, an expression she'd never seen on Haasim before, making him seem years older.

'We have operatives in several countries, people who are prepared to carry out operations when called upon. We need people who can clear the way for one of those operatives to be activated... or perhaps you would even be willing to carry out direct action yourself?'

She nodded eagerly.

'I'd love to be involved in any way.'

At that moment, Hassim knew that the indoctrination had succeeded.

He smiled then changed the subject.

'You told me you were heavily involved in politics back in England. Tell me more about that.'

'I said I was involved, I'm not sure about 'heavily'. I'm a member of the Labour Party, that's hardly the same thing, is it?'

He shrugged.

'Anyway, what's my politics got to do with anything?'

'Because someone climbing the political ladder could be extremely helpful in years to come. Are you intending to stand for public office?'

'Well, I had thought of standing as a local councillor and, who knows, maybe one day for parliament. I've already applied for a position as personal assistant to

Judith Snells, she's the Labour MP for Maidstone. If my application's successful, it looks like I might be able to start a month earlier than I'd expected.'

The side of Haasim's mouth curled into the start of a smile.

'We need people prepared to be patient for months, years if necessary, people who are in a position to work their way up the ladder of their chosen field.'

'So it would help the cause if I were elected as a Member of Parliament?'

'Are you serious? Think about where you'd be working. You could gain access to the heart of the British establishment. We could bypass security, and cause disruption at some of the UK's most iconic buildings.'

'You do realise my chances of becoming an MP are miniscule?'

'That would just be the icing on the cake. Whatever you end up doing could still be useful to us.'

Louise's face lit up.

'I could do that. I could change things from within.' She smiled. 'Count me in.'

'Working for us and striking against the UK establishment would be a perfect role for you. By assisting us, Allah will be pleased and you will be blessed.'

'How does it all work?'

'What do you mean?'

'How will you notify me who I'm supposed to be working with, what I'm supposed to do?'

'We'll discuss all that before you leave Afghanistan. I have your contact details and I'll make sure you're notified when and where you're needed.'

Louise sat back, a curious expression on her face.

'What will my position be? I don't just want to be a lackey, someone given the odd minor job to carry out when required.'

Haasim laughed and shook his head.

'You could be one of the most important people in our organisation Lulu,. You'll be a *sleeper.*'

As he said this, she could feel his grip tighten; he was obviously thrilled at the prospect. Looking down at his hands, she could see his knuckles whiten where he was holding her so tightly. Removing her hand from his grip she said, 'A sleeper?'

'Sleepers are operatives placed into influential positions in countries where the government is intolerant to Islam. They are absolutely crucial to our organisation.' He moved closer. 'When needed, sleepers are activated, either to carry out direct action, or to enable others. Do you understand what I'm saying?'

She nodded.

'Do you think you could do that?'

Louise's self-esteem was rising by the second.

'Of course I could. I've said I'm in, haven't I?' She was obviously elated, so Haasim was surprised to see her eyes fill with tears.

'What's wrong?'

'I'll miss everyone here. It's such an amazing place.'

'We'll miss you too.'

'I was so nervous when I first arrived. You hear such terrible things about Afghanistan on the news back home, especially about Kabul, but everyone has been so wonderful. I feel completely at home here.'

'I can't believe you've only been here a year. I feel like I've known you forever.'

She looked at him through her tears.

'More than anything, I'll miss you. It wouldn't have been the same without you, Haas.'

'Don't be daft,' he said, his face colouring. 'If you hadn't teamed up with me, it would have been someone else.'

'Maybe,' she smiled, 'but I'm glad it was you.'

'We've had some fun, haven't we?'

'We certainly have!'

They both laughed then slowly subsided into silence and stared into each other's eyes. Haasim suddenly became serious again.

'God will bestow his blessings when you become a sleeper. The work you will be tasked with is for the greater good. Always remember, God is great.'

He waited for a couple of seconds for the trigger to work then reinforced his point.

'You will be spreading Islam's message throughout the world.'

'Haas, I want to convert fully to Islam. I want to bear testament and become a Muslim woman. I want to dedicate myself to following Allah's teachings, to wear the Hijab...'

Haasim shook his head and interrupted firmly, 'No Louise, that can't happen. In your heart and in your private moments you can follow the teachings, you can read the Quran and pray whenever it's safe to do so, but to the outside world you must remain Christian. Suddenly converting to Islam would completely blow your cover. You would be useless to us.'

'But that means I'll be going against the teachings of Allah. I'll be following an alternative religion. I can't do that.'

He planted a reassuring kiss on her forehead.

'Don't concern yourself with that. Remaining as you have always been is a necessary evil to achieve the wishes of God, and to attain the long-term goals of the organisation. He will know that your actions are helping raise him to even greater glory and he will bestow his blessings accordingly.'

After Haasim left her alone to rest and recuperate,

Louise lay back, thinking about the dramatic change in her circumstances. She would no longer be simply an aid worker in Afghanistan, doing her bit to improve the lives of local people. She would be a sleeper, someone living and working back in the UK, carrying on with her life as if she'd never been away but prepared at a moment's notice, to carry out any actions asked of her.

Later that night, Louise had difficulty finding restful sleep. Each time she drifted off she had the same vision, a dream where she was walking in a wood and every fifty metres or so she caught the unnerving sight of her parents peering out of bushes, their eyes accusing her.

5

Boar Head Farm, Fletching, East Sussex
Tuesday 9th July, 2024, 3.45pm

Louise threw herself into the arms of her mother Debbie and they squeezed each other so hard she could barely breathe.

'Mum, it's so good to see you. I've missed you.'

Debbie broke the hold to look at her daughter and to wipe away tears of happiness.

'I was so scared when I heard you'd been shot. For heaven's sake darling, you could have been killed! Promise me that you're home for good, promise me you'll never return to that awful place.'

Louise gazed sadly at her mum. Holding her hands she said, 'Mum, I love Afghanistan, I love the people, I love their culture, so I can't promise that I won't return, but I'm home now, and that's what matters.'

Her father, Derek, had picked her up at Heathrow and was struggling into the kitchen with two heavy suitcases. He dropped them gratefully on the floor and beamed at his daughter.

'Thank God, we've finally got you back. Welcome home love, you've been sorely missed.'

Smiling fondly at him, Louise noticed how he seemed to have aged slightly in the short time she had been away.

'Thanks, Dad.' She looked around, surprised that her elder sister wasn't there to welcome her home. 'Where's Evie?'

Debbie glanced at Derek.

'She's been sent on a week-long training course. She tried getting out of it but her firm insisted she had to attend. I'm sorry, darling. Evie would have been here if she could, she had no choice.'

Louise knew her sister's blossoming career as a defence barrister was important to her, so it was no surprise.

'It doesn't matter, she'd have been here if she could. I'll get my suitcases upstairs and take a shower. I'll be down shortly for tea.'

'No, you won't,' said Derek. 'We're taking you out to a new Italian restaurant in Uckfield.'

'That sounds great. I will admit to missing a really good pasta since I've been away. Thanks dad, thanks mum. Love you to bits!'

6

Trafalgar Square, London
Tuesday 30th July 2024, 1.35pm

Louise sat on the plinth at the base of Nelson's Column, facing towards the National Gallery. The plinth was shoulder height and she had to hoist herself up to join the dozen or so people already seated there. She was dressed in white trainers, white skirt and red t-shirt. Her position, her clothes, everything was in accordance with her instructions. Louise was quivering with a mixture of nerves and anticipation but knew in her heart she was doing the right thing. This was what she truly believed in, and shortly she would be meeting someone who could help her play her part. In the next few minutes, she would meet her Harb Alsheueb handler for the first time.

Three days after arriving back in England, Louise had received a cryptic e-mail from Haasim. The planning had all been arranged before she left Kabul, when she created a new email account for herself, an account that only she and Haasim would know about. The text of the e-mail would seem completely innocent to anyone who happened to read it, but Louise had been supplied with the knowledge required to decipher the hidden meaning within.

The important part of the message read, *'Hoping to*

visit Trafalgar Square on my next visit to London. It's one of my favourite places, such a great view of the National Gallery from the plinth at the bottom of Nelson's Column. I loved the outfit you were wearing in that photo you sent me, can you wear it next time we meet? Got to go now, I need to be somewhere at 1.45 so I've only got 30 minutes to get showered and changed!'

Looking at her watch, Louise saw the time was 1.35; she was ten minutes early so to calm her nerves and pass the time she took a brush from her bag and combed through her long, wavy hair. There were about a dozen people sitting on the plinth, with another dozen standing close by. The remainder of the square was heaving with tourists of all nationalities on a gloriously hot July afternoon. Her eyes scanned the crowd for anyone who looked remotely Afghan.

The slim black man in chinos, white tee shirt and flip flops, sitting to her left, had been talking to a woman on his other side ever since Louise had arrived. Suddenly, he broke away from his discussion, turned to face her, held up his right palm in greeting and said, 'Assalamu Alaikum.'

Louise jumped. She knew that Assalamu Alaikum meant 'Peace be upon You' in Arabic; it was often used in Muslim society as a method of greeting or saying goodbye. She also knew the appropriate response, so she automatically said, 'Wa Alaikum Assalam.' ('and peace unto you').

'Miss Kenton, am I right?'

'Yes…sorry…how did you know my name? Do I know you?'

The man was about thirty, with short black hair. He smiled, placed his right hand on his chest and bowed his head.

'I'm Sulayman. Haasim told me you'd be here.'

Louise found herself tongue-tied.

'Oh…I wasn't…sorry, I was expecting someone…'

He laughed. 'Are you trying to tell me you weren't expecting someone that looked like me?'

Louise was flustered and Sulayman seemed to enjoy her discomfort.

'Muslims,' he tutted. 'They come in all colours. You've no idea which one will turn up!'

Pulling herself together, she returned the greeting by raising her right hand to her chest then glanced enquiringly at the woman sitting to his left.

Sulayman leaned backwards so the two women could see each other.

'My apologies, Louise, very rude of me. I should have introduced you. This is my sister, Kareema.'

Studying Kareema's face, Louise could see she was strikingly beautiful. She looked younger than Sulayman, possibly twenty-five, with long hair in braids and a dazzling smile. She was wearing a plain yellow dress, with sparkly yellow sandals. Louise smiled.

'Pleased to meet you, Kareema.'

'Pleased to meet you, Louise. We've heard a lot about you from Haasim.'

Sulayman leaned forward again, obscuring her view of Kareema.

'Do you like paintings, Louise?' He stopped himself. 'Sorry, can I call you Louise? Or would you prefer Miss Kenton?'

'Miss Kenton sounds far too formal. Louise is fine and yes, I like paintings. Why?'

He nodded towards the National Gallery. 'Let's take a walk, we have matters to discuss.'

They jumped down from the plinth and strolled slowly through the crowds then up the steps leading out of the square. Louise could now see that Sulayman was around 6'2' tall, and painfully thin.

On reaching the main entrance to the gallery, Kareema said, 'Okay, Suli, I'm off now. Good luck, Louise, we're thrilled to have you joining us.'

Leaning forward, she placed a peck on Louise's cheek, then did the same to her brother, before heading back down the steps to the plaza above Trafalgar Square. They watched her walk off through the throng of people gathered around street entertainers.

For the next hour, Sulayman and Louise wandered through the gallery, deep in discussion. She learned that he was from Nigeria and had been a senior handler for Harb Alsheueb for three years with one other operative under his control. He told her that she wasn't alone in her position, that they had sleepers in construction, the police service, prison service, judiciary, transport, and now she had joined them, they hoped to eventually have someone in Parliament. He praised her stoicism, retaining the outward appearance of a committed Christian while her heart belonged to Islam, and he assured her that Allah would understand why she was not always able to pray five times a day, and that she would not be punished. With every word, Louise's pride and certainty that she was doing the right thing grew stronger.

She learned that any e-mail messages she sent were to include the word 'curtains', which would confirm that the message was from her. At no time should she give away details of their meetings, nor was she allowed to discuss with anyone else the instructions he gave her and that included Haasim.

An hour later they left the gallery and were soon standing outside Charing Cross Station. Sulayman fixed her with a firm stare.

'Don't be concerned if you don't hear from us. You may not be spoken to again for several weeks, possibly several months.'

'Okay, I'm fine with that.'

'Whenever I need to speak with you about operational matters, it will never be over the phone or by email, it will always be in person.'

'Okay. Why's that?'

'For security. We don't want anything we discuss being read or overheard.'

For the first time, Louise felt a twinge of apprehension.

'Isn't it possible that by speaking to you I might draw the attention of the security services to myself?'

'No.'

'There's no chance that you or the other operative aren't already on a watch list somewhere?'

'Listen, security services like MI5 and the police Counter Terrorism Branch have way too much on their plates right now.'

She nodded, but still looked uncertain.

'They're already dealing with other active cells, Louise. They don't have sufficient resources to watch everybody, even if they are aware of them. I'm positive they have absolutely no knowledge of me or anyone I work with.'

'Good. I'm pleased to hear it.'

'You might be required next week but it's possible you may not be required for over a year. The main thing is to not to be afraid when the time comes.'

'I'll try not to be.'

'From what I've learned today, I'm certain you'll be ready for your deployment, whatever it is.'

'I will. I can't wait to be involved.'

'Until then, carry on living your life just like you always have and don't do anything differently. It's important you give nothing away regarding your true feelings about Islam. You must keep your devotion a secret from everyone.'

'My lips are sealed. I'll say nothing.'

'May Allah be with you. Assalamu Alaikum, Louise.'

Before she could reply, he'd turned on his heels, moved swiftly through the crowds and was gone.

On the train home, Louise went back over the incredible events of the afternoon with a sense of excitement unlike anything she had ever known. Looking around at her fellow passengers, she thought how surreal it all was. *If they only knew!*

Louise was welcomed back indoors by her parents, who believed she'd been seeing an old university friend in London, and Louise felt a slight pang of guilt when she had to fabricate details of their meeting. The three of them sat on the patio together in the late afternoon sunshine, sharing a large jug of orange squash filled with ice, and conversation turned to a discussion about Louise's time in Afghanistan and the current political situation there.

Listening to her parents talk, Louise knew that they broadly supported her views on the subject, but it suddenly hit her how appalled they would be if they knew the extent of her involvement with a radical branch of Islam. She had turned her back on the country that had raised her and kept her safe throughout her life; she would be imprisoned for many years if her actions were ever uncovered but most of all, she would bring shame upon her parents and be labelled a terrorist for the rest of her life.

7

Civic Centre, Uckfield, East Sussex
Thursday 17th October 2024, 11.30pm

The returning officer climbed the steps onto the stage and walked to the lectern. After thanking various people, reporting the number of spoiled papers and the total number of votes cast, she said, 'I can confirm that the following candidates have been duly elected as District Councillors for Wealden Council: Stephen Carroll, Arthur Rogers, and Louise Kenton.'

Louise was thrilled with her election. Together with her parents and sister, she celebrated well into the early hours. Before leaving for Afghanistan, she had campaigned on local issues for the Labour Party whenever she was home from university and had continued the work as soon as she'd arrived back home. This was her first step on a very long ladder, hopefully resulting one day in her election to parliament.

Louise had received no communication from Haasim in the three months since her meeting with Sulayman. She realised this wasn't because he didn't want to contact her, it was simply necessary. The various security services were interested in communications between Afghanistan and the UK, in particular communications between people known to have sympathies with proscribed terrorist groups, it was unlikely, but Haasim could possibly have fallen into that group. It was simple: there was nothing for the organisation to contact Louise about, so they hadn't.

Over the following months, Louise threw herself into her role as a District Councillor. She still worked during the day as personal assistant for Judith Snells, then spent most of her evenings and weekends phoning and emailing members of the public who had contacted her with specific grievances. She also enjoyed teaming up with other councillors to hold surgeries, an idea they had copied from MP's.

In her few private moments, Louise read the Quran and prayed as often as possible, normally when the rest of the family were out. Occasionally, she managed the required five times a day but not often. This was a part of her religion which Louise loved; it took her from the world she inhabited, into a world where she felt peace in her heart. Whenever she prayed, she immediately felt calm and at one with God, something she had failed to achieve in all her years as a Christian. She knew that the peace and serenity she achieved through prayer would remain with her for the rest of her life.

She was proud of her transformation. Her faith in Christianity had become a distant memory; she now knew the truth was to be found in the Quran, not the Bible.

8

Millennium Bridge, London
Wednesday 12th February 2025, 6.00pm

Louise was admiring the view of St Paul's Cathedral from the centre of the Millennium Bridge. Its huge dome rose imposingly from the jumble of buildings at the northern end of the bridge. A City Cruisers ferry passed underneath, and she watched as passengers on the rear of the ferry waved furiously at those standing on the bridge. Louise couldn't help smiling at their enthusiasm and returned their salutes with equal vigour.

She had received the first email for seven months from Sulayman at the weekend and found herself both nervous and excited. The timing of the meeting was fortunate, allowing her to finish work before making her way there. Leaning back on the handrail, she turned her gaze in the opposite direction, back to the south bank of the Thames and the Tate Modern Gallery, where she noticed Sulayman sauntering through the crowds towards her. On seeing her, he smiled broadly and within a few seconds was leaning on the rail next to her. She noticed he didn't greet her in Arabic like he had on their first meeting.

His face was expressionless, giving nothing away

about the importance of the meeting, simply staring blankly along the river towards Westminster.

'Hello Louise, how have you been?'

'Life has never been better, thank you. The job's going well and I'm now a District Councillor. In fact, they're talking about me applying for the next selection process to be a Labour Parliamentary Candidate!'

He nodded. 'I'd heard about your election.'

'Really?'

He glanced at her, then looked down at the river again.

'Think about it, Louise. We've naturally been monitoring your progress closely and the names of District Councillors are public knowledge. I'd heard that you'd become a Councillor, but not about your parliamentary prospects. That's wonderful news.'

'Early days,' she replied. 'So, why suddenly contact me after all this time? I thought they might have dismissed the idea of me working for them.'

He slowly shook his head, and his expression hardened.

'Instructions have come down from on high.' He stared into the water, his face a mask. 'Apparently an MI5 agent is paying far too much attention to two of our operatives, and the bosses want the situation dealt with.'

He turned to Louise, and for a second she thought his eyes seemed to be looking for a reaction, accusing her.

She felt a surge of fear: if Harb Alsheueb even remotely suspected her of betrayal, her life would be at great risk.

'But... you can't think it's me! I'm not an MI5 agent!'

Hearing the hint of panic in her voice, the expression on his face softened. He raised one eyebrow and gently shook his head.

'I'm not accusing you Louise. We know who the agent is. I'm here because the organisation wants you to confirm that you're ready for your first assignment.'

The fear was replaced by a pulse of excitement which coursed through her body. This was the moment she had hoped for, the moment she had longed for. She cherished the feeling of being wanted by the organisation. Fighting to remain calm, she said simply, 'Yes, I'm ready.'

Nodding towards the dome of St Paul's, Sulayman indicated for her to follow; this was a mannerism that Louise would see many times in the future. Initially they walked in silence, carefully sidestepping the crowds walking in the opposite direction.

'As I've explained, we already know who the agent is. Your role will be vital to our operation's success.'

'Don't leave me in suspense. What is my role?'

'To befriend her, persuade her that she's in danger then lead her to a given location.'

Louise found herself surprised that her first operation would be against another woman.

'I'd never considered that an opposition agent might be female.'

Sulayman didn't look at her and continued walking slowly, his eyes fixed on the mighty dome of St Paul's.

'Why not? Our enemies come in all shapes and sizes. A good tip to ensure your own safety is unless you're certain that someone is signed up to our cause, never speak openly to anyone and never trust anyone.'

He moved to block her path; his eyes locked onto hers as he said, 'Don't ever forget that Louise. If you're not 100% certain that they're a member of our organisation, don't trust them.'

'What, even my family and friends?'

'*Especially* your family and friends.'

For a second, it was as if a cloud had passed over the

sun, making her shiver, then she gave him reassuring smile and nodded.

'Okay, I understand.'

Sulayman moved out of her way and they continued walking. On reaching the end of the bridge, they walked up the long sloping ramp towards St Paul's which now towered over them.

'We'll provide you with all the details you need, including an address to draw her to. Once you've completed your task, you'll need to disappear and leave the next part of the operation to others. Can you manage that?'

Listening to his words, she experienced another shiver of excitement. The likelihood that the female agent would suffer a terrible fate due to her complicity didn't really register. Her training had kicked in: the cause was far more important than any individual. The operation was necessary for the protection of Harb Alsheueb, therefore whatever happened to this woman was necessary for the benefit of Islam; that was all that mattered.

Nodding thoughtfully, she said, 'I'm ready. I'll do whatever's required.'

He smiled, satisfied that she was another perfect product of the training regime. They had almost reached the top of the slope.

'I hoped you'd say that.' He pointed to a nearby café. 'Fancy a coffee and something to eat so we can discuss things further? My treat. I'm freezing and I'd rather give you more detailed instructions in comfort.'

Over the next thirty minutes, Sulayman explained that the MI5 agent was called Sarah Cairn, a junior agent targeting low-level terrorist suspects. However, the two operatives she was currently monitoring were pivotal to Harb Alsheueb's plans, because they were due to be carrying out an attack in the very near future. Cairn's activities were causing the organisation significant problems, so they intended to showcase their capabilities on two fronts: by taking her out and then carrying out the pre-planned operation almost immediately.

'Is she that much of a danger to the plans?'

'She might be, but probably not. It's mainly intended to shake up MI5, show them that we can operate wherever and whenever we want, and show them they can't stop us acting with impunity.'

Louise was shown a head-and-shoulders picture of Sarah, who could best be described as homely. She was about thirty, with short black hair in a side parting, small dark eyes, a tiny turned up nose, and thin lips. Sulayman stressed that there was no time to lose. Louise's first active service would take place the following Saturday at eleven a.m. in the Piccadilly branch of Waterstones Bookshop, in the West End.

Louise was to wear a suitable disguise, something to make CCTV identification difficult should the operation become compromised. She was then given details of how and when to approach Sarah, along with a plausible story to persuade her that she was in danger and the location to which she would lead her. Once she'd completed her task, she was to leave the premises; the operatives inside would do the rest.

As they left the cafe, Sulayman placed his right hand on his chest and passed an appreciative nod by way of thanks.

'Stay calm and you'll be fine. Your first job is always nerve-racking.' He handed her an envelope. 'You'll need this when you meet Miss Cairn. It's your new identity.'

'Thank you.' She placed the plain white envelope into her handbag.

'Assalamu Alaikum.'

'Wa Alaikum Assalam.'

He grinned at her and walked off back over the bridge without a backward glance.

As she walked back along Fleet Street and The Strand to Charing Cross Station, Louise thought about the changes in her life following her year in Afghanistan, particularly after she'd attended the meetings with Haasim. She had been convinced of the benefits of Islam before she'd even met him, but her relationship with him had taken her off in a new and wonderfully exciting direction. Her training had turned her from a woman who detested confrontation and violence to a woman prepared to do whatever was necessary for her cause, no matter what the cost to others.

Looking at the man sitting opposite her as the train sped through the Sussex countryside, she wondered what he would think if he realised that he was sharing his carriage with a sleeper, a member of an active Radical Islamist group, a terrorist soon to be carrying out her first operation.

9

Waterstones Bookshop, Piccadilly, London
Saturday 15th February 2025, 10.45am

As instructed, Louise arrived at Waterstones Mezzanine Café at 10.45. She was wearing black full-length culottes with black high-heeled shoes, a thick dark grey woollen jacket, a light grey scarf and blue thick-rimmed spectacles. Her long hair was completely concealed underneath a black woolly bobble hat, having been firstly tied in a tight bun on her head. It wasn't overly warm in the café and she wasn't the only person wearing a hat on such a bitterly cold day, so she looked far from conspicuous.

Louise was also confident that she looked nothing like her normal self. She'd come fully prepared for the final stage of the operation, carrying a small holdall containing her normal clothes to change back into after she'd completed her task, and an empty white plastic carrier bag.

The café was busy but not overcrowded and a few tables were still available. She knew the operatives were due in the café at eleven and Sarah Cairn was expected there with covert equipment to monitor their discussions. Louise hadn't questioned how Harb Alsheueb knew this would be happening, but Sulayman had hinted that they'd managed to place a mole within MI5, who was in a position to intercept her daily assignments, so they knew Sarah's movements each day before they happened.

She climbed the winding stairs to the café's counter, ordered a cappuccino and a toffee muffin then took a seat at a table for two next to the huge windows overlooking Jermyn Street. Within two minutes, she saw a slim Asian man in black jeans, a dark blue coat and a multi-coloured scarf ascend the stairs, order a coffee and sit at a table four metres away from her.

Five minutes later, an overweight white man in a maroon coat entered the cafe; his round face was ruddy, possibly from the cold outside. He placed his order, then joined the Asian man and sat down with his hot drink. They shook hands, leaned towards each other, and began to talk quietly but intensely together. Looking around at the rest of customers, she felt confident that these men were her colleagues. As she'd learned from her meetings with Sulayman, meeting in person was the favoured method to discuss operational matters.

Just after eleven, she noticed Sarah climb the stairs with a rucksack on her back and enter the café. Placing an order at the counter, she looked just like any other woman going about her business. Louise stared at her prey: alert, eager to carry out her duty and without any pity for her potential victim.

Sarah paid with cash for her purchases, which was unusual, then picked up her tray containing a hot drink and sandwich, before pretending to look around for a seat. Unsurprisingly, she chose a vacant table close to the two men, confirming Louise's suspicions that they were indeed the operatives.

She smiled to herself as Sarah placed her rucksack on the table instead of the floor. The top end of the rucksack pointing towards the two men, making her think it might contain a covert camera or listening equipment concealed at that end. Sarah had carried out the manoeuvre so calmly and casually that Louise was convinced no one else in the cafe would have thought it in the least suspicious.

It suddenly hit her that this was the point of no return. She was about to take her first real steps on behalf of Harb Alsheueb and it would be of immense value in combating MI5's operation. However, it would also have an untold impact on the woman sitting only a few metres away from her. This was her job though, and her training had taught her there was no room for sentiment. In any conflict there would be winners and losers: Sarah would be the loser, and it was important that the cause Louise believed in was the winner.

She knew the two men would not be giving anything important away in their discussions and that they would suddenly stand up and leave the café at 11.20. Once they were out of sight and while Sarah was collecting her things, Louise would make her move. At least that was the plan.

She had to admit that Sarah was good at her job. She was calmly reading a book, sipping her drink and tucking into her sandwich, not looking the least bit nervous or conspicuous, despite sitting close to two suspected terrorists, casually listening into their conversation on an earpiece, when her life could be on the line if her cover were blown. The irony was that, for Sarah that was exactly what was happening: her life was very much on the line.

As planned, at 11.20 the men broke off mid-conversation, stood up and left the café together. They walked straight past Sarah, trotted quickly down the stairs and headed out onto Jermyn Street.

Looking bewildered at this unexpected turn of events, Sarah quickly gathered her belongings and stood up to leave, then stiffened as she felt a firm hand on her shoulder; she looked around to see an attractive young woman with blue thick-rimmed glasses, wearing a black woolly bobble hat smiling at her.

'Hello, my name is Kelly Davies,' Louise said, adding in a hushed voice, 'MI6.'

Louise produced the fake identity card, complete with a recent passport style photo of herself which had been in the envelope given to her by Sulayman at their meeting near the Millennium Bridge. She had no idea how Harb Alsheueb had obtained the photo but had been very impressed with the professional look of the card.

Sarah looked understandably confused and carefully examined the identity card, causing Louise's heart to race. She was fighting to remain calm, her whole being alert to the huge risk she was taking. After what seemed ages but was probably only a few seconds, Sarah handed back the card, seemingly satisfied.

'How did your people know I'd be here?'

Louise returned the identity card to her pocket and indicated for Sarah to retake her seat, then sat down opposite her at the table. She looked grimly at the woman across the table.

'We've received information that Harb Alsheueb are monitoring your movements and we've intercepted emails indicating they intend to eliminate an MI5 officer.'

Sarah took a sharp intake of breath and put a hand over her mouth, her professional calm rapidly evaporating.

'Then why the fuck haven't you informed my department?' she hissed.

Louise rested one of her hands over the other as she

leaned across the table.

'Our investigations have shown that your department could be the root of the problem, so this seemed the safest way to alert you.'

'What are you talking about?'

'We believe there is almost certainly a mole within your department. We believe that the intended target is you, Sarah, but if we'd notified your bosses or anyone else you work with, we might have compromised ourselves and you by inadvertently passing that information to the mole.'

A look of horror spread over Sarah's face.

'Oh, my God…oh fucking hell…no!'

Louise placed her hand on Sarah's arm, in a convincing show of sympathy and concern.

'It's okay, stay calm, it's all under control. The reason those men left so quickly just now was because they're intending to lure you into a trap.'

'What do you mean, a trap?'

'They were hoping you'd follow them.'

Louise held Sarah's hand, giving it a reassuring squeeze.

'They intended to lead you into a quiet area of Green Park, where another operative would have discreetly dispatched you.'

Ashen faced, Sarah nodded her understanding of the gravity of the threat but said nothing.

'They're trained assassins, Sarah. You'd have been unlikely to survive.'

A determined look suddenly appeared on Sarah's face.

'I'd better phone in right away.'

She pulled a mobile phone from her rucksack, but Louise grabbed Sarah's hand before she could do anything.

'Think about it, Sarah. If you phone in now, the mole might learn that we're onto them, which could make things even worse. Leave it for twenty minutes and we'll get you to a safe house. Once you're there, we'll go through secure channels to arrange for your colleagues to come and collect you without simply phoning in through the main office.'

Sarah considered Louise's suggestion for a few seconds then finally nodded her agreement.

'Okay.'

She seemed to be losing control again; tears forming in her eyes, she looked utterly shell shocked. Louise got to her feet in a show of urgency.

'We need to remove you right now. They'll realise you're not following them once they've gone a few hundred yards. We don't need them coming back - could make things very awkward. Come on, let's get moving.'

Sarah stuffed everything into her rucksack. Fear rapidly overcoming her, she was now willing to place herself completely in 'Kelly's' hands.

'Where's the safe house?'

'Just ten minutes away. It's a flat on Golden Square.' Louise rested a hand on Sarah's shoulder. 'Are you sure you're okay?'

Without speaking, Sarah inclined her head towards the stairs, as if to say, 'let's get going'.

Louise nodded and they went down the stairs together, heading out of the café and into the bookshop, passing right through the ground floor and leaving via the main entrance onto Piccadilly.

They crossed the road and headed along Air Street. Watery winter sunshine was now filtering through the clouds, but it did little to warm them as they entered Golden Square, on one side of which was number thirty-two. A large insurance company owned the ultra-modern offices from the ground floor upwards, but Louise pushed open a gate on ground level made from heavy black railings, which led down to a basement. They descended a flight of iron steps to the front door of a basement flat, where they were completely hidden from the view of anyone at street level. Louise pressed the bell.

A deep, gruff sounding man's voice said, 'Hello?'

'It's Kelly,' she replied.

A buzzing sound indicated that the door was open. Louise pushed it ajar, offering Sarah the opportunity to enter first. As Sarah stepped across the threshold, she was immediately grabbed by an Asian man with a full beard who appeared from behind the door. He placed his hand over Sarah's mouth, grabbed her around the waist and bodily carried her inside. Her muffled attempts to scream were barely audible. Another bearded man appeared and put his hand out, barring Louise from entering.

The first man roughly pushed Sarah up against a wall.

'If you scream, I'll break your fucking neck.'

His partner yanked the rucksack from her back, removed the recording equipment and tipped the remaining contents onto the floor. After a swift check through the contents, he handed the rucksack to Louise.

'Lose this and lose it fast, then go home.'

Taking the rucksack, Louise felt like an actress in a spy movie; it all seemed surreal and weirdly thrilling. She lifted the rucksack onto her shoulders which worked perfectly with the holdall she was carrying, making her look like any other young tourist strolling around the West End of London.

She had no idea what would happen to Sarah. Would they beat information out of her first? Would they waterboard her? What exactly would they do before they killed her? Whatever the truth was, she found that she really didn't care. Sarah Cairn was an enemy of Islam and deserved what she had coming. Louise had done her bit and been faithful to the cause, which made her glow with satisfaction. Sarah was collateral damage, merely a consequence of Louise carrying out her duty.

Ten minutes later, she was outside the stage door of the Spartacus Theatre on Jermyn Street, which she had been told would be left unlocked. She had also been assured that CCTV would be turned off both inside and outside the stage door, and that the door would be unmanned.

The stage door had been difficult to locate, being an unremarkable set of glass double doors, with a tiny sign which was hard to spot. Once inside, she pushed the rucksack to the bottom of a wheelie bin full to the brim with rubbish. When the bin men collected it, the rucksack would be forever hidden somewhere in landfill or perhaps incinerated; either way, the security services would never find it.

There was a ladies' toilet just beyond the bin and Louise gratefully pushed open the door. She'd been desperate for a wee since leaving Waterstones, and the sense of relief as she sat in the scruffy cubicle, both physical and mental, was wonderful. Once finished, she changed into her own clothing and placed the disguise into the white plastic carrier bag. She enjoyed the feeling as she released her hair from the bun and brushed it until satisfied it was neat and tidy, before returning to the stage door.

Watching through the double doors as people passed by, she waited until a large crowd on a guided walking tour appeared, then calmly stepped out into the throng and walked with them for a short distance, before turning right at the junction into the crowds on Piccadilly Circus.

Satisfied with her disposal of the rucksack, she made her way along Coventry Street into Leicester Square, where she saw a road sweeper with his barrow. Holding the carrier bag aloft, she smiled and asked, 'Can I dump this in your bin please?'

'Fine by me.'

'Thank you.'

She forced the bag deep into the bin, then walked slowly away with a contented smile on her face. Having disposed of her disguise, Louise made her way to Charing Cross Station and caught the 12.42 to Uckfield.

Back at the farm, she was relieved to find that her father was out working in the fields and her mother had gone shopping in Brighton. She collapsed on the settee, mentally exhausted, and stared through the lounge window into the garden. Her elation at having completed her first mission was overwhelming: she felt more alive than she'd ever felt before.

Her first assignment as a sleeper was over; it hadn't been difficult and had been a complete success. What's more, she was certain that she would be ready to handle a more serious job when the time came. The misery and suffering of Sarah Cairn did not enter her mind, so complete was her indoctrination. Should Harb Alsheueb require her again, Louise would be ready, she wouldn't let them down.

10

MI5 Headquarters, London
Sunday 16th February 2025, 9.30am

Stephen Sallis, Head Officer at MI5, stood in front of the gathered agents, his face grim. He was a short man, 5'8' in his thick-soled shoes, early fifties, and everything about him was grey, save for the white shirt he was wearing. He waited for the final agent to enter the room and close the door.

'Ladies and gents, thank you for travelling in on a damp and cold Sunday morning. I know for many of you this should be a rest day and I apologise for the intrusion.'

He paced slowly around the room as he spoke.

'One of our own has disappeared off the face of the earth... and in our occupation that spells trouble.' He composed himself, the emotion clear in his voice. 'Sarah Cairn from C team had been working on two men believed to be attached to Harb Alsheueb. We know that she intended to carry out surveillance on them yesterday morning. They were hardly the most important targets, in fact I would describe them as low level, but she hasn't been seen since she left this building.'

A male agent raised a hand.

'Didn't she pass deployment details to her supervisor?'

'Good point. In fact, you've hit the nail on the head. Unfortunately, Sarah left no details of where she would be operating.'

This comment brought a murmur of disbelief from those in the room.

'As you are all aware, details *should* have been left with control and passed to her supervisor, neither of which happened. This was completely out of character. She is normally professional and dependable, but for some reason failed to carry out this simple task. It makes no sense at all.'

Sallis stopped speaking for a moment and cast his gaze over the faces before him.

'We do, however, know the names of the suspects she was monitoring.' He clicked a button on the remote control he was holding, and a large screen in the corner was illuminated by pictures of two men. Pointing at them, he said, 'Their names are Ali Yusef, originally from Pakistan, and Miles Harding, from Stratford-upon-Avon.

'We've no idea why nobodies like these two would be protected by their organisation to the extent of removing one of our agents. Our best guess is that they were imminently be deployed on some kind of attack, so we're having them brought in straight away. We've sent requests to the Metropolitan Police and hopefully both will be brought in sometime this morning under the Prevention of Terrorism Act, 2005.

'They won't anticipate being arrested today, which is very much to our advantage. This will not only enable us to disrupt their operation, it will also give us a chance to interrogate them about what's happened to Sarah. Unfortunately, if they remain schtum, we'll have a serious problem trying to find her.'

The room fell silent, save the sound of discontented murmuring, and the shuffling of bottoms on seats.

Rubbing his hand backwards and forwards vigorously over his hair, Sallis continued, 'Sarah was not an experienced agent, but she was extremely competent, her greatest strength was being renowned for not taking chances. So, until further notice, we must work under the assumption that she hadn't cocked up, but was somehow compromised.

'Until now, Sarah had only been monitoring Yusef and Harding's electronic footprints. We're sure that until this point she hadn't carried out direct physical surveillance on them, so she wouldn't have come into contact with them until yesterday morning. There doesn't appear to be any way they could possibly know she was watching them. Which begs another question. If Harb Alsheueb are responsible for abducting her, where did they get the information from that she was monitoring them in the first place?'

A female agent spoke up. 'I appreciate that she was very professional, sir, but it sounds like she's been identified by someone within Harb Alsheueb as carrying out surveillance.'

Sallis slowly nodded. 'That could be right, but like I say, she hadn't previously come within sight of them, so that is unlikely.' He sighed, looked up to the ceiling, then back down to the gathered agents. 'Look, I hate to say this, but it's possible we have been infiltrated by someone with sympathetic leanings towards Harb Alsheueb. For all I know that person, in effect a terrorist mole, may be in this room right now.'

Heads in the room began turning, with everybody looking furtively at those around them. Nobody escaped scrutiny, nobody spoke. The atmosphere had become decidedly edgy, which was exactly the response Sallis had hoped for. He was, after all, investigating the probable abduction of an agent and he wanted everyone on their toes.

Pointing at the images above his head, he continued, 'These two fuckers weren't operating alone, they've got the backing of a powerful organisation behind them. They would have been working under a handler and would almost certainly have had assistance from others in taking Sarah out.'

He was interrupted by a flustered young clerk bursting into the room without knocking. He was holding a sheet of paper in his hand.

'Sorry to interrupt, sir, but important news about Sarah has just come through from the police.'

You could have heard a pin drop as Sallis walked swiftly over to the young clerk, turned to the assembled agents and said, 'I'll be back in a few moments.'

He took the sheet of paper from the clerk and followed him out of the room, closing the door. Three minutes later, Sallis was back in the room and walked smartly to the front. He turned to face his colleagues with a sombre expression on his face.

'I'm afraid I have bad news. The body of a woman believed to be Sarah has been found on waste land near Welham Green, in Hertfordshire.' He glanced down at the sheet of paper before continuing with a noticeable break in his voice. 'She was naked, appears to have been tortured, and may have died from strangulation. A post-mortem will be carried out this afternoon to establish the precise cause of death.'

His voice had faded as he fought to control his emotions. He looked down at the paper with glassy eyes then returned his gaze to the room.

'Sarah was clearly onto something, and Harb Alsheueb didn't appreciate her attention.'

He placed the sheet of paper gently on the table then suddenly retrieved it and angrily screwed it up before hurling it across the room.

'I don't need to tell you how rarely one of our agents is killed on duty, so the gloves are now officially off with anyone who has links to Harb Alsheueb! It looks extremely likely that they tortured Sarah to find out how much she knew.' He shook his head. 'Christ knows what she went through.'

He was speaking now with raw emotion.

'Her death must not have been in vain! She was onto something, something they were terrified of us learning about. We need to get seriously stuck into those bastards and find out what the fuck it was!'

A female agent, one of Sarah's closest friends, began to cry, and after an understanding nod from Sallis, left the room. This gave him a chance to regain his composure.

'All Head Agents are to remain behind. The rest of you, please return to your duties and thank you for your attendance. I repeat, I'm sorry if you've had your rest day cancelled and to bring you such dreadful news, but we need everyone we've got working on this until further notice and I'm sure you are as keen as me to nail these bastards.'

Thirty officers rose to their feet, quietly filed from the room and the last officer softly closed the door. The only people left were Sallis and his four Head Agents, each one of them responsible for their own team of agents. They gathered in silence around a single table to receive instructions.

Sallis rubbed his eyes and grimaced, then composed himself before speaking.

'Tom, your team will concentrate on going through anything that Sarah was working on regarding Harb

Alsheueb. I want you to check through hard copy files, computer files, emails, everything. I particularly want you focussed on her informants. Arrange meetings with both ASAP. It's possible that one of them might know something that could unlock why this happened.'

Tom nodded and Sallis jerked his head towards the door. Tom made his way swiftly from the room, leaving Sallis with the other three. Sallis turned to the only female agent in the room.

'Sally, Sarah was looking at two low-level operatives. They shouldn't have had a clue we were onto them; therefore, she wasn't thought to be under any risk. I want your team to concentrate on tracing all known associates of Ali Yusef and Miles Harding. I want to know everything about them. I want any of their associates not prepared to be cooperative to be placed under severe pressure. If necessary, make their lives a fucking misery. Let's start putting the heat on these bastards. We need to let them know that if they want a fucking war, they can have one and they'll fucking lose!'

'Understood boss, I'll get right on it.'

The third Head Agent was now on the receiving end of Sallis's gaze.

'Bill, I want you to personally notify Sarah's family and friends about her death. You'll need to liaise with the police to make sure they don't duplicate this by doing it themselves – I think we should inform them ourselves. Once that's done, allow things to settle for a couple of days then get your team to concentrate on her private life. We all know that agents aren't supposed to speak about operations with friends and family, and we all know that some agents do. Fucking hell, I did it myself when I was a young agent. So, concentrate on speaking with Sarah's nearest and dearest, and see what you can glean from them. It might be that she's let something slip to a family member or friend, something that could help us.'

'Will do boss,' said Bill. He stood up to leave but was held back by Sallis's hand on his arm.

'Don't forget, be gentle,' said Sallis. 'They'll be even more traumatised than we are.'

Bill stared down at his boss, gave a single nod of his head and left the room.

This left just Sallis and the fourth agent, John Jarvis, sitting at the table. They had known each other for twenty years, admired each other's capabilities, and although not close friends, were certainly close colleagues. Sallis leaned forward on his forearms, closed his eyes, and gave a huge sigh. He could feel pins and needles in his right hand, and vigorously rubbed it with his left. For a few seconds, he sat slumped forward, then, pulling himself together, sat upright and opened his eyes.

'Sorry about that mate, I must be getting soft in my old age.'

John placed a reassuring hand on his shoulder.

'Don't be daft, we're all feeling the same. I could quite happily have burst into tears when I heard what those fuckers had done. She was a sweet kid and a bloody good agent.'

Sallis nodded. Although nobody else was in the room, he leaned in towards John and almost whispered, 'I didn't make too much fuss about it during the briefing, but the bosses have been concerned for a while that we might have been infiltrated by a terrorist group, and this more-or-less confirms it.'

John looked at his colleague in horror. 'Shit, that would be a fucking nightmare.'

'How many agents are under your supervision with more than five years' service?' asked Sallis.

'Five.'

'Good, with that amount of service, they're least likely to be our mole. I want you and those five agents to start checking through everyone who has joined us in the past five years. The remainder of your agents can continue working on whatever cases they're currently engaged on.'

He leaned back, closed his eyes and scratched the back of his neck.

'Check through all vetting procedures carried out when those agents joined, dig into their family lives and friendships.' He fixed John with a look of steely determination. 'If we're harbouring a rotten apple, we need to find who it is quickly, before we lose another agent.'

11

Boar Head Farm, Fletching, East Sussex
Monday 17th February 2025, 10.00pm

Louise was relaxing in the Lounge with her mum and dad watching late night TV, her mum in an armchair, her dad on the settee alongside Louise. He was engrossed in checking through a speech he would be giving at a venue in Brighton the following morning, to an international conference on the use of pesticides in farming.

The ITV News at Ten, with newscaster Melanie Holmes, began with breaking news.

'Good evening. In the past hour MI5 have announced that one of their agents has been murdered by the Harb Alsheueb terrorist group.'

Louise stiffened and sat forward, staring intently at the screen.

Derek happened to look up from his speech and was intrigued by his daughter's interest.

'What's up love?'

She forced a smile and lied.

'Nothing, I just want to listen to this story.'

He shrugged and raised his eyebrows, before returning to his speech.

On screen, the presenter handed over to ITV's crime

correspondent, Duncan Wilson, who was reporting live.

'I'm standing outside MI5 Headquarters in London's Millbank, where Director General Henry Green has just given a moving statement about the murder of one of their agents, Sarah Cairn.'

A picture of Sarah appeared on the screen and Louise gazed at the familiar face.

'Unusually, he gave details of her deployment, carrying out surveillance on two male members of the Harb Alsheueb group, a proscribed terrorist organisation. He described these men as 'low-level targets' who were not believed to provide a direct threat to Sarah. However, after leaving this building behind me at 10 o'clock on Saturday morning to carry out surveillance on them, nothing was heard from her again.'

He paused, as a convoy of police vehicles with blue lights flashing and sirens blazing drove by. Once the noise had died down, he continued.

'Yesterday morning at 8.15, Sarah's body was discovered by a woman out walking her dog on an area of waste ground near Welham Green in Hertfordshire. She had been subjected to torture before being strangled. All members of Sarah's family were informed before details were released to the press. We'll have more on this story later. Back to you in the studio.'

'Bastards!' said Louise's dad, who had stopped mouthing over his speech, and was watching the TV with a look of disgust on his face. Debbie also looked appalled and stared at the screen silently.

A strange, warm sensation poured through Louise. No sympathy for Sarah, or remorse for her actions, only satisfaction at a job well done. She had only one thought in her head: *the bitch got exactly what she deserved.*

Picking up the remote control, she turned down the sound on the television, an action that gained her parents' attention. Working hard to conceal the pride welling in her chest, she conjured up an appropriate response.

'That poor woman, what an awful way to die.'

Her father glanced over the top of his spectacles, 'Don't worry Lulu; they'll get the bastards. Our security services are the best in the world. It's just a matter of time before everyone involved is caught and convicted.'

Looking back at the screen he said, 'They want to shock us into a reaction. They're always hoping to start a holy war against the Christian West. What they've done to that poor girl shows the depth to which human beings can sink.'

He shook himself.

'Sorry I've been ignoring you both. Just a few more minutes and I'll be done. I really don't want to look an idiot giving this speech tomorrow.'

Louise maintained her mask of concern and empathy but was inwardly glowing with pride. On her first operation she'd managed to con Sarah Cairn into believing she was an MI6 agent, persuaded her that she was being taken to a safe house, successfully led her into a trap and ensured that she wasn't a threat to the organisation any more. She had perfectly executed her part of the operation.

She thought fleetingly about the terror and agony Sarah must have felt before the blessed release of death, but it didn't bother her one iota. This was war and Sarah Cairn had been the enemy. The brainwashing in Afghanistan had achieved its goal and left her an unfeeling shell; as far as Louise was concerned, Sarah's suffering and death was a job well done.

Now, however, she needed to be alone with her thoughts.

'I think I'll head off to bed and do a little reading before turning in.'

Her father looked up from his paperwork, smiled, and planted a kiss on her cheek. Louise walked across to her mother and gave her a hug before making her way upstairs.

'Night mum, night dad.'

'Goodnight Lulu,' they replied in unison.

The sense of achievement was immense; she felt so wired that she wanted to scream with elation. She bounded up the stairs two at a time and crossed the landing to her room. As she sat on her bed and slowly removed her jeans, she realised that she wanted more of this feeling and couldn't wait for her next deployment. Louise prayed quietly for five minutes, during which she could almost feel the blessings of Allah raining down on her.

That night however, at 3.30 in the morning, Louise awoke with a start to a sense of being watched. As her eyes adjusted to the dark, she could see a woman standing at the foot of her bed. Fear gripped her and she tried screaming but no sound came out. The figure spread her arms and looked imploringly at Louise, asking the same question over and over in Sarah Cairn's voice, 'Why…Why?'

Suddenly, Louise really did wake up, sweating and shaking. Sitting up, she stared into the darkness, but the room was empty, and she sank back into her pillow. However, she could no longer sleep and lay there wide awake until morning.

12

Covent Garden Market, London
Monday, 24th February 2025, 1.00pm

The crowds gathered in a neat semi-circle around the unicycling juggler then burst into rapturous applause as she finished her act. Louise joined in by politely clapping, while carefully scanning the rapidly dispersing audience for Sulayman.

She'd been more than a little concerned by the tone of Haasim's email; it was far curter and more business-like than those she'd previously received. What was even more unusual was that she'd only been given twenty-four hours' notice. The previous week's operation had been a complete success, so she had no idea why they wanted Sulayman to speak with her so urgently.

Sulayman turned up and without speaking took her into the gardens of St Paul's Church, next to Covent Garden Market, where he made sure nobody was nearby before speaking.

'We've got a problem.'

'What's that?'

'The operatives from Waterstones were arrested on Sunday morning. They were due to carry out an operation on Monday, but that's now been shelved.'

'What sort of operation?'

'That's none of your business, Louise.'

'I'm sorry,' she said. 'I heard on the news they'd been detained.'

'And it didn't bother you?'

'Not really. They don't know anything about me.'

'That's true, but our mole says they're using face recognition technology to find whereabouts Sarah Cairn and our operatives came into contact. They're checking CCTV.'

'Do they know where to look?'

'Not really. Fortunately, our mole conveniently 'lost' Sarah's deployment for that day, which makes it far more difficult for them to trace her.'

'That's good isn't it?'

'Yes, but they're deploying the technology straight into the West End, which is where they're guessing she was working.'

'Fuck! So they might trace me speaking to Sarah and leading her to the safe house. Is that what you're saying?'

Sulayman shrugged. 'Possibly, but remember, you were wearing your disguise. You'll be okay.'

'I hope so.' She cuddled her upper arms for reassurance. 'God I'm shaking.'

'I must remind you Louise, should you be arrested, say nothing, give nothing away and take your punishment. It will bring you Allah's blessing.'

'They won't catch me,' she replied, her self-confidence returning. 'I'm too careful.'

As they made their way towards the exit, she felt the same buzz of excitement as when she'd embarked on the operation in the first place. She was so proud to be a member of Harb Alsheueb, knowing she was involved in something far more important than herself.

'If either of us ends up being arrested, I want you to

know I'm glad to have served with you Sulayman. I wouldn't have wanted anyone else to have been my handler.'

He regarded her with a look of affection, a look she'd not from him seen before.

'Thank you, that means a lot. Don't worry yourself too much, Louise. We're not done yet... but be careful.'

They reached the gateway back into Covent Garden Market. Sulayman looked thoughtful.

'Remember, Louise, it's never over until it's over.'

She nodded. 'I'm fine.'

'If they come for you, say nothing. Stay loyal to the cause and all will be well.'

Louise didn't want to speak loudly and draw attention to herself, so she whispered, 'Assalamu Alaikum.'

Sulayman whispered in reply, 'Wa Alaikum Assalam.'

She nodded and walked off into the covered market.

13

Labour Party Head Office, London
Monday 19th May 2025, 2.00pm

Three months passed, and Louise had heard nothing more about her involvement in the abduction, torture, and murder of Sarah Cairn. However, charges under the Prevention of Terrorism Act had been laid against Ali Yusef and Miles Harding, who remained in custody awaiting trial. Her fears and worries slowly subsided and life returned to normal.

Louise walked nervously into the room, where the panel of three sitting Labour MP's smiled broadly at her. She took her place on the single chair facing them, feeling conspicuous. She took a few deep breaths to calm her nerves and then looked up confidently at the panel sitting in front of her. After a rigorous selection process, she was now being confirmed as a Labour Party Candidate at the next general election. The lady chair was first to speak.

'Good afternoon, Louise. The panel would like to congratulate you on your selection.'

Louise beamed with pride and replied, 'Thank you, I'm absolutely thrilled.'

The Lady Chair continued, 'The panel have decided

that the constituency you will stand in as Labour Party candidate at the next general election will be Mid-Sussex.'

Louise was genuinely elated at her selection but found herself crushed with disappointment at being given Mid-Sussex, a Conservative safe seat. She considered saying nothing but after all the effort she'd put in, she felt obliged to say *something*. Shuffling awkwardly on her chair, she started to speak.

'Thank you, Madam Chair. I'm obviously delighted at my selection, but I had hoped to be given a seat where I had at least some chance of victory.'

The lady chair looked at Louise with a wry smile.

'You've been recommended, Louise, because you're committed, determined, and work very hard indeed, but you must remember that you're still very young. Not only that, but the Mid-Sussex Constituency is local to where you live. Because of that fact and the extremely hard work you've put in as a District Councillor, the panel feel your selection could greatly increase our share of the vote.'

Holding the Lady Chair's gaze, Louise continued to fight her corner.

'Yes, I very probably will increase our vote share, but nowhere enough to get myself elected.'

This time, the lady chair spoke with an air of exasperation.

'If you prove yourself during this election campaign and keep working hard for the party, as you have already done for several years, another constituency with a greater chance of winning will eventually come your way. Stick with it Louise, your time will come.' She produced a strained smile then looked down at the papers in front of her with an air of finality.

Louise could see there was no point in pressing the matter and once her general questions had been answered, the meeting was called to a close. She stood up, shook hands with the three panel members and walked quickly from the room.

After leaving the building, she turned right onto Victoria Street, intending to head back towards parliament and her job at Judith Snell's office. Feeling a light tap on her shoulder, she turned around and was surprised to find herself looking into a pair of green eyes. It took her just a few seconds to recognise that they belonged to Adam Greenacre, the Labour MP for Erith and Thamesmead.

'Hi, Louise. I heard about your selection and wanted to pass on my congratulations in person.' He offered his hand, which she took and shook firmly. 'Could I buy you a celebration coffee?'

She found herself blushing; he really was rather good-looking.

'I'd love to say yes, Adam, but I really need to get back to work. Judith will be expecting me.'

'Actually,' Adam said somewhat sheepishly, 'I've spoken to Judith and she's more than happy for you to take an extra hour. So, what's your answer? Go for a coffee with a strange man from Kent, or tell him to sod off?'

Louise took a few seconds to compose herself and studied him carefully. He looked about thirty-five, with short, dark brown hair and the athletic build of a rugby player. Added to that, he was smartly dressed in a well-tailored dark grey suit, white shirt, red tie and shiny black shoes.

'Well, if you've gone to the bother of pre-planning it with my boss, it would be rude to refuse. I'd love to go for a coffee with a strange man from Kent.'

Adam grinned. 'Great! I know a lovely little café just around the corner from here.'

'Sounds good.'

'I hoped you'd say that, and keep your purse in your handbag, everything's on me.'

This was a blatant attempt to chat her up and having not had a relationship since returning from Afghanistan, she was perfectly happy to receive an approach from a very attractive man, even if he was at least ten years older than her.

The café looked inviting from the outside, with tempting pastries displayed on cake stands in the window. He opened the door for her then placed his hand in the small of her back to guide her inside, which sent an unexpected tingle through her.

Louise pointed at a Chelsea bun. 'One of those please, with a Mocha, no sugar.'

At the rear of the café, Louise settled down at a table for two, while Adam placed their order at the counter. A couple of minutes later he joined her, carrying their drinks and pastries on a tray.

'Here we are, Mocha with no sugar and a Chelsea Bun.'

Adam flashed her a smile and for the first time she noticed his beautifully even white teeth, and how striking his deep green eyes were.

'Thank you. A girl could get used to being treated like this.'

Adam sat down and raised his eyebrows.

'That's good because I was rather hoping that this wouldn't be our last drink together.'

Although they'd only just met, she felt herself falling for him. He was good looking, had a gorgeously deep voice, a classy dress sense and was a Labour Member of Parliament! What was there not to like?

'That suits me.'

Spooning a half teaspoon of sugar into his Latte and

gently stirring it, he looked deep in thought.

'Please don't think I'm a weirdo Louise, but I've been keeping an eye on your progress for a while now.'

He eyed her nervously, worried about how she would respond.

Louise was more than a little surprised to hear this. She'd seen him at a few meetings and events and, like most women, thought him rather dishy, but he'd never given any indication that he was interested in her.

'I'm flattered, but why would you be keeping an eye on someone like me?'

'I might as well come straight out with it... I've been keeping an eye on you because I think you're absolutely gorgeous.' He began to redden, looking suddenly like an embarrassed schoolboy. 'Sorry, I realise that's not a very good chat-up line, is it?'

Louise's heart leapt and she decided to make things easier for him. Leaning across the table, she held one of his hands in hers.

'I think it's a lovely chat-up line.' She squeezed his hand. 'And for the record, I think you're all right yourself.'

He beamed and blew a sigh of relief then stroked her hand with his thumb.

'Sorry, do you prefer being called Louise, Lou, or something else?'

She grinned. 'This will sound silly, but ever since university, all my friends have called me Lulu. Even my parents and sister call me Lulu now.'

'Lulu it is then.'

Thirty minutes later, they left the café. He'd learned that she was twenty-three and had grown up in Sussex on the family farm. She had quickly realised that she needed to protect her position as a sleeper, so had concentrated on her home life as much as possible. About her time as an aid worker in Afghanistan, she simply said that she had enjoyed the work very much, but struggled getting on with the Afghan people, and was utterly baffled by the Islamic religion. She also shared her joy at being elected as a District Councillor, and then her selection as parliamentary candidate.

Meanwhile, she had learned that he was thirty-eight, had been brought up in a village called Borough Green in Kent and had competed in the national pole-vault championships during his days at Loughborough University. He had been a Labour activist since he was sixteen and was proud to have been one of the party's youngest ever MP's when first elected to parliament.

He escorted her back to Judith's office, and they kissed for the first time then smiled sheepishly at each other.

'Thanks Adam, I've had a lovely time.'

'Me too. Perhaps now's a good time to exchange mobile numbers?'

'I hadn't even thought of that. Great idea!'

Two minutes later, numbers exchanged, they shared another quick kiss before saying goodbye. The fifteen-year age gap was irrelevant and hadn't even been mentioned.

She looked over her shoulder at him as they went their separate ways. He was a good catch, in more ways than one. Louise had made her mind up, even at this early stage, that she had to do everything in her power to make this relationship work. Not only was he charming, good looking and someone she could see herself being very happy to spend time with, but he could also prove perfect for her role as a sleeper should her own parliamentary ambitions fail to bear fruit. These two completely different opportunities co-existed in her mind quite naturally and didn't cause her any concern;

combining the two would bring excitement into her life in more ways than one, and she couldn't wait.

On entering the office, Louise found Judith sitting at her desk; she gave Louise a knowing look.

'Congratulations on your selection. How do you feel?'

Louise beamed with pride.

'Great, although I would have preferred a different constituency. I've got no chance in Mid-Sussex.'

'I wasn't talking about your selection as a parliamentary candidate. I was talking about selection by the hottest MP in the Commons!'

Louise flushed bright pink.

'Oh that, absolutely wonderful! And you're right, he is hot. Thanks for allowing me to be late back to work.'

Leaning forward, Judith said, 'Well? How did it go?'

When Louise had finished her account of their afternoon, Judith sat back with a look of smug satisfaction on her face.

'You could do a lot worse than Adam Greenacre. He's really going places that young man. He'll be a minister within a few months, maybe even in the cabinet. You're going to make many ladies around parliament extremely jealous.'

'You're probably right but for now he's chosen me, and I won't be letting him go anytime soon, so they'll have to lump it.'

They both laughed and Judith nodded.

'I hope he does well in his career,' said Louise, part of her mind still thinking about how this turn of events could be of use to the organisation. 'But I still don't understand why he's interested in *me*.'

Judith made a face.

'Because you're a very pretty girl, Louise. Just as importantly, you're ambitious, the same as him.'

She picked up her papers and switched seamlessly from idle chatter into work mode.

'Well, that's enough about your love life. I need you to take down a letter to the Transport Secretary.'

Louise stood up, shrugged off her coat then sat down with her pen, writing pad and Dictaphone. Smiling at Judith, she said, 'Okay, I'm ready, fire away.'

14

14 Barn Avenue, Hildenborough, Kent
Friday 30th May, 2025, 6.50pm

'Hi Lulu, come in. How was your journey?'

Louise's best friend Millie beamed with excitement as she held the front door open.

'Brilliant thanks. It only took forty minutes from Charing Cross.'

Louise leaned her case against the stairs and hugged her old school friend. Melissa, or Millie, as she was known by family and friends, was a buyer in the City and had done very well for herself, buying her beautiful three-bedroom detached house two months ago at the age of only twenty-three. Louise was mightily impressed and a little jealous.

'Wow, you've got a great place. I can't imagine I'll ever be able to afford anything like this.'

'Your time will come. After all, you're going to be a famous politician in the next few years!' Millie smiled sweetly at her friend. 'Now, tell me all about this hunky MP you've started dating. I looked him up on Google. Fucking hell Lulu, he's gorgeous!'

'There's not much to tell really. Our first date, if you could call it that, was in a café near St James's Park.'

'And how was it?'

'Amazing! We fell for each other almost immediately. Since then we've had three more dates - two meals out and the cinema.'

Millie leaned forward and narrowed her eyes. 'And?'

'And what?'

'Well? Have you?'

Louise pretended not to understand her friend, saying demurely, 'Have I what?'

'Don't play games. Have you shagged him yet?'

'I might have.'

'And?'

'And what?'

'Don't wind me up Lulu! Was he any good?'

Louise was enjoying Millie's desperation to find out more. She laughed.

'He was fantastic! We've only slept together once, but he was definitely the best.'

'You lucky cow. I haven't had a boyfriend for months.'

Louise changed the subject.

'It's so lovely being here. I've missed you since you left Fletching.'

Millie grinned.

'Come on, let's crash out in the lounge. We'll catch up, then get changed and head out.'

Louise was surprised by this.

'Oh, I thought we'd be eating in. Where are we going?'

'I've booked a table at the Tasty Bhaji, it's a great little Indian about a mile from here. If we walk, we can get as pissed as we like!'

Louise gasped as she followed Millie through to her lounge; it looked like something in a Homes and Gardens photoshoot, with its huge inglenook fireplace, complete with a dark wood mantelpiece covered with photographs of Millie with family and friends. The beige carpet looked thick and expensive, and the tan three-piece suite luxurious and inviting. They each settled down into an armchair just as Channel 4 News was starting.

The first item was about seven bodies found in the back of a lorry on the M6 in Lancashire, believed to be illegal immigrants who'd arrived in the UK by boat into Holyhead. Although it was an upsetting report, the friends weren't really listening, and carried on chatting excitedly about nothing in particular. But the second news item changed all that.

'Police investigating the abduction and murder of MI5 agent Sarah Cairn have today released CCTV images of a woman they believe may contain vital information.'

As the newsreader spoke, the screen was filled with pictures of Sarah and Louise sitting in the café at Waterstones. Although the images weren't close-ups, it clearly showed Louise producing her fake identity card to Sarah. It skipped to a few seconds of them in conversation, then skipped again to where they got up together and left.

Louise could tell the camera must have been sited high above the serving counter somewhere, because it showed the tables on the Jermyn Street side of the café. It would have been difficult to identify anyone from the images and seeing herself in action on a television screen sent a tingle of pleasure down her spine. The images had an almost hypnotic effect on her, until she suddenly became aware that she was no longer listening to what Millie was saying.

Forcing herself to snap out of it, Louise attempted to excuse her apparent rudeness.

'Sorry Millie, do you mind if we stop talking for a minute and watch this? It's a story Judith Snells is particularly interested in.'

Adrenalin was surging through her and she was working hard to remain calm. Millie was a little surprised at her friend's behaviour but nodded.

'Of course. I'll belt up.'

She reclined back in her chair and joined Louise watching the report.

The newsreader, William Percy, continued, 'On leaving the café, the woman walked ahead of Sarah, who appeared happy to follow. Their route was traced from CCTV camera footage, until they descended out of view to a basement flat in Golden Square. The woman reappeared within three minutes with Sarah's rucksack but Sarah herself had disappeared and was not seen again until her body was found on wasteland in Welham Green, Hertfordshire.

'At 3.20 next morning two men are seen to ascend the stairs from the flat struggling with what appears to be a heavy trunk.' Pictures of the two men struggling with a dark trunk appeared on the screen. 'The trunk was then loaded into a stolen transit van, which has since been found abandoned in St Albans. It is believed that Sarah was almost certainly inside the trunk, but it is not known whether she was dead or alive at that time. At this stage police do not know the identities of the two men and unfortunately the night-time CCTV images are of poor quality. A forensic search of the flat, which had been thoroughly and professionally cleaned, failed to provide any further evidence,'

A map of the route taken by Louise now appeared on screen, and several images of her in disguise were shown as she walked through the West End.

'The woman police wish to interview was next seen at Piccadilly Circus, then in Regent Street, before turning left onto Jermyn Street. She then disappeared off the face of the earth, and there are no sightings of her leaving either end of Jermyn Street, despite both areas being monitored by several CCTV cameras.'

Images of the woman and the map were replaced with the face of the newsreader.

'Police are asking for anyone who knows the identity of this woman, or indeed the identity of the men seen carrying the trunk, to contact the incident room on the number displayed on the screen.'

Louise had been utterly transfixed by the report; she felt exhilarated but also unnerved. The images hadn't been close-ups, or of particularly good quality, but she was convinced that someone might be able to identify her. She hardly dared look Millie in the eye just in case she'd recognised her. Having been so engrossed by what she was watching, she'd failed to hear Millie attempting to attract her attention.

'Lulu...Lulu...LULU!' The final call of her name was almost a shout and shook Louise out of her trance.

Trying to take control of herself, she concocted an excuse for her behaviour, expressing sympathy for Sarah.

'Sorry Millie. I've been following that story ever since they found her body. What happened to that poor girl is dreadful. How can people be so evil?'

Millie turned the TV off and rose from her chair, then walked across to Louise and stood behind her, running her fingers thoughtfully through Louise's long hair. After a few moments, she said cheerily, 'Right, that's enough sadness. We're going out and we're going to enjoy ourselves!'

Three hours later, after consuming large amounts of Indian cuisine and far too much red wine, the two friends slowly made their way along the quiet, almost traffic-free country lane towards Millie's house. The warm evening made it a pleasant walk, and Millie slipped her hand through Louise's arm.

Louise had really enjoyed herself. 'Thanks Millie.'

'What for?'

The truth was that catching up on old times, over copious amounts of wine, had been just what she'd needed to calm down after watching the news report, but she couldn't tell Millie that.

'For being such a great friend. It's been a wonderful evening.'

Millie smiled warmly and squeezed Louise's elbow. 'It was fun wasn't it?'

Louise noticed out of the corner of her eye that Millie was glancing at her every few seconds, as if she were wondering whether to say something.

'Something on your mind, Mills?'

'I was worried about you earlier. You seemed to be in a trance when we were watching that news report.'

Louise was instantly uneasy.

'Yeah, sorry about that. Like I said, I've been monitoring it for Judith. I suppose I've grown weirdly connected to the fate of Sarah Cairn.'

Millie nodded and the friends walked on in silence. Then, after a minute or so, Millie turned to Louise.

'Lulu.'

'What?'

'Remember Mustafa?'

Louise was puzzled; why would Millie be mentioning Mustafa after all these years?

'Of course, I went out with him for months.' She looked wistful. 'Blimey, Mustafa. Haven't thought about him for a while. Why are you asking?'

'I don't know, I think it was watching your reaction to that news report.'

'What do you mean?'

'It reminded me how strongly you reacted to the

mickey-taking that Mustafa had to put up with. You're really interested in anything to do with Islam, aren't you?'

Millie didn't elaborate. She seemed to be waiting for her friend's reaction.

Louise knew she had to think carefully before answering, and decided to inject humour into the conversation, hoping to deflect Millie from the direction she was heading.

'I'll tell you a secret, Millie. With Mustafa it was all about the sex!'

'You're kidding! Little Mustafa? He seemed such a…'

Louise laughed. 'You wouldn't have called him Little Mustafa if you'd slept with him.'

Millie stopped in her tracks, her mouth agape, then both girls collapsed in fits of giggles which nearly saw them at the bottom of a ditch. They continued to laugh as they began reminiscing about boyfriends from their younger days, wondering where they were now. Louise drew a silent breath of relief; she seemed to have thrown Millie off the scent. Boyfriends and schooldays remained the topic of conversation until they arrived back at Millie's house, and lasted until they went to bed.

In her room, however, the doubts resurfaced. Was Millie the tiniest bit suspicious about Louise's involvement in Sarah's abduction and murder? It was highly unlikely, but Sulayman's warning to 'never trust anyone' was ringing in her ears. In future, she would have to be extra careful around Millie, especially in her reaction to news reports.

15

Foyles Bookshop, Charing Cross Road, London.
Tuesday, 4th November 2025, 1.00 p.m.

An email from Haasim arrived on Friday 30th October, asking Louise to meet Sulayman the following Tuesday at Foyles Bookshop and he was now waiting for her, as expected, in a quiet area on the first floor. As she walked in he greeted her.

'Assalamu Alaikum.'

'Wa Alaikum Assalam.'

'Hi Louise, our operatives from the Waterstone's operation are being tried at the Old Bailey in January.'

'I know. I've seen it on the news.'

'Has anyone spoken with you about the CCTV images?'

'No, no one...,' she hesitated for a moment, 'although, my best friend Millie noticed my reaction when it was on the news, but that was ages ago and she's not mentioned it since.'

He raised his eyebrows but didn't speak, his silence urging her to go on.

Louise concentrated, trying to recall the events of the evening with Millie, then she explained everything that happened during her visit. Although she was speaking about her best friend, she left nothing out; loyalty to Harb Alsheueb and Allah was more important than anything, or anyone.

The silence was broken by the clicking sound of Sulayman running a finger along the spines of a row of books. He then turned to Louise; his face was troubled.

'That could be a problem. Keep me posted if she asks awkward questions in the future. I know she's your best friend, but we can't afford to take chances.'

Louise nodded, she would protect the cause to the best of her ability, at all costs, even if meant that at some stage in the future Millie became 'collateral damage.'

'And how's Adam?'

The mere thought of Adam lifted Louise's mood and made her smile involuntarily. She'd been certain that Harb Alsheueb were aware of her relationship with him, so wasn't surprised at Sulayman's question.

'He's great, thank you. We've only been together a few months, but this feels like the real thing.'

'Love can be a dangerous companion in our game. Are you still dedicated to the cause, Louise?'

'Of course!'

'You're sure? We're aware how falling in love affects people.'

'I would never desert my faith or the organisation for a man.' Louise looked around to make sure nobody else was nearby before raising her voice. 'I can't believe you're even asking me that question!'

Her indoctrination had convinced her that the main thing she should strive for in life, apart from loving God, was complying unquestioningly with the instructions of Harb Alsheueb. Only by doing that would she guarantee receiving the blessings of Allah.

Satisfied with Louise's response, Sulayman said, 'That's great. You've convinced me you're still fully committed. I'll pass that on.'

Ten seconds passed with silence between them.

'You won't hear from us for a while. They want you to cement your relationship with Adam while he climbs the parliamentary ladder.'

'I thought that might be the case.'

'Should he become a member of the cabinet, it might allow you access to secure government buildings, access that could have previously only been dreamed of.'

It was at this moment that Louise fully understood that her relationship with Adam would always be based on deception and the exploitation of his position for the cause. Strangely, the thought of carrying off such a deception didn't faze her; on the contrary, it excited her.

Ten minutes later their discussion ended. Sulayman reminded her she would be unlikely to receive an email for months.

'Assalamu Alaikum, Louise.'

'Wa Alaikum Assalam.'

They waved goodbye and left the bookshop through different exits.

She couldn't stop thinking about the joy she would receive from helping a terrorist cell strike at the very heart of government. That would be precisely what attending all those sessions had been preparing her for, and hopefully one day soon she would be given the opportunity to put her training to good use.

She knew her future actions on behalf of the organisation could quite possibly make history, indeed she hoped they *would* make history. Little did she know, at that moment in time, how dramatically her wishes would come true.

16

Hilton Hotel Restaurant, Park Lane, London
Sunday 8th February 2026, 9.10pm

The windows on the World Restaurant at the top of the Hilton Hotel had stunning views across the London skyline but Adam had eyes only for the woman sitting across the table. The waiter politely asked if they were finished and Adam nodded.

'Yes, thank you.' He offered his glass of red wine up to Louise. 'To us.'

She chinked glasses with his and smiled warmly.

'To us.'

The waiter was unobtrusively clearing away their plates and cutlery.

'Would you like to see the dessert menu?'

'Yes please,' said Adam.

'Certainly, sir.'

The waiter moved off expertly through the tables, leaving them alone.

Adam and Louise had only been together for nine months, but that had been long enough for them to become utterly besotted with each other. Despite the duplicitous life she was leading, Louise had genuinely fallen in love with him, and although they both had busy jobs, particularly Adam with his duties as an MP, they spent as much spare time as possible together. In fact, when they weren't working, they were rarely apart.

Louise continued to pray and read the Quran as often as possible when she found time alone. Her belief in the goals of Harb Alsheueb remained rock solid, despite her feelings for Adam. Being a sleeper had been far more stimulating than Louise had ever imagined, and she looked forward to her next active assignment. She was being required to manage two entirely separate lives and far from it being a struggle, she was loving every moment; it was as if there were two Louises, and they never really acknowledged each other.

The waiter reappeared, handing a dessert menu to each of them.

'I'll leave you alone for a few minutes to make your choices.'

'What do you fancy?' asked Louise, absent-mindedly perusing the menu.

Adam didn't reply but held out a hand towards her. She reached across and took it.

'I'm so glad a strange man from Kent tapped me on the shoulder that day!' She squeezed his hand. 'I do love you.'

He suddenly released his grip and reached into his inside coat pocket, leaving her staring at him, baffled. Suddenly, he stood up and moved around next to her, dropped to one knee, and held out a small red jewellery box with the lid open, displaying a stunning white gold ring with a large solitaire diamond. Several people at nearby tables stopped eating their meals and were discreetly watching developments unfold.

'Louise Kenton, I love you with all my heart. Will you marry me?'

With an involuntary yelp of pleasure, she dropped

off her seat to kneel on the floor in front of him, threw her arms around him and shouted, 'Yes, oh yes!'

The tables around them broke out in spontaneous applause, with a couple of customers standing up to provide an impromptu standing ovation. The couple kissed then Adam removed the ring from its box and carefully slipped it onto her ring finger, resulting in a further ripple of applause.

Seated once more, Louise couldn't stop staring at the ring. It was exactly the one she would have chosen for herself; it was perfect.

'How could you have known that was the type of ring I would like? We've never discussed it.'

He raised an eyebrow.

'No, but you've mentioned what type of ring you'd like to your sister, Evie.'

'So, you've been in league with my sister?'

'Yes, and it worked a treat didn't it?'

Reaching across the table, he tightly held both her hands in his, then leaned across and kissed her finger with the ring on it.

The waiter returned.

'May I offer our congratulations on behalf of the restaurant and staff? The manager has asked me to inform you that the desserts are on the house.'

'Thank you,' said Adam. 'That's very kind.'

Having chosen their puddings, Louise said, 'I can't believe we're actually engaged. Were you thinking of a long or short engagement?'

'I'd like it as short as possible; I'd marry you tomorrow.'

Her eyes sparkled with happiness.

'A short engagement it is. I'll start looking at venues. I can't wait to be your wife, Adam; our life together is going to be so wonderful.'

'And I can't wait to be your husband.'

Louise radiated joy, proud to be engaged to the man she loved so deeply. It was only later that night, when she had said her prayers, that the thought which had been dormant in her mind surfaced: that she would soon be one step closer to being in a position to take direct action against the British Government on behalf of Harb Alsheueb.

***

Boar Head Farm, Fletching, East Sussex
Saturday 14th February 2026, 12.45pm

'What?' Screamed Evie, 'You got engaged last week, and you're only telling us about it now! Where's your ring?'

Feeling embarrassed, Louise removed the ring from her jeans pocket and placed it on her finger. Debbie started crying and Derek clapped his hands with joy.

'I wanted to wait until we were together as a family before I said anything.'

Once Debbie had composed herself, she asked, 'When are you thinking about for the ceremony?'

'As soon as possible. We can't wait to be married.'

'That's wonderful,' beamed Derek. 'I'll speak to the vicar. Hopefully, he'll have a Saturday free before the end of summer.'

Louise had been dreading hearing those words, although she'd prepared herself for them. Throughout her time with Adam, her heart had remained faithful to Islam, although to the rest of the world she continued to present the image of a committed Christian. There was no room in her heart for the Church of England anymore, but her position in Harb Alsheueb required her to keep up the pretence. She still attended church with her mum and dad occasionally, playing the part of a Christian worshipper to the best of her ability, something she was finding harder and harder to do, but, as Sulayman had reminded her, it was a necessary evil to achieve the greater good.

Her prayers to Allah had, of necessity, become less frequent, mainly due to the amount of time she now spent with Adam, but she still prayed in private whenever she could and still read the Quran regularly. When Adam asked why she owned a Quran, she had lied to him, saying it had been presented by fellow workers at New Beginnings, when she had to leave Afghanistan early after her injury. Adam believed her story that she'd kept it because it brought back happy memories. He had no reason to question her and absolutely no reason to suspect that she may be using it to regularly pray to Allah.

17

St Andrew's and St Mary's Church, Fletching, East Sussex
Saturday 27th June 2026, 3.30pm

'Adam, repeat after me, 'I Adam…''

'I, Adam…'

'Take you, Louise…'

Adam dutifully repeated the familiar lines, word for word. Then it was Louise's turn. She repeated the same phrases and, if she faltered momentarily over some of the words, the assembled congregation either didn't notice, or put it down to wedding nerves. The ceremony proceeded without a hitch, culminating in the vicar proclaiming Adam and Louise husband and wife, then asking the couple to kneel in front of him.

'Those whom God has joined together, let no one put asunder.'

Any reservations Louise had been feeling had now disappeared and she couldn't have been happier. They were looking forward to their lives together in the house they had bought in Otford, Kent, convenient both for commuting into London and within easy reach of Louise's parents. They had enjoyed furnishing it and had slept there together for a couple of weeks prior to the wedding, despite her parents' mild disapproval.

Now it was their big day. The ceremony was over and the reception at a nearby country house was into its final hour. In thirty minutes, the bride and groom would be departing for Gatwick Airport, where they were booked into a hotel for the night, before flying out to Sri Lanka for their honeymoon.

As Louise left the ladies' toilet at the end of a long corridor well away from the reception area, an Asian man whom she didn't immediately recognise, stepped out in front of her. He held out an arm to block her passage.

'Hello, it's Louise isn't it?'

She stopped and looked at the man's face. He was over six-feet tall, skinny but powerful-looking, with scruffy collar-length hair and a long, thick beard but no moustache. Suddenly, a glimmer of recognition entered her head.

'I'm sorry. I can't remember your name, but I've a feeling we've met somewhere.'

Then it came back to her.

'Kabul! You were working for MSF, weren't you? Your medical centre was only a few doors away from where I was working.'

The man smiled with his mouth, but not his eyes; he seemed annoyed about something and appeared to be staring straight through her.

'My name's Ismail, Ismail Ahmed. I used to stand outside our Medical Centre, sometimes I saw you passing by.'

Embarrassed at not really remembering him well, she replied, 'I'm so sorry Ismail, I kept my head down walking to work. Best not to make eye contact with males when you're a lone white female on the streets of Kabul.'

'You're right of course, my apologies, I hadn't thought of it like that.'

'It's okay,' she smiled. 'I've just got married and I'm off on honeymoon. We're leaving in twenty minutes!'

She had begun to feel decidedly awkward and wanted to end the conversation.

'It's been really nice seeing you again, Ismail.'

She made to head back to the reception, but once again he blocked her path, this time by stepping in front of her.

'You've married that MP, Adam Greenacre, haven't you?'

Uneasy at the tone of his question, and aggressive body language, she replied, 'Yes, why?'

He moved closer, now deliberately invading her personal space.

'I take it you've told him about the meetings with Haasim, and those other lunatics during your time in Afghanistan?'

Louise went cold. *How could he possibly know that?* She held his gaze, uncertain where he was going with this.

The merest trace of a smile appeared on his face, the corners of his mouth turning slightly upwards.

'It would be terrible if anyone let something slip to Adam about your past... if he somehow learned of your shameful behaviour.'

His words were whispered, menacing.

She started trembling and felt her heart racing, then took in a gulp of air and forced herself to look directly into his cold eyes.

'Come on, Ismail, I was curious about the Islamic religion, that's all. I was raised as Church of England. Everything in Kabul was new to me, so I wanted to learn a different culture.'

He laughed and checked over his shoulder to make sure no one else was leaving the reception and heading towards them.

'Oh, really? And what about the six months of secret meetings, the training camps where you were schooled in the ways of radical Islam?'

Louise stared at him open-mouthed. *How the fuck does he know all this*? This man could ruin her marriage with Adam and derail her position within Harb Alsheueb in one fell swoop. She wasn't about to let either of those things happen without a fight, but for the moment, she said nothing.

Ismail pressed home his point.

'How would the security services view the wife of an MP who'd spent several months attending jihadist training camps?'

Anger now burned through her; she decided to go on the attack.

'What the fuck do you want?' she hissed. 'This is my wedding day and I won't have you ruining it!'

Ismail became equally angry, moving to within an inch of her nose.

'Go to Sri Lanka, enjoy your honeymoon, but when you return, phone me.'

He handed her a scrap of paper with his mobile number scrawled on it.

'I want ten thousand in used notes before the end of July, or the security services and your husband will hear all about your activities out there, including what type of training you underwent. If you pay up, I'll return to Afghanistan and you'll never hear from me again. If you don't, you'll lose everything.'

Louise was in shock. Her anonymity as a sleeper was being threatened, not to mention her marriage and even her freedom. Knowing she had no choice and playing for time, she growled at him, 'You'll get your fucking money, but once that's paid, if you ever try getting more, you'll regret it.'

He grinned, revealing the poor state of his dental care. At that moment, footsteps could be heard coming down the corridor. They both looked and saw Adam walking towards them.

Ismail turned to walk off, but after a couple of metres he stopped, turned his head to look over his shoulder and said cheerily, 'Have a lovely time Louise. Don't forget, give me a call sometime when you get back.'

He held out his right hand towards Adam, firmly shook his hand and said, 'Congratulations, you've got a wonderful wife, there!'

Adam looked puzzled.

'Sorry, we haven't been introduced.'

'I'm Ismail, I met Louise in Kabul. We were aid workers for two separate agencies and our offices were quite close together.' Turning towards Louise he said, 'I'd love to stay and chat more, but my wife is waiting and I'm running late. Have a great time on your honeymoon.'

He patted Adam on the shoulder and walked off along the corridor.

18

The London Eye, London
Friday 17th July 2026, 5.30pm

The pod climbed imperceptibly into the sky, revealing a stunning panoramic view of the capital. However, Louise was oblivious to her surroundings.

She had emailed Haasim two days after arriving in Sri Lanka. As well as using the code-word curtains, she'd added a separate code-word, nursery, signifying she had a problem and needed a meeting urgently. Haasim had replied with the location, date and time.

'What's the problem?' Sulayman hadn't bothered with any niceties when greeting Louise or asked about her wedding and honeymoon.

Checking they couldn't be overhead by the other people sharing the pod, she said quietly, 'A man called Ismail approached me at my wedding. He knows about the meetings I went to in Kabul and the training sessions I attended.'

Sulayman looked at the floor, deep in thought, his face inscrutable. He then looked out through the pod's windows towards the Houses of Parliament and slowly nodded his head.

She leaned in to whisper, 'He's blackmailing me. He's given me a mobile number to call him. Either I pay him ten thousand in used notes before the end of July, or he tells Adam and the security services everything about me, including my links to what he called 'radical Islam'.'

Sulayman looked grim, and for a few seconds remained silent.

'What time do you usually start work?'

Louise was surprised by this change of topic. She had anticipated questions about Ismail, about where she'd get the cash from, not a question about her work.

'Any time between eight and ten. Why's that important?'

'Arrange to meet him in Green Park at 7.30 next Thursday morning, a hundred metres from Hyde Park Corner. When he arrives, lead him to a secluded spot.'

'Okay. Why there? And what happens if he won't meet me that early?'

'Don't worry about that, he'll come. If he thinks you've got ten thousand in cash, he'll come no matter what the time is. I've dealt with greedy shits like him before.'

An awkward silence grew between them until she repeated her question. 'I'll ask again, why there?'

'Because that's the quiet end of the park and there are plenty of trees and bushes to provide cover. He'll understand that the wife of an MP wouldn't want to be seen handing over that amount of money.'

She searched his face for a hint of what would happen to Ismail.

'Do I actually bring the cash for him?'

The hint of a smile played on his lips.

'You needn't bother.'

She realised what that meant and once again excitement surged through her. The thought of being involved in the eradication of another enemy gave her a buzz, especially an odious individual like Ismail, but she still had concerns about her own safety.

'I won't be able to contain him for long before he susses that something's up, so what's the plan?'

Sulayman was visibly relaxing; he suddenly seemed to be enjoying himself.

'Just meet him where I said, the rest will be taken care of. You'll have plenty of time to get to work, have a cup of tea and be seated at your desk by 8.15.'

That night Louise was woken at 4.30 in the morning by something and initially couldn't work out what it was. As she slowly came to, she could hear a faint voice outside her bedroom window. Someone was in the garden. She thought about waking Adam, but he was fast asleep after a late-night working through his red box, so she decided to look for herself.

Climbing quietly out of bed, she crept over to the window, opened the curtains and looked outside. The sun was rising, casting a weird glow over the garden, the trees throwing long shadows like fingers stretching across the lawn. There was nobody there and the voice had stopped.

Assuming it was just a dream, she climbed back into bed, only for the faint voice to start again. She sat up and strained to hear, she was unable to make out the words, but it was definitely a female voice, a familiar voice. Then with horror she recognised who it belonged to - Sarah Cairn.

She shuddered; how could she be hearing Sarah's voice? It wasn't possible but she could definitely hear it. Sitting absolutely still in bed, she strained her hearing even harder, until she was able to pick out words: it was the same phrase repeated over and over, 'You'll pay... you'll pay... you'll pay'.

Louise felt she was losing her mind. No matter how hard she tried to relax and ignore the voice, she couldn't make it stop, so, unable to sleep, she got up and went downstairs where she turned the TV on and stayed there until morning, curled up in a ball on the sofa. She was still there when Adam came down at 6.30.

'I wondered where you'd got to. Everything okay, love?'

She stretched her aching muscles from where she had slept awkwardly and smiled reassuringly at him.

'Yes, I'm fine. I woke up early and couldn't get back to sleep, so I decided to get up and make a coffee rather than disturbing you.'

'Why couldn't you sleep? Something worrying you?'

'No,' she lied, memories of the voice still echoing in her brain. 'Everything's great, just one of those things I suppose.'

19

Green Park, London
Thursday 23rd July 2026, 07.30am

Ismail arrived on time. He was strolling down the central footpath one hundred metres from the Hyde Park Corner entrance, when he heard Louise calling.

'Over here, Ismail.'

He walked towards the voice and found her sitting on a bench, partly concealed among trees and bushes. Sulayman had been correct, this end of the park was indeed quieter; there appeared to be nobody else nearby. Louise still felt vulnerable though as she hadn't seen anyone who might be her backup, meaning she had no support should Ismail become aggressive, or even violent.

Ismail sat down beside her and came straight to the point.

'Have you got my money?'

It was a cool morning, yet he had a film of sweat glistening on his forehead and had a wild look in his eyes, he seemed desperate. His voice shook.

'I want my fucking money.'

Louise was taken aback by this instant anger and aggression; she was frightened but determined to be strong.

'Yes, I've got your 'fucking money', but I want one guarantee first.'

His face contorted with anger.

'Look, I've already told you, pay up and you'll never hear from me again.' He tugged at her arm, spinning her round to look at him. 'Now, where's my fucking money?'

At that moment, a young couple appeared around the bend of the footpath holding hands, giggling about something. They would be passing the bench any moment, so Ismail released her arm, realising that for a few seconds at least, he would need to behave rationally and remain calm.

As the couple passed, the man leaned over and kissed his partner sweetly on the lips. She responded by reaching into her handbag and pulling out a black handgun with a silencer fitted to the barrel. She quickly covered the gun with a tee shirt, hiding it should any passers-by look in their direction.

Pointing it at Ismail, she said with a heavy West African accent, 'Please come with us Ismail. One wrong move and I'll blow your brains out.' The woman's partner was a huge muscular man, and he roughly manhandled a terrified Ismail to his feet.

His voice faltering, Ismail asked, 'Who the fuck are you? What do you want? You've got the wrong person.'

The woman smiled.

'No, Ismail.' She waved her free hand towards Louise. 'Thanks to this young lady, we know that we've definitely got the *right* person.'

Her partner turned to Louise. 'Get off to work. You can leave him to us.'

Louise was enjoying witnessing Ismail's plight. Looking at him one last time, she smiled broadly, waved goodbye and said, 'See you later Ismail, good luck!'

Her last sight of Ismail was of him being frogmarched out of the park through a gate onto Piccadilly, where a large black car had pulled up. The rear passenger door swung open and Ismail was pushed forcefully into the back seat. The man closed the door and the car pulled away. The pair returned to holding hands, and strolled off calmly down Piccadilly, looking for all the world like an ordinary couple.

Louise was relieved to see that the area was still quiet, with no other pedestrians in sight. The whole incident had taken less than three minutes. She walked through the park towards Buckingham Palace, then crossed the Mall before walking through St James's Park to Westminster, and work.

A serious problem had been resolved. She knew what would happen to Ismail, that he would never threaten her or anyone else in the organisation ever again. She didn't feel bad about this; on the contrary, she felt deeply satisfied. He was an enemy of Islam and Harb Alsheueb, an evil bastard who was more than happy to destroy her life. But she had beaten him to the punch and destroyed his.

20

One Tree House, Pilgrim's Way, Otford, Kent
Saturday 27th March 2027, 9.20am

'Pregnant? That's wonderful!'

Adam gave his wife a cautious hug as she told him the news shortly after emerging from the bathroom.

'I can't believe we're going to be a family!'

They kissed, walked together from the kitchen to the conservatory and sat down on a settee. Adam was ecstatic, but then looked thoughtful.

'What about your selection as candidate for Mid-Sussex? The election will be this year sometime. Are you happy to still stand? What about your career?'

'What's wrong with me being a pregnant candidate? There's no law against it.'

'You're right, no reason you shouldn't, but you might need to cut down a little on the doorstep canvassing.'

Leaning her head on his chest, she said quietly, 'I'd love to do all that, but I've been thinking about things since the day we met, and I've come to a decision. I don't think I want a career in politics anymore.'

'Don't be silly, you've worked so hard.'

'I mean it. I see the long hours you work! I enjoy my

job as Judith's PA and giving up on my career would fit more easily around being a mum.'

'But...'

She cut him off.

'I want you to know that everything at home is being taken care of. Now you're in the cabinet you'll need all the support I can give.'

He stroked her hair, and with a crack in his voice said, 'You'd give up your own career to support me?'

She smiled and nodded.

'Yes, I want everything out of the way in order to give your career the foundation it deserves.'

'You are wonderful, thank you so much. If you're sure...'

'Look, in a few years, you could be Home Secretary, maybe even Chancellor of the Exchequer. After that, who knows?'

'I love you so much,' he said, kissing the top of her head.

'Love you too,' she replied, nestling into him.

Adam gently released her and stood up.

'I'd better get going, my surgery is at 10.30.'

'That's fine. Get out there and climb that ladder.'

He pulled her to him, then patted her stomach softly and bent down so his face was next to her tummy.

'Goodbye little one, we'll chat again when I get home.' Standing up, he blew a kiss, whispered, 'Love you,' and left.

But Louise had a reason for giving up her career which she couldn't share with her husband. His promotion to Minister six months earlier had come as a complete surprise. The incumbent had been sacked after porn had been found on his computer inside the House of Commons, causing a raft of newspaper headlines that hadn't been great for the party. She wanted to concentrate fully on her role as a sleeper, and his new position had relegated her own personal ambition for a political career to the back benches.

Adam's parents had beamed with pride on hearing of his promotion and Louise was genuinely thrilled for him. His career was in the ascendancy: he was now Secretary for State at the Department for International Trade. She couldn't have been prouder, or happier.

At the same time, and just as importantly for Louise, his promotion to Cabinet Minister meant Harb Alsheueb would probably be contacting her soon. She now had the prospect of being a mother to Adam's child, whilst at the same time having the ability to cause great harm to the government as a result of his blossoming career. The separate threads of her life couldn't have been more in conflict, but Louise did not see it that way – to her they formed a single yarn; however much she loved Adam and their unborn child, they could never compete with the love in her heart for Allah.

21

Ecclestone Square, London
Thursday 16th September 2027, 9.30am

For mid-September it was a stiflingly hot day, with the temperature in the upper twenties. Louise was seven months pregnant, and due to finish work at the end of the following week. An email had arrived from Haasim on Monday 6th, and she was waiting for Sulayman, pacing up and down uncomfortably in the sun.

He emerged from behind a crowd of tourists on a guided tour and sauntered up to her.

'Assalamu Alaikum.'

'Wa Alaikum Assalam.'

'Hi Louise, it's been a while. Good to see you again.' He looked at her bulging stomach. 'It can't be long until the birth. How have you been keeping?'

She proudly stroked her belly. 'Not too bad, thanks. I've enjoyed being pregnant and escaped with hardly any morning sickness, but this heat...'

He made a sympathetic face then got down to business.

'Adam is now Minister in the Department for International Trade.' He didn't elaborate or comment.

Louise knew what was coming, and it sent a thrill of

anticipation through her whole body. She jumped in before he could say any more.

'I'm prepared to do anything you need.'

They walked together along a path beneath some trees giving some welcome shade.

'Before you ask, Louise, we have no intention of harming Adam; to be blunt, your position as his wife could prove extremely useful in the future.' He stopped walking and turned to face her. 'When do you go on maternity leave?'

'The end of this month. Why?'

'We need you to place a device inside your husband's department.'

Louise was delighted and terrified in equal measure. She'd expected involvement in a small operation somewhere, but hadn't anticipated such a dramatic turn of events so soon. To plant a device in a secure government building, with all the risk involved in completing a task of that magnitude. This would be her first solo direct action and she was determined she wouldn't be found wanting. Her training had more than just prepared her; it had made her eager for this moment.

Sulayman brushed some early leaves from a bench and sat down. He patted the space next to him.

'How many times have you visited Adam's department in the past?'

She thought for a moment. 'Only twice, why?'

'What's the security like?'

'It's pretty good but not great, particularly if you're well known to the security staff. The first time I visited, I saw someone get waved straight through.'

He nodded, smiling, clearly satisfied with her answer.

'Can you invent a reason for visiting next Thursday or Friday?'

Louise thought for a moment. 'Yes, he's away on a

trade conference in Birmingham. He leaves at ten on Thursday morning and doesn't return until Friday lunchtime.'

'Sounds perfect. Can you think of an excuse that would get you in?'

'I suppose I could turn up and ask to speak to him around 10.30; when they say he's already left; I could ask to use the loo.'

'That sounds ideal. The device is small, under a kilo. It will be completely sealed and 100% waterproof, so we thought a toilet cistern would be a good hiding place. It'll have an inbuilt timer, set to detonate nine days after you plant it.'

'Exactly nine days?'

'Yes. If you're intending to be there at 10.30 on Thursday, that sounds as good a time as any. I'll ensure it's set to detonate at 10.30 nine days later.

Louise looked puzzled. 'That's a long delay. Why nine days?'

Sulayman's face showed he had been anticipating the question.

'This is the first in a series of attacks, which will gradually grow in size and impact. We thought if the device is planted during a Thursday or Friday, the explosion would be on the weekend of the following week, meaning minimum casualties but maximum effect.'

'Why not the weekend immediately after it's planted?'

'The police will stupidly assume that it was planted within the previous forty-eight hours, so they'll waste loads of time going through CCTV for the Thursday and Friday before the weekend.'

'So low casualties are the way forward from now on?'

He laughed a somewhat mirthless laugh. 'Oh no, not

at all! This first explosion is intended to shake them up, make them worried about security at government buildings, but follow-up attacks will be for maximum impact *and* maximum casualties.'

'But surely that means they'll step up security at other government buildings, making it harder for us to carry out attacks in the future...'

He held up a hand to stop her speaking.

'Leave future plans to others, Louise, you just concentrate on the job I've given you. What are your thoughts?'

'It sounds feasible to me. Adam's not normally at work over the weekend, so an explosion on a Saturday or Sunday would be perfect. If there's a change of plan, I'll let you know.'

A young woman pushing a toddler in a pram strolled past, singing 'Baa Baa Black Sheep' to her little boy. Louise automatically rubbed her stomach with both hands. Once the woman was out of earshot she asked, 'How will you get the device to me?'

'If you're going to Adam's department for 10.30, make sure you're sitting on a bench near St James's Park Cafe with an open bag by your feet at 10.15 next Thursday morning. We'll get someone to discreetly drop the device into your bag. Once you've got it, make your way straight to Adam's department.'

Louise gave Sulayman a thoughtful stare, before saying with determination, 'I'll be there next Thursday. You know I won't let the organisation down.'

He raised his right hand and nodded, acknowledging her bravery.

'I know how frightened you must be. I remember the first time I had to plant a device. It was in Mogadishu and I was scared stiff, petrified.' He inclined his head and whispered empathetically. 'It's much easier second time.

Trust me, you'll be fine.'

He was right, she was frightened, in fact she was terrified, but she was also thrilled and determined she wouldn't be found wanting.

'If Harb Alshueub trust me enough to handle the task, then I'll complete it.'

'Assalamu Alaikum Louise.'

'Wa Alaikum Assalam.'

Sulayman walked quickly away, leaving her sitting on the bench, looking just like any ordinary, pregnant woman. He looked back and shouted, 'Don't forget, 10.15 next Thursday, good luck.'

22

St James's Park, London
Thursday 23rd September 2027, 10.28am

Louise sat on a bench close to the cafe. As planned, she left a shopping bag open with three items of clothing inside. There were several members of the public around but nobody noticed the young Asian woman in the dazzling blue dress sit down beside her on the bench and place a small brown package, about the size of a bag of sugar, into the shopping bag of the woman sitting next to her. The Asian woman stood up and said softly, 'Good luck,' before walking off.

Louise climbed to her feet, the bag in her hand, then walked through the park and across Horse Guards Parade. Her senses were heightened and she was aware of every sound, as if she were hearing them for the first time: the wind in the trees, the crunch of her feet on the coloured asphalt of the parade ground, pigeons cooing on the ledges of buildings. She was also aware of every person who passed her.

It was a cool morning but every now and then the sun's rays peeped through gaps in the buildings and warmed her face. She was experiencing a high that few people ever attain. She'd been anticipating feelings of guilt for the destructive tsunami she was about to unleash on her husband's workplace, but the only emotion she actually felt was a heady determination. Her brainwashing had altered her mind to the point where she genuinely believed blowing up her husband's department was the right thing to do, so she blithely continued on her way.

Despite the low temperature she could feel dampness under her arms by the time she arrived at the Department for International Trade. As Louise walked into the building, she was greeted by two security guards Adam had introduced her to months ago.

She greeted them with a false smile.

'Hi Steve, hi Colin, how are you?'

Steve spoke first. 'Hello, Mrs Greenacre, haven't seen you for a few weeks. Is everything okay?'

'Fine thanks, but can I have a quick word with Adam?'

'Sorry,' said Colin, 'he left twenty minutes ago.'

She pretended to be confused and disappointed.

'That's odd, I thought he wasn't leaving until eleven. I've walked here from work because I found a pen I that's very special to him in my bag – it's been a lucky charm for him throughout his career and I thought he'd like to have it with him.'

The guards looked sympathetically at her and Steve said, 'Looks like you've had a wasted journey.'

She shrugged in mock annoyance and dumped her bag on a table. Holding her bump, she said, 'I'm bursting for a wee. Could I just nip to the ladies? I'll only be two minutes.'

Colin said, 'We shouldn't really, not unless you've got business in here, or you're with your husband of course.'

Steve shook his head and glared at his colleague.

'For Christ's sake Colin, she's a minister's wife. What

is she gonna do?' He turned to Louise. 'You can go through, but we'll need to check your bags first.'

Anticipating this, Louise made light of it.

'It's only clothing in the shopping bag, but the items are... rather personal.' She found herself blushing despite herself.

Chuckling, Steve nonetheless stepped forward and opened the top of Louise's shopping bag, causing her heart to leap into her mouth. If he found the device, it would be game over. He looked in and could only see clothing, which she had placed carefully over the device, completely concealing it at the bottom of the bag.

She voluntarily opened her handbag and started rummaging inside to distract his attention. He left the shopping bag and gave her handbag a cursory look inside. Satisfied with his checks, he gestured for her to pass through the scanner without putting her bags onto the conveyor belt.

'I won't look too closely if it's personal items, Mrs Greenacre. On you go, we wouldn't want to keep a pregnant lady waiting for the loo. I remember what my wife was like when she was expecting.'

Picking up her bags, she smiled sweetly at them and passed through the scanner, setting off an alarm and illuminating red lights. This wasn't surprising, because apart from the device, she had a set of keys and a mobile phone inside her handbag. The alarm caused a further security guard to swiftly appear, but Colin raised a reassuring hand, indicating all was well.

Louise realised she had been holding her breath and exhaled in relief. She then climbed the stairs to the first floor, where the ladies' toilet was situated. As she pushed the door open, she was disappointed to see someone already in there; a chubby middle-aged lady was washing her hands.

Louise walked over to the mirror above the wash basins and stood next to her. She removed a lipstick from her handbag, looked into the mirror and started applying it. The woman began waving her hands under the dryer, all the time watching Louise in the large wall mirror, she had a penetrating stare, which unnerved her. She was paying far too much attention for someone she'd never met; it was as though she sensed what was going on. When the woman finished drying her hands, she turned to Louise and looked down at her tummy.

'Looks like baby's coming soon. When's it due?'

Greatly relieved that she was seemingly only interested in her pregnancy, Louise flashed the woman a pleasant smile and replied, '1st of November, about six weeks' time.'

'Lovely! Your first?'

'Yes.'

'Boy or girl?'

'A little boy.'

'Well, good luck. You won't regret it. My children have brought me more happiness than I could ever have imagined.'

The woman smiled again, turned away and walked out, leaving Louise alone and shaking with stress.

When she was certain the woman had left and wasn't coming back, Louise checked each of the four cubicles carefully, making sure none of them was occupied and she was completely alone. Once this was done, she went into the second cubicle from the left, closing and securely locking the door. Before she did anything else, she pulled on a pair of rubber gloves she'd brought with her. Removing the clothing on top of the device, she lifted it out and held it for the first time. It was a little smaller than a kilo bag of sugar and a little lighter. It looked so harmless.

Luckily, the toilets hadn't been updated for several years, allowing her to remove the cistern lid and carefully place the device into the water at the bottom. She'd done some research and found that most cisterns held around five to six litres; the device took up the space of around three-quarters of a litre of water, meaning the toilet would still flush normally, so it was extremely unlikely to be discovered before it detonated.

Louise replaced the cistern lid with trembling hands and experienced a surge of fear at the sound of the lid settling into place. She then checked and double checked that the flushing mechanism still worked and made sure everything in the cubicle looked exactly the same as when she entered. She was now drenched in sweat and used toilet roll to wipe her forehead dry, using the flush yet again to wash away the paper. Leaving the toilet with one last look around, Louise composed herself and headed back downstairs.

By the time she passed Steve and Colin, Louise was feeling much calmer and managed a relieved smile, which was interpreted by them as the result of her loo stop.

'Thanks gents,' she said. 'That's much better.'

Steve waved her back through the scanner, which once again caused the alarm to sound.

'Take care, Mrs Greenacre. See you again soon.'

'Bye Miss,' added Colin.

Louise could feel herself shaking, something she hoped wasn't visible to anyone else; her legs felt like they were wading through treacle and could barely support her weight. She returned their smiles and walked through the door into the welcoming coolness of the street outside which made her feel instantly better. It was all over, she'd done it. She had completed her first solo mission. So far it had been a complete success, and she was ecstatic.

23

One Tree House, Pilgrim's Way, Otford, Kent
Saturday 2nd October 2027, 10.47am

'Lulu! Get in here quick!'

From the urgency in his voice, Louise knew that something dramatic must have happened and she had a good idea what that something might be. She rushed from the kitchen through to the conservatory, where she found Adam pacing backwards and forwards, speaking on his mobile phone. Feigning innocent interest, she went over to him.

'What's the matter?'

He didn't answer but waved his hand at the settee indicating for her to sit down. He was deep in conversation with someone.

'Is anyone hurt?' he asked, on the phone.

Louise could hear a female voice at the other end. Adam responded to whatever the woman was saying: 'Right... right... are the press there?' Again, she could hear the female voice, but was unable to make out her words. 'Okay, I'll be there as soon as possible... okay... thanks for calling.'

He ended the call, flopped down onto the settee alongside Louise and pulled his wife towards him.

Holding her close, he spoke directly into her ear.

'There's been an explosion at the office, up on the first floor somewhere. There's a huge amount of damage and I need to get there as quickly as possible.' He held her face in his hands. 'I don't want you to worry, but it looks like it might be a terrorist attack.'

Louise played the part of the shocked and supportive wife to perfection.

'Oh my goodness! Is anyone hurt?'

Despite her expression of concern, Louise's main feeling was actually one of deep satisfaction that the device had exploded as expected and was causing the disruption and disorder Harb Alsheueb had hoped for. She'd done her job, and done it well.

Adam looked grim.

'They don't know at the moment but two security guards are unaccounted for. Sorry darling, my car's been ordered. It'll be here in a few minutes and I need to get changed.' He kissed her bulging stomach.

She nodded and squeezed him tightly before letting him go.

'Take care darling.'

He tried to smile but she could see the worry and sadness in his eyes. He stood up and moved swiftly from the room and she could hear his footsteps running up the stairs and then the wardrobe door being slid open.

Louise relaxed back into the comfort of the settee and stared straight ahead, shaking with a mixture of nerves and excitement. Her gaze shifted to the scene outside the bi-folding doors, to their beautiful garden; it was her favourite view from the house and in the early autumn was a riot of colour. But she couldn't concentrate on the plants; all she could see was the moment she planted the device in the cistern, playing over and over in her head.

The thought suddenly hit her that if the missing security guards, Steve and Colin, were dead, that would make her a double killer. She imagined the devastation that would cause to their families and for the briefest of moments she felt a flicker of sympathy, but her training kicked in once more, erasing any feeling of shame or remorse, leaving her feeling nothing but pride in a job well done.

Adam raced back downstairs and Louise stood to meet him.

'My car's here. Don't wait up, I'll probably be needed all day and most of the night.'

He kissed her fleetingly on the lips, turned and almost ran through the hall and out of the front door to the drive. She followed him through the hallway and waved goodbye from the doorstep before quietly closing the door.

Back in the conservatory she opened a door leading into the garden and stepped outside, drawing a deep breath. Her mind was now calm. Harb Alsheueb would be pleased with her, but she was even more pleased with herself. Walking across the patio onto the lawn, she turned to look at their wonderful house.

She knew how lucky she was to live in such a beautiful place; how much she loved her husband, and that he loved her; she knew the action she'd taken was not only against the law, but was also against everything she had been brought up to believe in; more importantly though, she knew that her planting of the device, along with whatever damage and injury it had caused, was for a greater good. She felt at peace.

24

Whitehall, London
Saturday 2nd October 2027, 12.15 pm

Adam stepped from his ministerial car outside Temple Underground Station.

'That's the closest I can get you Minister,' said the driver. 'The whole of Whitehall, The Houses of Parliament, and most of the surrounding roads are on lockdown according to the radio.'

'Thanks for trying, Martin. I'll walk from here.'

He set off along the Thames Embankment, turning right up Northumberland Avenue towards Whitehall Place. The air was pleasantly warm as he hurried through the hordes of people, some going about their ordinary business, others converging to find out more about the events unfolding nearby.

Ten minutes later he was joined by his personal secretary Stuart Quigley at the outer police cordon, 150 metres from the site of the explosion. Despite showing their parliamentary and ministerial passes, they were prevented from going any further. The young police officer explained that the whole area was now a crime scene and access to the area could only be granted by the senior investigating officer. He radioed for a more senior officer to attend and speak with the minister.

Five minutes later, Adam heard the words 'Mr Greenacre?' He turned and saw a middle-aged man in a smart blue suit, who had approached from inside the cordon, leading Adam to assume he was a police officer. The man extending a hand to Adam was slim and clean shaven, with a face that gave little away.

'Yes, I'm Adam Greenacre,' he replied. 'And you are?'

'Detective Chief Superintendent Mark Dawes from Counter Terrorism Command. I'm the OIC here.'

'Pleased to meet you.'

'Thank you for coming down, Minister. How were you made aware of the incident?'

'I was called by a member of my staff. She was heading out for a day's shopping with friends, heard the explosion and ran to see what had happened. She saw my department building with all the windows blown out.'

'Ah yes, we've spoken with her.' He checked inside a small notebook he was holding. 'Samantha Berkeley, am I right?'

Adam nodded, 'Yes, that's her. She seemed very shaken. Is she okay?'

'She's fine, Minister. One of my officers has taken her to Charing Cross Police Station to complete a statement.' He became thoughtful, then asked quietly, 'How well do you know the security staff in the building Mr Greenacre?'

'Please, call me Adam.'

'Okay. How well do you know the security staff in the building, Adam?'

'I know them pretty well. They work a shift system, earlies, lates, and nights, so over time I've bumped into all of them several times.' He frowned, wondering where this was leading. 'Why do you ask?'

The detective looked Adam in the eye.

'I'm afraid we've found the body of a female in security officer uniform, and a male security officer has been taken to St Thomas's hospital. His left leg was blown off just above the knee, he's likely to lose his right hand, and he has multiple fractures.'

This struck Adam like a thunderbolt. He didn't know the security staff well, but they'd all been pleasant enough to him since he'd become the minister and had become part of his daily routine. He shook his head, 'How the fuck could someone do this?'

Dawes sighed. 'I've been dealing with terrorist incidents for eight years Minister, and one thing I still haven't worked out, is why apparently normal people become capable of committing atrocities like this.'

He stood looking up at the buildings towering around him before continuing, 'Minister, please follow me. The press are gathering and I'm certain they'll have plenty of questions for us both. Please be careful where you're walking. There's debris everywhere and the entire building and surrounding area is now a crime scene.'

Adam and Stuart were led through the cordon and up Whitehall Place to the front corner main entrance of the building. The damage from the explosion was suddenly apparent; it was extensive with almost every window broken on the lower two floors. Adam looked over towards the main entrance. There was rubble on the stairs where a wall appeared to have been blown out and part of the ceiling was hanging down, giving an unnerving view through to an office on the first floor at a twenty-degree angle.

They were led through to the outer cordon on Whitehall, where three TV crews, several journalists, and a separate pen of photographers were gathered, together with dozens of members of the public.

On seeing DCS Dawes and Adam, the journalists appeared to lose all sense of decorum, launching a barrage of questions, shouting each other down, desperately trying to be heard. The police press officer on scene calmed the situation, assured them that they would all get their chance then pointed to a female journalist on the front row, who became the first to pose a question.

'Detective Chief Superintendent, do you have any idea what the cause of this explosion was?'

Dawes pulled his shoulders back. 'It seems almost certain that it was some kind of improvised explosive device. Our forensic teams will be carrying out a thorough investigation but because we have a rough idea where the seat of the blast was, I can confirm that we are treating this as a possible terrorist incident.'

A male TV reporter asked, 'Where exactly was the seat of the blast and can you give details of casualties?'

'The seat of the explosion was on the first floor, somewhere inside the ladies' toilet. We're currently unable to say exactly whereabouts in the toilet, which was quite large with four cubicles and two hand basins. I'm unable to give precise details of casualties, but I can confirm there has been at least one fatality.'

A female TV reporter raised her hand and was pointed at by the press officer.

'Minister, if this is a terrorist incident, does that suggest that security at your department was unduly lax?'

Adam replaced Dawes at the microphone.

'Security is very tight at the Department for International Trade, as it is in all government buildings. Everyone attending has to empty out their pockets and have their bags searched, then they pass through security scanners, just like going through departures at an airport.'

The reporter persisted, 'Then how did the device get through?'

Dawes took control once more.

'The investigation is only just beginning. It's impossible for the minister to answer that question. Hopefully, we'll be able to provide you with more answers in a few days.'

The questions continued for twenty further minutes, before the press officer called a halt to proceedings. Dawes led Adam and Stuart down to a forward control vehicle, resembling a large silver pod. They climbed the steps to enter. Once inside, Dawes indicated for them to take a seat either side of a tiny table, then moved to a small kitchenette area and made coffee with hot water from a large urn.

Adam looked around; there were three uniformed officers monitoring a bank of screens and consuls, one of them was an Inspector, and it was he who was directing police units to their postings by radio.

Placing the drinks on the table in front of Adam and Stuart, Dawes sat down alongside them.

'Please call me Mark, I can't stand formality.'

They both nodded, and Adam took a sip from his cup. 'What happens now, Mark?'

Dawes' face was expressionless.

'I'm afraid I have several difficult questions for you both. Are you happy to crack straight on with answering them now, or would you rather wait until later?'

Adam looked at Stuart and said, 'I'm happy to get on with it, what about you?'

Stuart nodded. 'Yes, now is fine.'

'That's great. Firstly, have you employed any new members of staff in the past few weeks?'

'No,' answered Stuart. 'The newest arrival has been the Minister and he's been with us over a year.'

Dawes noted down the answer. 'What about CCTV, where is the hard drive located?'

Stuart answered again. 'In a basement room that's only accessed by myself, my deputy, or the security supervisor.'

'What's the coverage like?'

'The whole of the exterior, inside the main entrance and part of the ground floor.'

'So, we should be able to recover the recordings?'

Nodding, Stuart said, 'No problem. An explosion on the first floor won't have damaged anything in the basement.'

Dawes again noted down the answer then turned to Adam.

'Have you received any threats in the past few weeks?'

'No, nothing at all.'

'Can you think of anyone who might wish you harm?'

'No... why are you asking this? Surely the attack was on a government building, not on me personally?'

'In all probability yes, but you're the head of that department, so why have they targeted your building, over any other government department?'

'I've no idea... random selection?'

Dawes shrugged, tilting his head to one side. 'It's possible, yes.'

A further fifteen minutes of questions and answers seemed to have satisfied Dawes, and he thanked them for their time.

Placing a hand on Dawes' elbow, Adam asked, 'When will we be allowed back into the department, Mark?'

'Not until it's been declared structurally safe and the forensic teams are finished. Sorry Adam, there's a huge amount of work to be done. It'll be several days at the very least.'

Having thanked Mark for everything he was doing, Adam and Stuart left the control vehicle and walked off towards Parliament, where Adam anticipated being busy all day and most of the evening, dealing with the fallout.

25

`One Tree House, Pilgrims Way, Otford, Kent`
`Sunday 3rd October 2027, 7.30am`

Closing down his computer, Adam walked through to the kitchen, filled the kettle with water and flicked the switch. He leaned back on his chair, stretched his aching limbs and rubbed his tired eyes. He'd been awake all night going through emails and posting on various social media platforms, which were buzzing with news, views and general discussion about the explosion. Everyone wanted to know Adam's thoughts, and everyone had a view of their own.

During the day he'd managed to squeeze in a short call to Louise, giving her brief details of what had happened, and reminding her that he would be very late home.

He eventually arrived home shortly after 1.50 in the morning, then decided to stay awake and work through the night. He needed to closely monitor what was happening, including updating the public via social media. There was nothing to be gained by waking Lulu and worrying her; in her condition, she needed all the sleep she could get. So he delayed speaking with her until taking in her morning coffee, which he would be doing in a few minutes' time.

The spoons chinked in the mugs as he stirred firstly his own coffee, then his wife's. He removed two slices of bread from the toaster, buttered them then smothered them in marmalade, just how she liked it. *This will earn a few brownie points,* he thought, *she loves breakfast in bed.* He lifted the tray and quietly crept up the stairs.

'Good morning darling, rise and shine.' Adam stood over her carrying the breakfast tray.

Louise was half awake. She hadn't slept well, which was hardly surprising considering she'd caused an explosion at her husband's place of work, and had been following the story throughout the previous day. Yawning loudly, she sat up and stretched her arms above her head.

'Good morning, how was everything last night?' She patted the duvet, gesturing for him to place the breakfast tray over her lap.

He gave her a tired smile, handed her the tray and sat down beside her.

'The department has been badly damaged. A female security officer is dead and another is so badly injured they'll be affected for the rest of their life.'

It was roughly what Louise had been expecting. She'd always known that her involvement might result in her being responsible for the suffering of others. She wasn't too bothered about having murdered someone, but was a little surprised to find herself feeling a twinge of sympathy for the injured security guard.

She managed to produce a tear or two. 'I know. I've seen the news reports, isn't it awful. Their poor families, how are they coping?'

Adam realised, to his shame, that having been busy dealing with the fallout from the bombing for nearly twenty-four hours, he hadn't really considered the families of victims. He'd assumed the police family liaison officers would handle that type of thing.

'I've no idea, I'll try finding out this morning.'

Louise sipped her hot coffee, enabling her to mask her true feelings and manufacture some more convincing tears.

'Have you been up all night?'

He rubbed his tired eyes with the palms of his hands.

'Yes, and I'll be required for interviews all day. Not only that, but the police want to speak with me again.'

'Why?'

'I don't know. Come to that, I wouldn't be surprised if the PM wanted to speak to me again, too. He had me in for twenty minutes yesterday, wanting to know chapter and verse.'

'Why don't you try getting a couple of hours' sleep now? You'd feel much better for it.'

She wiped the tears away with the sleeve of her nightdress and reached for a tissue on the bedside table. Keeping up the pretence of shock and grief was proving harder than she'd imagined, but keep it up she must.

'Sorry love, I haven't got time to sleep. My car's coming at 8.30 and I probably won't be home again until late.'

He leaned forward, held her tight and kissed her on the cheek. 'Don't worry. Adrenalin and bucket-loads of coffee will keep me going. I'll be fine.'

She held his embrace, her mind spinning. It was the first time she had truly experienced the strain of the double life she was leading. She loved Adam so much and so deeply, yet she'd carried out a terrorist attack on his place of work. The place where he was respected and trusted, where he was the Minister, the boss.

However, Harb Alsheueb would be delighted with her, and Allah would be sending his blessings cascading down from heaven. She must love Allah above any person, that's what her training had taught her, and she honestly believed that her planting of the device had been for the furtherance of his glory.

26

SO15 Headquarters, Bayswater Road, London
Monday 4th October 2027, 9.00am

Detective Chief Superintendent Mark Dawes climbed onto the slightly raised stage and stood facing the packed briefing room. They were gathered at SO15's brand new operational headquarters building, Virginia Square, in response to the terrorist attack two days before.

'Good morning ladies and gentlemen, thank you for your attendance.' He paced slowly backwards and forwards before addressing the hushed assembly.

'The attack on the Department for International Trade on Saturday came completely out of the blue. I have had extensive discussions over the weekend with MI5, and they assured me they had received no intelligence whatsoever to indicate a potential attack. I don't need to tell you how unusual that is. There is normally intel pouring in from informants, or a raised level of electronic communication between suspects on watch lists before such an attack. Not on this occasion, though.'

A young detective Sergeant opened the briefing room door, looking terribly embarrassed as he slipped in. He moved quickly around the edge of the room and stood leaning against the wall at the back of the room, concealing himself as well as possible behind colleagues.

DCS Dawes glared at him, looking more than a little irritated.

'DS May, thank you for your attendance, but when I say the briefing is at nine, it means nine, not two minutes past. For goodness sake, we're investigating a terrorist attack. See me in my office afterwards.'

DS May looked suitably chastised.

'Yes sir. I'm really sorry sir, I missed my train.'

Dawes ignored the apology and continued speaking. 'Over 1,300 people work in the Department for International Trade, around 200 of them are trade negotiators for the UK government. Despite it being an incredibly important location, CCTV only covers the building's exterior, the main entrance lobby, and a few corridors on the ground floor.' He leaned forward, lifted his cup and sipped his tea, before saying, 'DCI Gravely.'

Malcolm Gravely was a sunny natured detective who had been born in Trinidad and Tobago. Despite having lived in the UK for over 20 years, he had retained his strong West Indian accent. He looked up from his note taking.

'Yes sir?'

'You will head up Team 1. Your team will be responsible for obtaining, reviewing, and evidencing where necessary, all CCTV from the Department of International Trade, plus any other CCTV within a 100-metre radius, is that understood?'

Gravely looked distinctly unimpressed with his posting, but nevertheless dutifully said, 'Yes, sir.'

Pursing his lips, Dawes started tapping the knuckles of his clenched fist on the table in front of him, his gaze sweeping from left to right across every person in the room then back again.

'Ladies and gents, we are almost certainly looking at an inside job.' He stopped tapping the table, and probed his right ear, as if clearing a blockage. 'By inside job, I mean that someone who works in the department or a member of the security staff must have helped the bomber to gain access. Even then it's baffling, because everyone who enters the building passes through the security scanner, which would have undoubtedly picked up the device.' He ran his fingers through his hair. 'DCI Jarvis.'

Mandy Jarvis raised her hand.

'Here, sir.'

Dawes smiled at the deceptively genial looking woman with grey hair sitting at the back of the room. They had been young officers together, then colleagues in SO15 for many years.

'You will head up Team 2. Your team will be responsible for running checks on all personnel in the department and all visitors to the building. I want their vetting status checked and double-checked. It's possible that a sleeper has slipped in under the radar,' he scratched his neck thoughtfully, 'and if that's the case, I want them traced as soon as possible. Is that clearly understood?' Dawes had no idea just how prophetic his words were.

Nodding her head, Jarvis said loudly and clearly, 'Yes, sir!

Dawes then called out, 'DCI Pope.'

Phil Pope, known as 'PP' to everyone, raised his hand. 'Here ,sir.'

'You will head up Team 3. Your team will carry out interviews on everyone who works in the building, starting with all security staff, moving on to departmental staff and finally all visitors we can trace who visited the building in the past month. Understood?'

Nodding, Pope said, 'Yes sir, I'll get right on it.'

Dawes moved back behind the table and pulled the chair out.

'Detective Superintendent Morris will now give details of casualties and damage, followed by a comprehensive intelligence update.' He nodded at Morris and sat down.

The mixed-race man in a crisply pressed black suit who now took centre stage was overweight but not obese, with spiky grey hair which were at odds with his shiny round face and double chin. Karl Morris turned to face the gathering with a warm smile, but this faded when he started speaking.

'The device exploded somewhere inside the ladies' toilet on the first floor. Initial forensic reports suggest it was probably housed inside one of the cisterns. This obviously raises several questions, the greatest of which is how the fuck did it get there? Not only did it get past the security guards, who search absolutely everyone, it also got through the security scanner which would definitely have picked it up.'

He rubbed a hand over his chin and down across his expansive jowls to his throat.

'There were two main casualties, a female security guard named Caroline Havers, aged thirty-seven, who was killed instantly as she patrolled outside the toilet door and a male security guard named Ian Harper, aged fifty-two. This poor sod had his left leg blown off above the knee, lost his right hand where it was severed by brick shrapnel, leaving it hanging off his wrist, and as if that weren't bad enough, he has four broken ribs, a shattered pelvis, and a broken right femur. He's currently critical, but expected to survive, although whether he will want to carry on living considering his injuries, is another matter entirely.'

There was an angry murmuring around the room

and several expletives could be clearly heard. Dawes scanned the room, not in a critical way but nodding his head in understanding. Morris gestured for his colleagues to calm down, then, once order was restored, continued speaking.

'In addition to the security guards patrolling on the first floor, two other guards at the main entrance received minor blast injuries and shock. There were also three female members of the public passing the building who were hospitalised after being hit by flying glass and debris. Luckily, they were not seriously injured and were allowed home after treatment. There were dozens of other members of the department working in the building at the time of the explosion, mainly in offices on the upper floors, but luckily no one was near the seat of the explosion. They all escaped without serious injury, although several suffered shock.'

He poured a glass of water from the jug on the table and took a gulp.

'Currently, we have no idea which group was behind the attack, but because it was almost certainly carried out with the assistance of someone working inside the department, or perhaps a frequent visitor, we don't believe this was a lone wolf. The Harb Alsheueb group are rapidly growing in size and capability and to my mind this has their M.O. written all over it.'

He breathed in deeply and walked from one corner of the room to the other.

'The interesting thing about this group, according to MI5, is that they don't believe in carrying out suicide bombings, running people down with motor vehicles, or maniacs armed with knives or guns shooting or stabbing pedestrians, which as you all know have been the preferred methods of attack for radical Islamic groups for many years.'

He wagged his finger from side to side. 'Oh no, Harb Alsheueb don't believe in those old-fashioned methods, they believe in using individuals to carry out attacks independently, having firstly received comprehensive training and instruction at one of their camps. They plant their devices then make good their escape, leaving them free to strike again in the future. It's a more risky but more cost-effective strategy.'

An officer raised his hand. Pointing at him, Morris said, 'Yes?'

'Sorry to interrupt sir, DI Dave Howarth, Parliamentary Protection. You were wondering how they gained access without being detected? Well, there are several access points over the rooftops of these old buildings. Have they been considered as possible entry points?'

'Good question. The short answer is yes, we are aware and they have been considered. They've all been checked and appear to have remained closed for several months, if not years. However, I'd be happy to speak with you privately immediately after this briefing, just in case your troops know something we don't.'

A female officer opened the door, 'Chief Superintendent Dawes, there's an urgent phone call for you sir.' Dawes climbed to his feet and left the room.

Morris continued, 'I'd wager a month's salary that Harb Alsheueb were behind this attack because it's got all their hallmarks,' he raised his eyebrows, 'but as you're all aware, I'm not infallible, and I've been way off the mark in the past.'

A small ripple of laughter swept through the officers, before silence engulfed the room once again. Dawes re-entered the room and took his seat.

Twenty minutes later, Morris finished his intelligence update. He'd gone through everything with a fine-toothed comb, leaving everyone in no doubt that this would be an extremely difficult investigation. However, he finished with an encouraging message.

'Assuming the bomber entered through the main entrance, they'll have been filmed on CCTV and that means we should be able to trace them.' He moved to the front of the stage and spoke with determination. 'The bastard who carried out this despicable and cowardly act will not get away with it. We will identify them and we will get justice for Caroline and Ian.'

Dawes rose to his feet, thanked Morris and addressed the officers once more.

'Don't forget people, someone who has easy access to that building is almost certainly responsible. Be diligent, be thorough and don't discount anyone, and I mean *anyone*. We're almost certainly looking for a sleeper, someone who's been activated after months, maybe years of waiting patiently. Any questions?'

The room fell silent, save for the sound of people picking up their papers and checking their mobile phones.

'Right, let's get to work.'

27

Charing Cross Police Station, London
Monday 4th October, 2.20 pm

Detective Sergeant Andy Taylor and Detective Constable Michelle White were part of Team 3, instructed to carry out interviews on everyone employed in the targeted building, as well as people who had visited in the past month. Their specific brief was to interview all security staff employed at the department by the security company H5T over the previous six months, including those who'd left the company in that time and any visitors who may have accessed the building without going through security.

Two of the H5T officers instructed to attend the police station to answer their questions were Steven Millerman and Colin Carson. They were waiting in a small side room on the ground floor of the Police Station and one of them was more than a little concerned about the questions he might face.

Steve looked down at his hands and twiddled his thumbs then slowly lifted his head to look at Colin.

'They'll be looking to screw one of the security staff over, you mark my words. The old bill will try their best to make it look like we allowed the bomber in.'

Colin shrugged. 'Stop worrying. We've nothing to hide so I don't know what you're getting in a flap about.'

His right knee jerking nervously, Steve's irritation was clearly showing.

'For fuck's sake Colin, what I'm trying to say is we're completely on offer here. How many times in the past when a major crime has been committed has the inside person turned out to be a security officer?'

Colin looked blankly back at Steve. 'So what? How the fuck does that make us on offer? We've done nothing wrong.'

Steve's exasperation was noticeable in his voice.

'You just don't get it, do you? The bomber must have come through security recently, which means the bomb came through security, too. Just think about it. Whenever there's been a terrorist attack or a robbery on a secure building in the past, it's nearly always a security guard that was the person on the inside, the person who enabled them access.'

'Agreed, but like I say, we've done nothing wrong.'

'Well, someone let the bomber in, and chances are it was one of our staff.'

'But we know everyone employed by H5T. You surely can't be suggesting one of them is in league with a terrorist!'

Steve shrugged. 'All I know is we're going to be questioned separately. We're going to face some very difficult questions, and we're going to be made to feel fucking uncomfortable.'

Colin leaned backwards on his chair. 'I can only think of three people we've let through the scanner without checking their bags or turning their pockets out. But if we admit that, it'll really piss off our bosses.'

Blowing out hard, Steve mirrored his colleague and rocked back on his own chair.

'It'll more than piss them off. We could be looking at disciplinary action, even the sack.'

'Maybe.'

Steve thought hard. 'I remember we let your sister straight through once when she was desperate for a wee, and I remember letting my cousin's teenage son Jake in when he'd popped in to say hello. He needed the toilet, too. Who was the third one?'

'Louise Greenacre, a couple of weeks ago. Remember, she was heavily pregnant and bursting for the loo just like my sister. We let her through without a proper search.'

Steve looked up to the ceiling, recalling the memory.

'Oh yeah. But you can't be suggesting the minister's wife was responsible, that's fucking ridiculous.'

'I'm not suggesting that, but there are thirty members of H5T staff employed in the department. We're only two of that thirty and we've let three *people* through in the last six months. How many more might the others have allowed through?'

'We can't deny letting any of them through, that would be completely fucking stupid. They'll be going through CCTV in detail so they'll be able to see for themselves whenever that's happened. Thank Christ I looked in Mrs Greenacre's bags, at least we can say for certain that the device wasn't in there.'

28

One Tree House, Pilgrim's Way, Otford, Kent
Thursday 7th October 2027, 10.00am

Louise opened the door and showed the two plain-clothes officers through to the lounge, where they sat down on the white leather settee and introduced themselves, insisting that she addressed them by their first names.

Adam had set off for work at six but before he left, he reassured a worried Louise that the police asking to speak with her was purely routine, as she had visited the department recently. She, of course, knew different; Adam's confidence was badly misplaced and they had very good reason to speak with her, they just weren't aware of it. Her husband may have been unworried, but for Louise this would be anything but routine.

Despite her conviction that she had done the right thing in planting the device, her nerves had been in shreds since she'd received a phone call the previous day from the investigating team, stating they wanted to question her about visits to her husband's department. The brainwashing she had received may have relieved her of any concerns about the rightness of her actions, but it didn't stop her worrying about their consequences. She emphatically did not want to go to prison.

Louise, however, had so far managed to maintain her composure.

'Would either of you like a cup of something?'

Despite her best efforts, Louise's voice had a distinct wobble in it, a fact which was not missed by Detective Sergeant Andy Taylor.

'I'd love a coffee please.' He leaned forward. 'Are you okay Mrs Greenacre?'

Fighting to control herself, Louise forced a smile and said cheerily, 'I'm fine thanks. It's just that I've never been interviewed by the police before, and I've certainly never been questioned about something so important. I think the nerves have got to me.'

Detective Constable Michelle White gave her a sympathetic smile.

'You've nothing to worry about, Mrs Greenacre. We're just here to ask you a few questions about your past visits to your husband's department, that's all. We'll be out of your hair in around half an hour, is that okay?'

Lifting herself out of her armchair Louise nodded.

'Of course, that's fine. I'll pop to the kitchen and make your drinks. Sorry, I didn't hear what you wanted, Michelle.'

'Coffee please, neither of us take sugar.'

'I won't be a minute,' replied Louise cheerily, then made her way through to the kitchen. Once safely out of sight, she leaned heavily on the worktop and breathed out hard. Despite her best efforts, nerves were getting the better of her; her hand was shaking so much that she had trouble spooning coffee into the mugs.

Five minutes later she returned to the lounge with three steaming mugs of coffee. She'd used her time alone in the kitchen to regain control of her emotions and settle herself down.

'Here you are.' She handed each officer a mug. 'Now then, how can I help you?'

Michelle opened a folder, flicked over a couple of pages, carefully perused whatever was written, then looked across at Louise.

'How many times have you visited your husband's department, Mrs Greenacre?'

'Please, call me Louise.'

Michelle said, 'Okay then, Louise.'

Louise paused a moment, as if to recall the details.

'I've visited three times. The first time was when Adam got promoted to Minister. He was so excited about his new position and wanted to show me around. The next time I went there to meet him as he finished his morning's work, and we went to lunch together.'

The nerves began to build again, as she came closer to the subject of her final visit. Her mind was playing tricks, telling her that the officers knew more than they were letting on. Did they know about the training camps in Afghanistan? Did they know about her meetings with Sulayman? Had they been monitoring her emails? Had they been following her? How much did they actually know? The pressure was building inside her head, and she could feel the beginning of a migraine, but she was determined to remain outwardly calm. Pulling herself together, she said, 'The final time was about two weeks ago.'

Michelle quickly pounced on the fact that Louise hadn't expanded on this comment.

'What was the purpose of your visit on that occasion?'

Louise understood why they were interested in her latest visit and replied confidently, 'I'd got an hour of downtime at work, and needed some fresh air. Adam had left his pen behind, so I thought I'd walk over, hoping to catch him before he left.'

Michelle looked confused. 'Left for where?'

Louise's mouth was dry. She picked up her cup, sipped her coffee as casually as she could manage, and gently placed it back down on the coaster.

'He was going to Birmingham on a trade conference. It was his biggest international conference since becoming a Minister, so I thought I'd drop his pen off. It's a bit of a lucky talisman for him.'

Michelle nodded. 'A nice idea. Did you go through security and up to his office?'

Louise could feel herself getting hotter. This was a leading question. It felt like they were stalking her - wolves slowly moving in for the kill. Were they intending to arrest her? Would she be leaving her house in handcuffs? Taking steady breaths to regain her composure, she said, 'He wasn't there, he'd left before I'd arrived.'

The detectives exchanged glances. Michelle was busily taking down notes, so Andy Taylor used her silence to take over the questioning.

'So you had no reason to enter the building, is that correct?'

He leaned forward, staring pointedly. Louise smiled, calmly took another drink and spoke with phony laughter in her voice.

'It's a bit embarrassing, but I was absolutely bursting for the loo.' She patted her swollen belly. 'In my condition when you've got to go, you've *really* got to go!'

Grinning and nodding at her reply, Andy asked, 'Were you searched, and did you and your possessions go through the scanners on each visit?'

Louise paused again as if to recall exactly what had happened.

'On the first two occasions yes, but on my recent

visit they felt sorry for me because I was so desperate.' Once again, she gave the appearance of accessing her memory. 'I remember my bags being checked, but I wasn't physically searched, and my possessions didn't go on the conveyor. Everything went through the body scanner though.'

Both officers picked up their cups simultaneously and sipped their coffees. Andy lifted his chin in a clear instruction to Michelle and she responded by taking over the questioning once more.

'So, you went to the ladies' toilet. I assume you used the one nearest to the main entrance?'

Louise nodded. 'Yes, that's right.'

'Where is that?'

'It's on the first floor. Up the stairs, turn left, first door on your right.'

'Has your husband made you aware that the first-floor ladies' toilet was where the bomb exploded?'

Louise swallowed, feeling quite nauseous. These questions sounded designed to lead her into a trap.

'Yes, he's told me everything about the explosion.'

Andy leaned forward once again.

'Think hard now, Louise. Did you see anything that looked out of place in the toilet? Did you see anything that looked unusual? Or perhaps you noticed something that looked as though it had been tampered with?'

Blinking almost continuously, Louise was working hard to prevent herself from bursting into tears.

'No, it looked like any other toilet. There was nothing unusual about it.'

'Was there anybody else in the toilet?'

'Yes, a rather plump woman washing her hands.'

'Did you recognise her?'

'No, I'd never met her before.'

This appeared to catch the interest of both officers

and Andy shuffled slightly on the settee.

'Could you describe her?'

This time Louise really was forcing herself to remember.

'Like I said, she was rather plump, about fifty, quite short, and had short red hair with flecks of grey in it.'

Michelle was scribbling down the description furiously. Looking up, she asked, 'What was she wearing?'

Louise screwed up her eyes as she recalled the woman's clothing.

'A blue trouser suit I think, with a white blouse.'

'Was she behaving oddly at all?'

This was an excellent opportunity to throw them off the scent, and she grabbed it with both hands.

'Actually, I found her behaviour a little unnerving.'

Michelle asked, 'In what way was it unnerving?'

'She kept staring at me in the mirror. It was all rather weird.'

Once again, the detectives exchanged glances.

'Did she say anything?' asked Andy.

'Yes. She asked when my baby was due and whether it was a boy or girl.'

'Anything else?'

'She said something about how much joy her children had given her then dried her hands and left.'

Andy changed the direction of questioning.

'How many cubicles were there in the toilet?'

'Four as far as I can recall... yes, I'm fairly certain it was four.'

'And which one did you use?'

Louise had been anticipating this question and was ready for it.

'The end one on the right, the one nearest the sinks. Why? Is that important?'

'No reason. We just need to make certain we've got all the details right.'

Smiling inwardly, Louise knew she had just won a small battle. However, the toilet was the location where the bomb exploded, and having visited it meant she would have to remain a suspect along with everyone else for a while. That was something she would just have to live with. The important thing was that she'd done her duty for Islam, and for Harb Alsheueb. She could live with feeling uncomfortable and being under suspicion because it was unlikely they could ever prove it was her.

Michelle continued the questioning.

'Do you know who the security officers were on duty at the front entrance when you entered on the most recent occasion?'

'I only know them as Steve and Colin.'

The questions continued for a further fifteen minutes, but Louise gradually began to feel easier about how the interview was going and started to relax. She had successfully deflected their questions and was rather pleased with herself. When they eventually finished, Louise walked them to the door where they thanked her for her time, got into their car and drove away.

After closing the front door, Louise walked through to the conservatory and sat looking at the family photos on a large wall collage. Her supreme confidence in her own abilities had taken a severe knock. She'd managed to see the police off on this occasion, but would they now be looking deeper into her past? The thought that they might start asking serious questions regarding her year in Afghanistan filled her with dread. This had been her first involvement in solo direct action, yet she was already under suspicion and being questioned in her own home. Any further operations would surely only increase the spotlight on her.

Ten minutes later, she began to think more rationally, her training once again giving her reassurance. No matter how much the police interview had unsettled her, it was worth it: she had done her duty, completed her mission and fulfilled the orders from Harb Alsheueb. Allah would be delighted.

Someone had died and someone had been dreadfully maimed because of her, but those facts were not her concern. The shockwaves it sent through the British Establishment would eventually provoke a response, which was precisely what Harb Alsheueb intended. She had become convinced that the suffering of the victims and their families, no matter how terrible that had been, was a price worth paying. She wasn't upset and felt no remorse, she was simply proud of how well her first operation had gone.

29

Golden Square, London
Thursday 23rd March 2028, 12.15pm

Louise returned to work after only six months on maternity leave. She reasoned that Harb Alsheueb would be far more likely to contact her once she'd resumed her normal routine. Adam was surprised by her keenness to return, but they could easily afford a nanny, so he hadn't questioned her decision too much. One week later she'd received the expected email from Haasim, requesting a meeting.

Sulayman approached in the spring sunshine from the opposite side of the square. He smiled and nodded from ten metres away, then walked over and sat beside her on a bench.

'What can I say? Great job last year.'

Despite the praise, Louise couldn't suppress a sense of irritation. She'd not heard a word from the organisation since the attack.

'That was nearly six months ago and I haven't heard a thing from anyone since.'

He held up his hands defensively.

'You knew you'd only be contacted when necessary. You were told from the start it would be infrequent.'

She shook her head, unimpressed.

'I put my life and liberty on the line, then I get ignored!'

He gave her a sympathetic look. 'I understand, and I've been instructed to pass on the gratitude and good wishes of Harb Alshueub. You have proved yourself a very capable soldier.'

Her hostility softened.

'Well, it's a little late in coming but thanks anyway.' She shifted uneasily on the bench. 'So, why the sudden need for a meeting today?'

Sulayman ignored her question and appeared to be looking at a young couple crossing the square.

'By the way, congratulations on the birth of your little boy. How old is he now?'

'Oliver's four and a half months. He was born on 3rd November. What's that got to do with anything?'

'There are rumours that Adam could be considered for a top post soon, is that right?'

She could sense the possibility of another operation and her former annoyance was replaced by mounting excitement.

'Yes, it might not happen for a year or two, though. Why?'

'Our bosses were very happy with your work. It caused precisely the disruption, uncertainty and chaos they were hoping for,' he brushed some tree blossom from his thigh, 'and they now have another deployment in mind for you.'

Louise's eyes widened. Sulayman continued to look into the distance.

'You seem very settled back in the UK and you're happily married with a baby. Do you think you're still capable of completing another operation?'

She was shocked that he'd even asked the question

and nodded vigorously.

'Definitely. I love Adam and Ollie, but that's different. There's no greater love than my love for God.'

He raised a hand in acceptance of her loyalty.

'You are a true follower of Islam and a very brave lady.' He turned to stare at her. 'Are you ready to hear the details, or would you like time to think about this?'

She hadn't anticipated this but wasn't going to pass up the opportunity of hearing more about the operation.

'I want to know.'

'Do you remember the 7/7 bombings in 2005?'

'Of course, everyone in this country remembers them. Three tube trains and one bus were blown up and there were over fifty fatalities. It was one of the biggest attacks by any terrorist group on the British mainland.'

He looked impressed, raising his eyebrows in surprise.

'That's right, you've been doing your research. But never mind the British mainland, it was one of the most successful operations anywhere in the history of direct action. It made all western governments sit up and take notice for many years afterwards.'

Louise looked concerned. 'But... those men were suicide bombers! You're surely not suggesting I kill myself!'

Laughing, he said, 'Things have moved on since then. There won't be anyone committing suicide in these bombings. We've learned it causes far more disruption when operatives survive. It causes havoc with Counter Terrorism Command and the security services. Knowing that perpetrators are still out there after they've carried out an attack really does their heads in.'

'Bombings? You said bombings. So, they're planning more than one explosion?'

'Yes.' He paused for a moment as a couple holding

hands walked past within earshot then once they were clear he continued, 'There will be six explosions over a two-hour period. The devices will be planted in six shopping centres by six operatives, in six separate locations throughout England.'

A ripple of excitement tingled down her spine. This time the purpose was not only maximum disruption but maximum casualties. She had always known that people dying could be a necessary consequence of her actions, yet some strange force inside told her she still wanted to carry out the deployment. After all, she'd been responsible for the deaths of three people already.

'How big will the device be?'

He held up his hands fifteen centimetres apart. 'A little under a kilo. The same as the one at Adam's department.'

'Will I be expected to work with anyone else?'

'No, the thinking these days is that all operatives work individually which ensures that if one is caught, the others should still get through and complete their missions. If they are subsequently interrogated, they will have no knowledge of anyone, apart from their own handler.'

'When will the operation take place?'

'Friday 5th May. We thought they'd appreciate the symmetry. The last set of multiple bombings were on 7/7, these will be on 5/5.'

Nerves were beginning to kick in but her curiosity overcame them.

'Where would I be expected to plant mine, I mean, in which shop?'

'Your choice, but we thought somewhere around here. Maybe Regent Street or Oxford Street, somewhere to make maximum impact.'

He brushed away some more blossom from his arm

and turned his gaze to her.

'You should be aware that there's plenty of CCTV in the area, so you'll need to completely alter your appearance again, but you've already proved you can manage that, haven't you?'

She thought back to her disguise when dealing with Sarah Cairn.

'Yes.' Changing the subject, she asked, 'Is there any further news about that?'

He shook his head. 'No, it's all calmed down now. I think you can forget about being arrested for that one. We've even managed to keep our operative inside MI5 following their internal investigation.'

Louise had a minor problem with the proposed date.

'May 5th is a working day for me and I haven't got any annual leave left. What time of day are we talking about?'

'Lunch time. Your device will be the first to explode, it will detonate at 1.30. The others will be every twenty minutes after that. Sorry Louise, you'll have to think of an excuse for work.'

Sulayman rose to his feet and inclined his head to one side. She stood up and walked alongside him around the square.

'Each operative will be handed their device at a nearby location. In your case, you'll be picked up by a black cab from outside the front of St Martins-in-the-Fields at one o'clock. The device will be on the rear seat of the cab.'

'That doesn't leave me long, does it?'

'The timer will be set to detonate thirty minutes after you collect it, so you won't have much time to get to wherever you've decided to deploy it. Then you'll need to conceal it without being seen and get as far away as possible before it explodes.'

Louise was worried about the shortness of the timer.

'The last timer had a nine-day delay so why does this have such a short one?'

'If it's planted in Regent Street or Oxford Street the shop is likely to be very busy. It won't be hidden in a cistern like before and the chances of it being discovered on the shop floor are too high for a long delay.'

Looking at her watch, she nodded her understanding.

'Okay, I'll be fine. I'm excited and honoured that Harb Alsheueb are trusting me again but I can't pretend it doesn't scare me.'

He kicked a stick off the footpath in front of him.

'There's one more thing you need to know.'

'Okay, but hurry up, I need to get back to work.'

'Once this deployment is concluded, there will be another long break before you are used again.'

'If they've got five other operatives, why are they using me on this operation?'

'Because you've already proved you're capable of carrying out a deployment without being caught. Some of the other operatives are untested.'

'Okay, and after this operation?'

'They want to leave you sleeping while Adam continues up the parliamentary ladder.'

'He's already Minister for International Trade. He's already in the cabinet, what more are they hoping for?'

He shrugged. 'I've no idea, let's wait and see.'

It was blindingly obvious to Louise that they had a specific plan in mind, but weren't prepared to give her the details.

'Okay. When the time comes, I'll be ready and I'll do whatever is required.' She glanced at her watch. 'Look, I'm running late, I've really got to go.'

Sulayman nodded and smiled. 'Assalamu Alaikum.'

She placed her right hand in the centre of her chest. 'Wa Alaikum Assalam.'

'Bye Louise.' He waved an arm in the air as he departed.

As Louise rushed from the square and walked swiftly back to work, her mind was turning cartwheels.

30

St Martin's-in-the-Fields Church, London
Friday 5th May 2028, 1.00pm

The woman in the long green dress and short cream coat was spotted by the taxi driver, who pulled up alongside the kerb at the bottom of the steps leading down from the church. She carried a large tan handbag and a plain plastic carrier bag; on her head she was wearing a Salmon coloured hijab and her eyes were hidden behind black thick-rimmed spectacles. Louise had left work at 12.20, walked quickly to Trafalgar Square then made use of the ladies' toilets in the Crypt Café underneath St Martin's-in-the-Fields Church to change into her disguise.

She deliberately lingered for fifteen minutes inside the cubicle, to ensure that anyone who had seen her enter the toilet dressed as Louise Greenacre wasn't still around to witness her leaving dressed as an Islamic woman. Once out of the cubicle, she kept the front of her hijab pulled modestly forward, trying her very best to hide her features from any CCTV cameras once she walked outside.

She felt a wonderful sense of relief to be dressed as a Muslim woman again. This was her first chance to dress and feel the way she wanted since she'd left Afghanistan and one day she hoped to be able to wear Islamic clothes all the time.

The taxi driver waved away a group of French tourists, who were eagerly inquiring at the front passenger side window whether he was available for hire and beckoned her over.

'Louise?'

She looked uneasily around, fearful of being heard, and nodded.

He unlocked the rear doors and she climbed inside. She immediately noticed the small package on the back seat, wrapped in dark brown paper and covered with clingfilm. Sitting down beside it, she thanked the grossly overweight driver for being on time and said urgently, 'Regent Street, as quickly as you can please.'

Her nerves were jangling; this operation was much higher risk than her first deployment but she was determined to do her duty.

'I'll drop you off at the Piccadilly Circus end. The traffic's not too bad so we should be there in five or ten minutes.'

The weather was chilly for the time of year, with dark clouds rolling angrily across the sky but fortunately it hadn't started raining. Despite the temperature, Louise had begun to perspire on the short walk up Whitehall and felt embarrassed about the faint scent of body odour she was sure was emanating from her. She had experienced a similar sensation during her previous assignment. Perspiring like this was unusual for her, and was a clear sign of her nerves.

Since the meeting with Sulayman six weeks ago, Louise had experienced a mixture of anticipation and deep unease. Getting a decent night's sleep had proved difficult and she had been unusually short tempered with work colleagues. She'd managed to remain calm around

Adam and Ollie, although there had been a couple of occasions when Adam had asked if she was all right, saying that she was being rather quiet.

The reasons for her broken sleep varied. Sometimes she heard the faintest whisper of someone talking while she was in bed and, although she couldn't make out the words like last time, she was certain the voice belonged to Sarah Cairn. On two separate occasions she was convinced she'd glimpsed Ismail looking at her through a crowd, once outside Westminster Underground Station and once on the Strand. On both occasions she had frozen to the spot but when she looked again, he'd gone. Then there was the recurring dream which haunted many of her nights. She was back in the training camp in Afghanistan, when she noticed that one of the instructors was a face she knew well: it was Millie. Each time something like this happened, she had to snap herself back to reality and tell herself that her real training would triumph.

She pulled the sleeves of her coat down over her hands, and picked up the parcel, placing it gently into her handbag. Just doing this made her feel sick with apprehension, fully aware that she was now responsible for an object with the capacity to kill dozens of people, an object that would detonate in less than thirty minutes.

Questions had been chasing each other through her mind since she'd woken up that morning. Would the device be stable? Had the timer been set correctly? What if the operation had been infiltrated by the security services?

Now she was sitting with the lethal object by her side, and the questions remained unanswered.

Louise brought herself back to the present and gazed out of the window, as the taxi drew into the kerb close to the junction of Regent Street and Piccadilly Circus. It was ten past one. She leaned in through the front passenger window to thank the driver with a noticeable quiver in her voice.

'Wish me luck.'

The driver merely shrugged and grunted.

'Listen lady, I'm just happy that parcel is someone else's problem now.' His forehead was dotted with beads of sweat, but on seeing the fear on Louise's face, he softened and smiled.

'You're a very brave lady. May God shower his blessings upon you.'

With that, he put the vehicle into gear and pulled away.

Sucking in a couple of deep breaths, Louise fought hard to calm herself and control the shaking in her hands. Looking at her watch, she saw it was 1.12, meaning the device would detonate in only eighteen minutes, possibly slightly earlier, possibly slightly later. Finding a decent location, placing it there, then getting as far away as possible, all had to be accomplished by then; she certainly didn't have time to waste on nerves.

Louise walked swiftly up the great curve of Regent Street, heading towards Oxford Circus. She kept the covering of her hijab well forward on her face, her head looking down at the pavement to avoid full-face images being recovered from CCTV at a later date.

As Regent Street's curve straightened out at the junction with Vigo Street, she spotted a very large ladies clothing shop on the right-hand side. She had never heard of the store before, which appeared to be brand new. The sign above the shop said 'Clothes Bazaar' and it looked extremely busy, with dozens of customers eagerly checking through the shelves and rails inside.

Holding her shoulders back and fighting the urge to drop the device into a bin and run for her life, she crossed the road at the traffic lights, walked twenty metres towards Oxford Circus and stepped from the pavement into the warmth of the shop.

Louise moved swiftly to the rear of the store, taking care not to draw any attention to herself and soon located the perfect place for hiding the device. A box unit of open-ended shelves against a wall had piles of tee shirts in various colours and sizes on each shelf, which would make it easy for her to conceal the device at the rear of one of the piles. Checking around, she waited until nobody was nearby, then feigned interest in a navy-blue tee shirt, holding it against her body and checking it for size.

She then used the garment to carefully remove the device from her handbag, and covertly wrapped the device inside it, placing it behind a pile of tee shirts on the shelf. It was completely hidden from view and unless six or seven navy-blue tee shirts were selected in the next ten minutes, it would remain hidden until it exploded. She looked at her watch: it was 1.21, leaving only nine minutes to get clear.

A sheen of sweat had formed on her forehead, which she wiped away using the sleeve of her coat. What if the device exploded early? Her legs were decidedly unsteady, her breathing had become ragged and her thought process foggy and unclear, but her training and instincts kicked in and Louise walked out of the store, all the while remembering to keep her head down, making sure the hijab was pulled forward to obscure her face.

Having crossed at the traffic lights to the opposite pavement, she continued along Vigo Street, before turning left into Burlington Arcade, which led down a gentle incline to Piccadilly. Once there, she crossed the road and turned right, heading for Green Park.

As she approached the park gates, there was a loud

thud in the distance and she felt the ground vibrate; she knew beyond doubt that the device had detonated. Her heart soared to know she had completed her second mission and although she was well aware that she had caused untold pain and suffering, she felt immensely proud of herself. She had done her duty and would undoubtedly receive Allah's blessing because of it.

The weather was deteriorating and light rain had begun to fall. Once inside the park, Louise moved towards an area near the centre of the park where she had observed, on a lunch hour visit three weeks previously, there was no CCTV. Finding a quiet spot underneath a tree heavy in leaf didn't prove too difficult. As the rainfall gradually increased, the park, although still fairly busy, was rapidly emptying. The tree she had selected provided plenty of cover, both from the downpour and prying eyes.

Louise checked around to make sure she couldn't be seen through the overhanging branches. Once happy that she was well hidden, she quickly removed the hijab, took off the cream coat, and detached the bottom half of the dress, which she had prepared by cutting it in two around the waist and securing it with Velcro. This revealed a knee length red skirt, which she'd been wearing underneath her dress. She then removed the spectacles and placed everything into a blue carrier bag that she produced from her handbag.

From the white carrier bag, she took a red, three quarter length hooded coat that perfectly matched the skirt she was wearing. The rain was falling harder but Louise wasn't bothered in the slightest, in fact it was a blessing. Her transformation was complete - she'd got away with it. After brushing out her long hair, she tied it into a ponytail and pulled her hood up against the rain, something that would further help to conceal her identity from CCTV. She then walked purposefully from the park through the gate opposite Buckingham Palace and made her way across the Mall into St James's Park.

Once there, she stuffed the carrier bag containing her disguise into one of the large refuse bins outside the toilets, covering it with other rubbish from the bin. That bin would be emptied later in the day by the park's refuse collection team and her disguise would disappear forever.

Fifteen minutes later, she arrived at work.

30

Just after 2 O'clock, Louise sneaked in through the rear door of the office in Gayfere Street, close to the Houses of Parliament. It was an entrance she rarely used. Judith wasn't due to arrive at work until between 2.30 and 3 O'clock that day, having held a morning surgery in her constituency. It tended to be just her and Judith in the office on a Monday because the assistants and researchers only worked on Tuesdays and Thursdays. The building was shared by several other MP's, who also had offices there but staff of the different MP's rarely mingled.

However today, as Louise stepped inside, she was greeted in the dark wood-panelled corridor by about a dozen of the staff from different MP's, excitedly talking together in small groups, many looking at breaking news on their mobile phones with looks of horror on their faces.

Approaching one group, Louise asked innocently, 'What's going on?'

A beautiful black woman who she knew to be the personal assistant for another Labour MP said, between glances at her mobile, 'There's been explosions at shops in three different cities. One in Liverpool, one in Manchester, and one here in London!'

Louise gave a convincing impression of someone in shock. 'Oh my God, whereabouts in London? I heard a loud bang about half an hour ago.'

Without looking up from his phone, one of the men answered, 'Clothes Bazaar in Regent Street.'

'Clothes Bazaar?' she asked, pretending to have never heard the shop's name.

'I know,' said the woman who was the first to speak, 'It's new to me, too.'

Pulling her phone from her handbag, Louise googled 'Explosions London,' while asking, 'Are there many casualties?'

The second man replied, 'No reports of any fatalities yet, but apparently dozens are injured.'

'That's terrible,' said Louise, shaking her head as if appalled at the news. 'Let's just hope no one has actually died. How can anyone do such a thing?'

Leaving the group in the corridor, she unlocked the door to Judith's office, walked inside and firmly pushed it closed. Sitting down at her desk, she blew out hard. The operation had proved to be far more intense and nerve-racking than she'd expected; she was utterly exhausted. Carrying out such tasks for the cause were a necessary part of who she'd become, it was what she'd signed up to, what she longed for, but the mental and physical toll were far more brutal than she had imagined.

She was still breathing heavily and looking into space ten minutes later, when the door opened and Judith walked in. Taking in the scene, Judith asked, 'Louise, what's the matter?'

Louise hadn't realised she was showing her emotions so obviously. Controlling her breathing, she looked up through tired eyes.

'Haven't you heard about the bombings?'

Judith furrowed her brow and nodded, 'Yes, I've

been listening to the radio in the taxi from Victoria. Four explosions in four different cities.'

'Four? I've only heard about three.'

'There's just been one reported in Portsmouth. Many injured according to reports. Is that what's upsetting you?' Judith seemed genuinely surprised.

Taking in a huge lungful of air, Louise composed herself. She was mentally worn out, but she still needed to play the empathy card.

'Sorry, I was just thinking about the victims and their families. Isn't it awful?'

Nodding slowly, Judith seemed to be agreeing with her. She sat down in the chair behind her desk and looked steadily at Louise.

'I understand it's very upsetting, but we can't afford to let something like this affect our ability to carry out our work. Whenever there's a terrorist attack in the UK, no matter where it happens, everywhere around Westminster is quickly locked down. Our working environment will become difficult enough Louise, without letting emotions get the better of us.'

Louise was taken aback by Judith's lack of compassion, but at least it meant she wouldn't have to keep up the pretence of being so upset.

'I'm sorry Jude, I guess it's just with it coming so soon after that explosion at Adam's department. I'll be fine, it won't happen again, I promise.'

She smiled at her boss, pulled herself upright in her chair and said, 'Right, we need to go through your diary for next week, and I need you to sign a couple of letters.'

32

One Tree House, Pilgrims Way, Otford, Kent

Apart from a brief mobile phone conversation with Adam as she finished work at five, Louise hadn't been called upon to display false horror over the bombings too often, as she had been working non-stop. She was still a little surprised at Judith's reaction: a great boss but almost devoid of emotion. Louise smiled to herself, imagining what a great servant she would have been for Harb Alsheueb. She seemed like a completely different person from the one who had engineered Louise's first meeting with Adam.

By eight that evening, she was expecting Adam home at any moment. She was still buzzing with the thrill of successfully completing the operation but was desperate to speak to him. She knew that seeing him and discussing it with him would enable her to perform the secondary role in her life, that of an empathetic and supportive wife.

Just before leaving work, she had been standing with others when she heard a radio broadcast giving full details of the latest numbers of casualties. The numbers had certainly made Louise take notice and she needed to ensure she responded appropriately, placing a hand over her mouth and gasping to reflect the actions of those around her. Six victims had been killed at the Regent Street explosion and many others had suffered life-changing injuries; some of the victims were children. Two had died in Liverpool, three in Manchester and four in Portsmouth.

There had been two more attacks, one in Norwich killing one person and one in Gloucester, killing three. This brought the total number of fatalities to nineteen, a number that was expected to rise because of the serious injuries many had suffered. The most recent news report gave the total number of injured as 212, of which sixty-seven were at Clothes Bazaar in London's Regent Street. Louise was pleased she'd played her part in a successful operation but for the first time since she'd become a sleeper, she experienced a flicker of unease about the extent of suffering she'd caused.

However, any self-doubt only lasted a few seconds then the training once again took over: victims were merely collateral damage. The same mantra played over and over in her head, that 'their suffering was necessary for the benefit of Islam, the greater good.'

She heard a car pull up on the gravel drive and ran expectantly to the door. Adam walked in, looking haggard and weary. He took her in his arms and hugged her like he would never let her go.

'Bastards,' he whispered in her ear. 'They've no respect for anything other than fucking Islam.' He pushed her back to arms-length and looked hard at her, a look that almost made her fearful he knew something.

'How could anyone be so evil that they were prepared to plant a bomb in a shop? I mean, what the fuck's going on in their heads?'

Just for a second, Louise felt a rush of anger at him for daring to insult Islam, but deep inside she knew this was the type of response Harb Alsheueb were hoping for. They wanted a reaction; they wanted people to feel disgust; they wanted an outraged western government to respond with indignation, with aggressive rhetoric, and hopefully with military force. That would be the ultimate success.

Her job for now though, was to play the distraught but supportive wife.

'I've been so upset Adam. I was so shaken at the office when I heard the news, that Judith had to tell me to pull myself together. I just couldn't help thinking about those poor people, and some of them were children!'

Adam's eyes were moist with tears; he sighed, closed his eyes and tilted his head back.

'We're so lucky. We live in a great country. Maybe that's why they feel the need to attack us, attack our way of life, because they don't have the same freedoms that we enjoy. Who knows what's going on in their sick fucking heads?'

His voice had risen and taken on a harshness which she had never heard before. The palm of her right hand was resting against his left cheek, as unspoken thoughts passed between them. She rubbed his cheek softly.

'Oliver is asleep, but I bet he'd still love a goodnight kiss from his daddy.'

Adam forced a smile, breathed in heavily, kissed his wife on the forehead, and headed upstairs.

33

SO15 Headquarters, Bayswater Road, London
Saturday 6th May 2028, 9.00am

Assistant Commissioner Sarah Maidment glanced at the officer sitting next to her. DCS Mark Dawes met her gaze and responded with a brief nod, at which she rose to her feet.

The briefing room at Virginia Square was packed with Counter Terrorism Command officers and Metropolitan Police senior management. Sarah was one of the highest-ranking female officers in the Met since Commissioner Cressida Dick retired; she cut a striking figure in her uniform, with her spiky blonde hair and piercing blue eyes.

Waiting patiently until complete silence had been established, she cast her gaze over the room.

'Good morning everyone, can you all please ensure that mobile phones are turned off.' Tapping her glass gently with a pen several times to enforce her point, she raised her voice. 'That means *off* ladies and gents, not on vibrate or silent... off!'

Several officers fidgeted uncomfortably, as they searched through pockets and bags to locate their devices. When everyone had settled down, Maidment sat on the edge of the table facing towards the gathered officers.

'Yesterday's terrorist attacks were the most well organised and well-coordinated in the UK since the 7/7 attacks in July 2005, but they were far more widespread.' She paused for dramatic effect, something that in the circumstances wasn't strictly necessary.

'The latest news is that there are twenty-four dead and 207 injured, but seventeen of those injured are described as critical, so the death toll is expected to rise.' She lifted herself off the table and paced to and fro across the slightly elevated stage. 'All indications point to this being the work of Harb Alsheueb but MI5 had no prior knowledge that a major attack was being planned.'

A male officer raised his hand and Maidment pointed at him.

'I find that hard to believe Ma'am. It's only a year since the attack on the Department for International Trade, and the threat level is still 'Severe'. Surely, if they weren't worried about an attack, it would have been reduced, so they were clearly concerned about something.'

'Well, that's what they're telling me. An attack was anticipated *somewhere*, probably in Westminster, possibly on another government building or perhaps even an attack *on* a minister, but explosions at shopping outlets throughout the country targeting totally innocent members of the public came out of the blue.'

She once again looked round the room, her expression severe.

'The press are all over these attacks and believe me, the public will be expecting answers and results. Therefore, and I apologise wholeheartedly for doing this, annual leave is cancelled for SO15 officers with immediate effect.'

Her comment brought a groan from some members of her audience, and a sympathetic nod of understanding from Maidment, who held her hands out and shrugged.

'I know, I know, it's unfair that you and your families should suffer, but just imagine what the families and friends of the victims are going through right now. That should help put everything into perspective.'

She gestured towards Dawes. 'You will shortly receive your postings from DCS Dawes. I'll be expecting maximum effort and complete professionalism from every one of you. This was a brazen attack on our democracy, on hundreds of innocent people going about their lawful business. It's an attack on every one of us, on our very way of life. Let's bring the perpetrators of these crimes to justice as soon as possible because, be in no doubt whatsoever, the eyes of the world will be on us.'

She sat down and nodded towards DCS Dawes who rose to his feet.

'Before I give out the postings, I have further information about casualties. Of the twenty-four fatalities so far, seventeen were adult females, four were adult males, and three were children, the youngest of which was only three years old.'

He paused to let the details sink in. The expressions on the faces of his audience showed that they fully understood the enormity of his words and shared his disgust.

'Of 207 injured, 152 were adult females, thirty-seven were adult males, and eighteen were children, the youngest of whom was an eight-month-old female baby, who had to have her left arm amputated.'

This revelation brought gasps, and some muttered swearing.

Fifty minutes later the officers shuffled soberly from the room. They had heard graphic details of the victims' suffering and the enormous damage caused at each location. Everyone had received their postings and been left in no doubt about the magnitude of the task facing them.

34

One Tree House, Pilgrim's Way, Otford, Kent
Wednesday 2nd August 2028, 7.00pm

Louise was seated on a high stool, resting her left elbow on the breakfast bar, as she looked through her kitchen window at the branches of trees on either side of her driveway, moving gently in a summer breeze. A glass of blackcurrant squash was in her right hand as she recalled her meeting with Sulayman earlier in the day. She was concentrating hard, running everything that they'd discussed over and over in her head.

The meeting had taken place in the Crypt Café of St Martin's-in-the-Fields Church, next to Trafalgar Square. Sulayman had been unusually late, and when he arrived, had offered no explanation for his lateness. He looked troubled and without greeting her said, 'Have you been contacted by the police in the last few weeks?'

'No, not since the two detectives came to my house and spoke to me about the explosion at Adam's department. Nobody has approached me following 5/5. Why?'

'You must have heard about the arrests last Wednesday. Everyone involved in the Portsmouth, Norwich and Liverpool jobs were picked up within a few hours of each other.' His voice was expressionless, but he was clearly on edge.

She shrugged her shoulders but said nothing. She had heard about the arrests on the news, but as each operative and handler was separate, hadn't been overly concerned.

Staring at her in exasperation, Sulayman said, 'For fuck's sake Louise! Three operatives and three handlers, each pair totally unconnected with the others, arrested in three separate locations on the same fucking day, and you act as if there's nothing to worry about!'

'But if all these pairs are separate, what has this to do with me?

He rolled his eyes. His message clearly wasn't getting through.

'It's highly likely that someone in Harb Alsheueb has blabbed, someone very high up, because only the top brass knew details of more than one operative.'

Suddenly the realisation hit home – hard.

'So... you're saying the police might know about me?' Tears quickly formed in her eyes. 'Oh no... oh please God no! What am I going to do?'

He glared at her and put his finger to his lips.

'Stay in control Louise and for God's sake keep your voice down. We can't afford to draw attention to ourselves.'

Fighting back tears, she nodded.

'If they'd known it was you who was responsible for the Regent Street device, you'd be in custody already.'

Her voice quivered with nerves. 'So, how did they trace three of our teams at once?'

He put his hands out with palms facing upwards and shrugged.

'We don't know. Whoever knew those three pairs would surely have known all six. If it's a whistle-blower, it must be a very high-ranking member of the organisation, but if that's the case, why hasn't he given up all six pairs, including us? That's the question we need the answer to.'

Sulayman was waiting for her to speak but she didn't respond. She could think of nothing to say.

He tapped the table and stared into space. 'The only other explanation is that the arrests were coincidental. Now that's extremely unlikely, but not impossible.'

His words had given her a glimmer of hope. 'That's what I'd assumed had happened when I heard the reports. So there is a chance I might be okay then?'

'To be honest, I don't know. The whole thing doesn't make sense. But that scenario is unlikely, probably a million-to-one.'

'That's just perfect,' she whispered. 'Just what someone wants to hear when they're three months pregnant.'

Sulayman was briefly taken aback. 'I'm really happy for you. I had no idea you were expecting again. That's quite soon after your first, isn't it? Congratulations, anyway.'

Louise rested her elbows on the table and placed her head in her hands.

'Good wishes will be a lot of help when I'm serving life imprisonment!'

He needed to divert her away from her sense of misery, so changed tack.

'The reason for this meeting isn't about the arrests, it's to ask you a question.'

'What question?' A slight wobble in her voice gave away her unease.

He leaned forward. 'Are you absolutely certain you've spoken to no-one about your association with us?'

'What's that supposed to mean? Of course, I haven't! Why on earth would I?'

'The organisation regards you and your position with Adam as pivotal. They regard you and me as their dream team and they really don't want us arrested as well.'

'I can assure you, apart from receiving the emails from Haasim and the meetings with you, I haven't mentioned a thing to anyone.'

'Fair enough, I thought that's what you'd say.'

'There's no danger of me saying anything,' Louise said, the irritation sounding in her voice. 'You can send that message back up the food chain from me.'

Satisfied he'd got the answers he needed, Sulayman left the cafe, after wishing her good luck with the birth.

Louise was finishing her glass of squash as she watched Adam's car pull onto the drive. He climbed out of the rear seat carrying his red briefcase and smiled at her through the window. She raised her glass to him and watched him walk to the front door.

35

SO15 Headquarters, Bayswater Road, London
Thursday 3rd August 2028, 9.00am

'Settle down people and listen up. All electronic devices off.'

DCI Barney Briscow stood in front of the assembled officers. He was a crusty old-school detective: a heavy drinker, heavy smoker and, at the age of fifty-seven, still liked the company of younger women. His behaviour had got him in trouble with senior officers many times during his career, but he was highly respected among the junior ranks, especially officers under his direct command. He worked hard, played hard, and often got results where others failed. Standing at 6'4', with thick salt and pepper hair, tanned complexion and a great physique for his age, he cut an imposing figure.

Eventually the murmured conversation ceased and all eyes focused on the man standing before them. Reaching up with his right hand, Barney Briscow rubbed the back of his neck before speaking.

'Three suspects from the explosions in Portsmouth, Norwich and Liverpool, were yesterday evening charged with Murder, Possession of an article for Terrorist Purposes and Membership of a Proscribed Organisation.

Their handlers were separately charged with Conspiracy to Murder, Membership of a Proscribed Organisation, and Preparation of Terrorist Acts. If convicted, none of them are likely to see the light of day for thirty years.'

His words were met with a small round of applause and tapping of desk tops. DCI Briscow nodded appreciatively and waited for the celebrations to die down.

'The bomber in Liverpool was a thirty-two-year-old Somali female named Rashida Nahir, the bomber in Portsmouth a twenty-six-year-old Nigerian male named Ehan Okafor. However, the bomber in Norwich was a twenty-five-year-old English born male named William Sanderson.

'He graduated from Cardiff University with a degree in English Literature then took a gap year travelling to South Sudan to help at a primary school. It's believed that this was where he may have first experienced the Islamic religion.'

He stroked his throat and raised his head thoughtfully before continuing.

'Prior to leaving for South Sudan, he was known by friends at university to be very much an atheist. However, during his fourteen months in South Sudan he appears to have become fascinated by the devotion of Islamic worshipers, then was gradually lured into joining them at prayer meetings. Over just short of a year, he was slowly indoctrinated and radicalised. It's known for certain that he attended training camps during the final eight months of his stay in the country.'

Briscow blew his nose and took a sip of water.

'None of the suspects were known to ourselves or MI5. They weren't on any watch lists, none of them had ever been in trouble with the police. They all held down normal jobs and appeared to be leading respectable lives.'

His face screwed up with anger and his words came out slowly. 'They were all fucking sleepers. So, the three remaining bombers, and maybe even their handlers, could be sleepers too. Ordinary citizens living ordinary lives, holding down ordinary jobs. One of them could be sitting in this room right now.'

Officers shifted restlessly in their seats; a low rumble of unease could be heard spreading throughout the room. Briscow's comments had had the desired effect.

Turning to the young detective constable sitting in the corner, Briscow said, 'Pictures please.' He pushed a key on his laptop and the screen above them illuminated, with CCTV images of suspects for the Manchester and Gloucester bombings. All the suspects were Asian looking males, three for the Manchester bombing, and three for Gloucester.

'I can tell you now, we don't have much evidence against any of the suspects shown here.'

He paused, then a picture of Louise in her disguise appeared on the screen.

'However, this female is strongly suspected to be our target for the Regent Street attack.'

The images of her in different locations were flicking over as a slideshow while DCI Briscow continued to speak. He pointed at the screen.

'These pictures show a female wearing thick black spectacles, a sort of peach coloured hijab, a long green dress which I've been advised is called an Abaya, short cream coat and black shoes.'

The room fell silent, all eyes seemingly transfixed by the pictures in front of them.

'As you know, the device planted in Clothes Bazaar had a delayed timer device, from fragments retrieved, we know that the type of timer used had a one-hour maximum. This means it could only have been planted there up to one hour before it detonated, making our job slightly easier than it had been at the Department for International Trade explosion.

'CCTV of every person who entered and left that store up to an hour before the explosion has been followed from street to street after they left Clothes Bazaar. This work has taken three months and thousands of hours. However, it seems to have been worthwhile, because this woman was traced all the way to Green Park, where she was seen to enter the park through the entrance by the Ritz Hotel and Green Park Underground Station. She entered the park and disappeared out of CCTV range,' he paused and took a sip of water, 'but the interesting thing is that, despite checking all CCTV cameras surrounding the park, she doesn't seem to have left. This would suggest that she knew where a CCTV dead spot was within the park, changed her clothing then exited the park dressed completely differently.'

Officers were gripped by Briscow's presentation, and by the blurred images on the screen.

Spreading his arms out wide, his palms facing upwards, he shrugged and said, 'Why would any normal person do that? Unless they'd just done something seriously wrong, something like blowing up a fucking shop!' He relaxed his arms and sat on the edge of the table.

'Unfortunately, hundreds of people were leaving the park at that time because it had started raining. At least a hundred women could have been the suspect, so tracing them all would be impossible.'

He gripped the edge of the table with both hands.

'Someone, somewhere, will know who this woman is,' he raised a finger at the screen, 'and we urgently need to trace that person. These images will be released to the press in time for the six o'clock news bulletins tonight.

Once that's done, we're hoping for a swift identification and arrest.' He swept his gaze across the room. 'Any questions?'

A female officer raised her hand. 'Would it be possible to use CCTV to follow each woman into the park then check to see when and where they left the park? It's a huge amount of work but if we can identify the one woman who isn't seen to enter the park, but is seen to exit, it could be worth it.'

'Thank you, that's an excellent question. The answer is we're already doing that, but several other people walked through the CCTV dead spots in the central area of the park and changed their appearance because of the rain. They put on raincoats, cagoules with hoods, raised large umbrellas and pulled them down low over their heads, some people even put on waterproof leggings. You name it... We're hopeful we'll get a result, but it's by no means certain.'

The officer nodded her head.

'Right then, any more questions?'

This time the room fell silent.

'Thank you all for your attendance. We've got half of these fuckers in custody, but the others are still out there. Let's find them.'

36

14 Barn Avenue, Hildenborough, Kent
Saturday 21st October 2028, 12.20pm

Millie opened the front door to Louise and the friends came together in a crushing hug. She'd left an open invitation for Louise to visit anytime she fancied and this weekend Adam was busy in Luxembourg at a trade conference, while Oliver was spending most of the weekend with Adam's parents, who absolutely doted on him. They had insisted on him sleeping over on Saturday night, saying that Louise needed a break and could have a good night's sleep for a change. Louise had initially been uncertain about the arrangements, unsure whether she felt happy about leaving Oliver with his grandparents at only eleven months, but their persistence finally won her over.

Millie and Louise had met a few times for drinks and meals after work but this was the first chance they'd had since her last visit to spend real time together. In addition, Louise was nearly six months pregnant and this would be her last opportunity to see her best friend, other than after work, before the birth. Millie hadn't said or done anything more to make Louise believe she suspected her, so fears on that score had faded.

Louise remained uneasy however, about photographs and CCTV images of her circulating on social media, in press reports and on the television news. It seemed incredible to her that nobody had come forward and identified her as the woman who'd planted the bomb in Regent Street.

The disguise had clearly done its job effectively, and as the weeks passed, she found it harder than ever to believe the images of the woman wearing the salmon-coloured hijab could actually be her. It certainly didn't look like her, but millions of eyes had been scrutinising her features, leaving her with the nagging fear that someone, somewhere, would spot the likeness.

Their lunchtime meal was spent discussing the possibility of Adam one day becoming Prime Minister and what impact that would have on her current lifestyle - and their friendship. Louise wiped her mouth with a paper napkin.

'Nothing could derail our friendship. We've been through too much together.' She raised her glass of elderflower cordial and they clinked glasses.

Millie smiled. 'I'm pleased to hear that. Right, let's get the washing up in the dishwasher then we'll have a wander through the fields to a pub to walk off our...' She suddenly stopped herself. 'Lulu, I'm so sorry, I hadn't thought about your condition.'

Louise laughed. 'It's funny how people go overboard when you're pregnant. I'm not ill, Millie, I don't have a 'condition'. I'm just pregnant, I'm still able to walk. In fact, a walk sounds great.'

Carrying the plates through to the beautiful kitchen, Louise passed them to Millie, who loaded the dishwasher.

'Hey, Lulu.'

'Yes?'

'Have you been following the story on the news

about the female suspect for the London Bombing?'

Louise froze. She could feel the familiar sick feeling in the pit of her stomach.

'Yes of course. It's hard to avoid. What about it?'

Millie placed the last of the cutlery into the dishwasher, put the powder into the drawer, closed the door and turned the machine on.

'Well, this is going to sound daft, but haven't you noticed that she looks weirdly like you?'

Trying hard to keep her voice level, Louise replied, 'That's crazy, she looks nothing like me.'

'She's got your exact walk and you're the same height and build.'

'Yeah, me and thousands of other women.' She turned to look at her friend, all her earlier anxiety flooding back.

Millie continued to tease her.

'Yes, but what with your known sympathies with Islam and association with a Muslim at school, you'd better hope that you're not on some list of 'persons of interest' somewhere!'

She made speech mark signs with her fingers and laughed. But Louise couldn't laugh; she couldn't even manage a smile.

'That's an outrageous thing to say!'

She fought to stem the tears which were beginning to form and Millie at once felt contrite.

'Hey, Lulu, chill. You know I'm not serious. It's just that when I saw those pictures, you popped into my head. Maybe it was because of that chat we had last time about Mustafa. I didn't mean to upset you.'

Millie's mention of their previous conversation had the opposite effect to the one Millie intended. It brought back all Louise's anxiety about her friend, and now it was ten times worse. Her words had unsettled Louise far more than anything she had experienced since becoming a sleeper. She needed to know more about Millie's real thoughts.

'You didn't honestly think that bitch on the footage was me did you?' she said, snivelling slightly and wiping the tears from her face.

'I told you – of course not, you muppet! It was just a stupid thing to say and I wish to God I hadn't.'

Louise had now mastered herself enough to smile ruefully at Millie.

'Sorry to overreact. It's probably the hormones. But to think that anyone might mistake that woman for me, well, it makes me sick.'

Millie took Louise's hand. 'No, it's me who should be saying sorry for being so thoughtless. Let's not say any more about it. Forgive me? After all, we've known each other for ever and you're my best friend in the whole world.'

Louise gave Millie's hand a squeeze.

'Okay, you're forgiven, but you're paying for drinks at the pub to apologise.'

'It's a deal. I'm happy to pay for every drink we have. After all, you're only on soft drinks aren't you, being preggers?'

As she prepared for their walk, Louise's mind replayed the conversation. Was Millie sincere? Had it all been a wind-up? How could she be sure? She knew that Millie had a wicked sense of humour, but this was all a bit close to the truth. On the one hand, Millie was her closest friend but on the other, if she really had noticed a strong similarity and if she mentioned it to anyone else, this could be the end of her anonymity and of her freedom. She might be acting paranoid, but then again, sometimes paranoia is justified.

37

Wrapped up warmly against the chilly weather, they left Millie's house for their after-lunch walk. A thirty-minute stroll across the fields took them to the Harvest Bell pub, sitting on a bend in a peaceful country lane, where they obeyed the politely worded notice and removed their mud-caked trainers before entering.

During the walk, Louise spotted a ring of trees sitting on the brow of a hill, about a hundred metres from the footpath, surrounded by a crop of newly planted winter wheat. She felt drawn to the place but her attention was distracted by Millie, who continued to apologise for her earlier comments about Louise's likeness to the mystery woman. Her well-meant words had the opposite effect on Louise, who found herself increasingly worried about Millie's true feelings.

Inside the pub, they were greeted by the familiar clinking of glasses and sounds of laughter and managed to find a small table for two by a window overlooking the rear garden. Once settled with their drinks, Louise couldn't stop herself from raising the subject once more.

'I still can't believe you would connect me in any way with that bloody woman who planted the bomb. Did you seriously think she looked like me?'

'Oh Lulu, I've said I'm sorry and I really am. I

wouldn't have mentioned it if I'd known it would freak you out. I was just so taken aback when I saw the footage and thought it was an odd coincidence, what with your interest in Islam and Muslim causes...'

'I just hate the idea that people might be watching those images and be thinking the same as you. It's so disgusting.'

'I'm sure they're not, and anyway, what does it matter? No one is going to connect you with that nutter. Now, can we stop talking about this? It's spoiling the afternoon and I want to enjoy our time together.'

Louise realised that pushing the matter any further would be counterproductive. Her rational mind was telling her to accept Millie's reassurances; that her friend had no real suspicions of her. But it was difficult to relax and another part of her mind was asking, *'Yes, but what if...?'*

Over the next hour they discussed the problems of running a household, their jobs, and Millie's love life and marriage prospects. They reminisced and laughed, enjoying each other's company, the awkwardness of their earlier conversation seemingly a distant memory.

Their return route to Millie's house led out through a rear gate in the pub garden, onto a footpath through open countryside. The path around the first field took them a quarter of a mile away then they tramped through a small area of woodland, before entering a dome-shaped field surrounded by more woodland. At the top of the field was the ring of trees which had so fascinated Louise on their outward journey.

'Millie.'

'What?'

'I'd love to visit that ring of trees. It looks like a magical place.'

'Really?' Millie seemed distinctly unimpressed. She

looked over towards the ring of trees, then back to Louise.

'You do realise we'll get plastered in mud crossing the field?'

'Yes, but I've loved those sorts of places ever since I was a little girl. Surely you remember the one on our farm, we played there endlessly?'

A smile appeared on Millie's face and she nodded.

'Yes, I remember we used to play Star Wars until it was dark.'

Louise gave her friend a playful, mischievous grin. 'Come on, let's walk up there.'

Millie still looked doubtful. 'That means walking across the field. The farmer is a particularly mean old bugger. He goes ape-shit at anyone he finds straying from the footpaths, especially if they're trampling his crops.'

'Isn't there a footpath that leads up there?'

Millie shook her head. 'No, it's strictly out of bounds to the public.'

The disappointment was clearly visible on Louise's face, then she had an idea and grabbed her friend's hand. 'Come on Mills, one last hurrah, one last time disobeying the rules before we become too middle aged and respectable!'

After a moment, Millie laughed. They exchanged a conspiratorial look, beamed at each other, then set off at a brisk pace across the muddy field, their trainers sinking into the sticky soil, and trampling the winter wheat as they went.

Ten minutes later, they managed to find a way through the banks of stinging nettles and small bushes forming the perimeter of the ring. Once inside, hidden underneath the canopy of the trees, they clambered over a pile of stones, formed many years ago when the farmer had dumped them, having cleared his field of debris before ploughing. They were enchanted to find that in the centre of the ring was a dark, still pond. It was about fifteen metres wide with worryingly steep sides. No sounds seemed to penetrate the trees and the air had a chill which made them both shiver.

'Wow!' said Millie. 'What an amazing place. It's like something out of a Harry Potter film. It would have been wonderful playing in here if you were a child.'

Looking around her, Louise nodded.

'Yes, but you can see why the farmer doesn't allow people access. If a child fell into that pond, they'd struggle to climb out up those sides.'

Louise felt herself shiver again then, running her fingers through the leaves of a fern, said, 'I don't understand how a pond could form on top of a hill. Where does the water come from?'

Millie rolled her eyes. 'Don't you remember your geography from school? It's a kettle hole, formed when a glacier retreats. They often hold water and, being shaded throughout summer and autumn by the trees, this one probably never dries out.'

To prove her point, she found a lengthy dead branch, and tested the depth of the water.

'Blimey Lulu, it must be two metres deep in the middle!'

'Oh yes, you're right. I remember kettle holes now.' She smiled at Millie. 'This is such a brilliant place. Come on, let's have a look round.'

They walked through the trees and bushes around the perimeter of the pond, pushing aside brambles and tangled undergrowth, until they reached a fallen tree with a few of its upper branches dipping into the water. Dappled sunlight managed to find a way through the canopy and danced on the pond's dark surface, giving it an almost otherworldly appearance.

'This is wonderful,' breathed Louise, looking up through the branches.

Glowing with happiness, Millie nodded her agreement. 'It's better than that Lulu, it's magical. I'm so glad you persuaded me to come here.'

Millie was the first to sit on the tree's horizontal trunk, which was the perfect height. For one idyllic moment, time stood still for them and the memories of the fun they'd had together playing inside the ring of trees on the farm at Fletching flooded back. Louise stood behind her and affectionately rubbed Millie's right shoulder with her left hand; Millie responded by looking up and smiling at her friend.

Louise returned her best mate's smile, leaned forward and drew the knife concealed in her hand across Millie's throat, causing a spurt of blood and an instant look of terror and disbelief on Millie's face. Her hands clasped around the gaping wound in a futile attempt to stem the flow of blood and save her life. Pitiful gurgling and choking sounds continued as she slid from the tree trunk onto the ground, where she lay writhing on her back, her eyes staring up at Louise, imploring her, pleading for help.

Louise stood motionless, watching the horror show of her friend fighting for survival. But as the last few seconds of Millie's life slowly ebbed away, something snapped in Louise's mind and she found tears pouring from her eyes. Millie, wonderful Millie, beautiful Millie, the best friend a girl could ever have. They'd been inseparable from the moment they met in primary school, yet she had just sliced her throat open as if she'd been cutting into a watermelon. She managed to gasp out a few words through her sobs.

'Millie, Millie, I'm so sorry, I love you so much.'

Millie couldn't respond; she had stopped moving

and now lay staring up into the trees, the final moments of her life draining away. After another minute, Louise noticed the silence; her friend's eyes had become glazed and lifeless... Millie was dead. Her long brown hair mingled with the leaves on the ground around her head, the blood seeping from her throat soaking into the grass and earth; her arms had fallen uselessly to her sides, her legs were bent, pushed tightly together and rolled over to the left.

Louise dropped to her knees next to Millie's body. She stared in disbelief at the friend whose life she had just taken; the friend who possibly, but only possibly, suspected the truth of her involvement in terrorist activities; the friend whom she loved so much, but who could no longer be allowed to live, because allowing her to retain her freedom may have resulted in her own arrest and imprisonment. She let the tears flow until she had no more tears left to cry.

Pulling herself together, she took her mind back to Afghanistan and the training sessions which had convinced her that violence was sometimes necessary and acceptable, training which had never failed her in the past, but which she was now, for the first time, beginning to question.

Looking down at the body which had once contained the soul and spirit of her lovely Millie, Louise again experienced an almost physical shock, as if something inside her had split apart. For the first time in years, she felt doubts about Harb Alsheueb forming in her mind, as if the clouds were parting, allowing her to see light and shade once more.

She sat on the damp ground, breathing in the cool, moist air and forced herself to face what she had become. She began to see the months of training she had undergone as the brutal indoctrination it really was. But with that dawning realisation came fear and horror, as she recalled the actions she had already taken on behalf of Harb Alsheueb.

It had taken the loss of someone dear to her to enable her to feel the loss and pain she had caused others. Her love of Allah and commitment to Islam remained undimmed, but she suddenly saw the movement which had used her for what it really was: a hate-fuelled corruption of her true faith.

But it was too late for poor Millie and that crippled Louise with grief. However, if she were to continue with her own life and attempt to make reparation for her past actions, she now had a more urgent problem: hiding her friend's body. Luckily, they were well hidden within the ring of trees; nobody could see her through the overhanging branches, bushes and nettles. It looked as though nobody had bothered visiting the place for a very long time, so it was highly unlikely that she would be disturbed.

The pond was the obvious place to hide Millie's body but she couldn't risk her floating back to the surface. For the next twenty minutes she gathered stones from the pile and forced them inside Millie's clothing to weigh her down. Throughout the process she struggled to see where she was walking and what she was doing every time she forced another stone into Millie's clothes, she was blinded by tears.

Eventually, she'd filled Millie's sleeves, jeans and coat pockets as best she could, confident her friend's body couldn't possibly return to the surface. After removing Millie's house keys from a pocket, she knelt down behind the top of her friend's head, wiped away the tears which blurred her vision, then bent down and planted a kiss on Millie's cold forehead.

Standing up, she moved around to Millie's feet,

firmly took hold of both legs, and began dragging her to the very edge of the slope down into the pond. She then moved around to her side, placed both hands under her left hip, lifted and pushed hard. Millie rolled quickly down the slope, making a soft splash as she entered the pond. Within two or three seconds she had slipped beneath the water; bubbles briefly broke the surface then they stopped... Millie was gone.

38

Louise bent down and picked up the small, serrated steak knife, which she'd removed from Millie's cutlery drawer before they'd left the house; she stared at it, hypnotised by the deep red liquid that had begun to congeal on its blade.

Dragging herself back to the moment, she drew her arm back and swung it in an arc, releasing the knife from her hand at the top of the swing then watching it spin through the air, before entering the centre of the pond with a tiny splash. She crouched at the pond's edge and plunged her hands in the surprisingly cold water, washing small amounts of blood from each hand before standing up and shaking them dry.

Having checked the ground where Millie's body had lain, Louise kicked dead grass and loose soil over the whole area, then spread a little extra soil where blood had flowed, before placing a couple of dead ferns across the disturbed ground. She'd left nothing to suggest the horror which had occurred thirty minutes before.

Brushing herself down as best she could, Louise peered out through the bushes and looked down the slope across the field towards the footpath; nobody was in sight. Her heart was pounding as she took one last look towards the pond, the final resting place of her dear friend, Millie. Taking a deep breath, she turned and walked through the bushes and nettles, before stumbling down the hill across the field. Luckily, she managed to re-join the footpath without anybody seeing her.

Instead of walking along the road and entering Millie's house through the front door, Louise used a short-cut that Millie had shown her on her last visit, cutting across a field and down a quiet alleyway which led to the garden, allowing her access to the house through the back door with little chance of being noticed by neighbours. She removed her trainers before entering; if the body should ever be found, she certainly didn't want mud containing splashes of Millie's blood to be found in her home.

She quickly collected her things together, but wasn't thinking straight, realising with a start that she couldn't simply go home. Adam's parents weren't expecting her until the following day and there was always the chance that Millie had mentioned to neighbours that she was staying for the weekend. If that was the case, they might notice her leaving a day early, giving her awkward questions to answer.

In her panic and grief, she had overlooked so many potential problems. From that moment onwards, she told herself she would consider every possible outcome carefully before taking action.

Later that evening, Louise phoned Adam's parents to check up on Oliver, then she contacted Adam. In both calls she fed them the story that she was having a great time with Millie, that they were about to watch the film 'Notting Hill' while enjoying a Chinese takeaway. It had taken all her strength to sound cheerful, but somehow she'd managed it.

Putting the phone down after ending the call with Adam, she slumped into an armchair, emotionally drained. It was unnerving being alone in Millie's house, surrounded by photos of her with family, friends, boyfriends and of course, with Louise herself. It was the sight of a photo of the two of them out on the town, that broke through her defences and the tears began to flow.

Next morning, after an interminable night during which she tossed in her bed, replaying the scenes in the wood, daylight finally arrived without her having a single minute's sleep. She dressed, cleaned her teeth in the bathroom and put her toiletries bag into her suitcase.

Louise then went through all the downstairs rooms, checking then double checking that the house was neat and tidy, leaving it exactly as when she arrived. She took one last look at the photographs on the mantelpiece: pictures of Millie at different ages, always happy and smiling, full of fun, full of life. Then, feeling wretched, she lifted her suitcase out through the front door. As she did so, Louise was horrified to see Millie's next-door-but-one neighbour working in his front garden.

She thought quickly, looked back towards the house and called out, 'Thanks for a great weekend, Mills. I'll call you this evening.'

Closing the front door, she pulled her suitcase to the end of the drive, then turned and waved towards the lounge window, as if Millie were returning her wave from inside.

Walking past the gardening neighbour, she cheerfully greeted him with, 'Good morning, lovely day,' as her suitcase made that familiar 'clickety-click' sound across the joints between slabs in the pavement. By 9.30 she was at Hildenborough train station, awaiting the next train to London.

Two hours later she arrived at the home of Adam's parents. She squeezed Oliver so tightly that he started to cry, making her release her grip. She held him at arms' length and smiled through misty eyes at her son. Her mother-in-law laughed.

'Come on Louise, you've only been apart for one day. Nothing terrible has happened.'

But Louise knew that was not true.

39

Boar Head Farm, Fletching, East Sussex
Friday 3rd November 2028, 7.35pm

Derek showed Millie's parents, Susan and Bill, through to the lounge, where Louise was waiting with her mother, Debbie. They rose to greet them, exchanging hugs and murmuring words of sympathy. Millie had been missing for nearly two weeks; the police were baffled by her disappearance and becoming extremely concerned for her welfare.

Susan and Bill had called round to talk about the situation with the Kentons, having known them ever since Millie and Louise became friends at school. They sat together on the settee, holding hands tightly, and sharing tearful glances. Debbie and Derek sat on the armchairs, while Louise kneeled on the floor, alongside her mother.

Derek moved forward to the edge of his chair.

'What's the latest news? Do the police have any leads yet?'

Millie's parents once again exchanged a glance, before Susan said, 'No, nothing.' Tears were welling in her eyes. 'Millie, my beautiful girl, what's happened to her?'

'I'm sure she'll turn up,' said Debbie. 'There has to be some rational explanation.'

Susan shook her head. 'I hope so, disappearing like this without a word is totally out of character...' She broke down, unable to finish what she wanted to say. Bill put an arm around her shoulder and she buried her head in his chest.

He continued where Susan had left off.

'She's not been into work. None of her bank cards have been used and all her social media accounts have been silent. It just doesn't make sense.'

Debbie looked at her daughter. 'Lulu's been interviewed by the police twice, and they might want to speak with her again.'

All eyes turned to Louise. She needed to say something and looked from person to person.

'The police are fairly certain I was the last person to see her. They think she may have been abducted shortly after I left her house.'

Her eyes rested on Susan and she prayed to her God that her expression would be seen as one of anguish, not guilt.

'She saw me off at the front door and waved goodbye through the window. Her neighbours saw us waving to each other but after that, nobody knows what happened to her.'

Genuine tears formed in her eyes and rolled down her cheeks.

'They're saying that was the last time anyone saw her.'

Susan released her husband's grip and leaned over the arm of the settee to wrap her arms around Louise.

'There there, Lulu. You've been such a wonderful friend to Millie. I hope the police have been gentle with you.'

Louise returned the gesture, wrapping her arms around Susan, and nodded. 'They've been very considerate.'

Susan released her grip and sat back on the settee, struggling not to cry.

Louise felt she should say something positive.

'I've come up with an idea to help widen the search.'

Bill looked keen. 'Go on, what is it?'

'Julie Hards, a friend of ours from school, has created a website called 'Find Millie.com.' It's somewhere that people can share anything posted on the various social media platforms. The more people we can make aware of what's happened, the more chance we've got of finding her.'

'Thank you, Lulu,' said Bill, 'that's a great idea.'

Smiling warmly on the outside, Louise was feeling wretched at her cruel deception of Millie's poor parents.

Two hours later, during which time they had gone over old ground again and again, Susan and Bill said goodbye to the Kentons, climbed into their car and drove away.

Louise and her parents continued to discuss Millie's disappearance for a further hour after Millie's parents had left, then made their way up to bed, where Louise lay in her room feeling utterly empty.

40

Tunbridge Wells Hospital, Pembury, Kent
Saturday 10th February 2029, 05.00am

'Come on, Louise. One more push and you'll be well on the way to your baby being born.' The midwife sounded cheery, adjusting her hijab slightly as she spoke, but Adam noticed her share a concerned glance with her male colleague.

'I can't,' sobbed Louise. 'I'm so tired.'

The sweat on her forehead was running into her eyes. She'd been in labour for seventeen hours and was exhausted.

Adam used a small towel to dry her forehead, rubbed her shoulder reassuringly, and leaned over until his face was close to hers.

'Come on love, one final push, it'll soon be over.'

'Easy for you to say!' she growled.

She started crying, gripped Adam's hand as the next contraction started, and pushed as hard as she could. A blood curdling scream rang out and her face contorted. Pushing with every ounce of strength she possessed, Louise howled with the effort and pain. She kept seeing Millie's lifeless face in her mind's eye, which made her howl even more.

The female midwife suddenly said, 'Okay Louise, you can stop pushing. I can see the top of baby's head.' Once again, she exchanged a worried look with her colleague. After a few seconds checking the monitors she issued a simple but calm instruction: 'Get a doctor.'

With that, the male midwife, a painfully thin man with a completely shaven head, smiled at Louise and said, 'I'll be back in thirty seconds. You're doing great,' before rushing from the room.

Still panting from the effort and trying to regain her breath, Louise looked on the verge of panic.

'What's wrong? What's happening to my baby? Is she all right?'

'There's nothing to worry about, but baby's heart rate has dropped, so we're calling for the doctor as a precaution.'

Adam stroked his wife's hair.

'It's all right darling, everything's under control.' But deep inside he didn't believe that for a minute.

The male midwife re-entered the room and spoke reassuringly to Louise. Adam beckoned his colleague to join him out of his wife's earshot.

'What the fuck's happening? Tell me the truth.'

The woman leaned in close, whispering directly into Adam's ear.

'The baby is too far down the birth canal to revert to caesarean section, so it will have to be born naturally, but baby's head is too large and your wife is struggling.'

Adam's eyes widened, 'So, what happens now?'

'That's the doctor's decision, not mine. They might let your wife have one more attempt at giving birth naturally, then it would almost certainly be a forceps delivery. Don't worry, it's perfectly routine.'

Adam did not look reassured.

'What does that entail?'

'The doctor inserts a set of grips either side of the head and baby is literally pulled out.'

'How is that possible if she's too small?'

'Your wife may have to be given an episiotomy before the forceps are used.'

Adam knew what that entailed and the worry registered on his face.

'Oh, I see … okay, just do whatever you have to.'

The midwife smiled reassuringly. 'An episiotomy sounds grim, Mr Greenacre, but it's not that unusual.'

Adam looked frightened but nodded his understanding.

'Just keep reassuring your wife. You've done a brilliant job so far; you've been saying all the right things. She needs your support more than ever now and hopefully it will all be over in about twenty minutes.'

Two minutes later the on-call doctor, bearing the name badge, 'Dr Ismail Shah, Paediatrician,' entered the room with his hair dishevelled and a disoriented look on his face. He'd obviously just been woken up in the side room where the night duty on-call doctors sleep and didn't look overly impressed at being disturbed at five o'clock in the morning.

He greeted the female midwife with 'Assalamu Alaikum.'

She replied with, 'Wa Alaikum Assalam.'

Even through her suffering, Louise was pleased to learn she was being helped by two fellow Muslims.

He swiftly examined Louise just as her next contraction started and told her, 'Push hard, give it everything you've got!'

Adam glanced at the monitors and saw that baby Alice's heartbeat had dropped alarmingly. Louise tried to push, but total exhaustion had overcome her, and the contraction passed without any further progress. Dr Shah also noticed the drop in baby's heart rate and said that she needed to be delivered in the next few minutes. After carrying out the episiotomy, he quickly explained to Louise and Adam how the forceps delivery would work, and that it would happen on her next contraction.

Louise squeezed her husband's hand tightly.

'I'm frightened Adam. What happens if our baby won't come out?'

She'd begun to wonder whether this was God's punishment for what she'd done to Millie, to Sarah, to Ismail, and to so many others. Adam cradled her face in his hands.

'Everything will be fine sweetheart. In a few minutes we'll be holding our beautiful baby girl.'

The next contraction started and Dr Shah positioned himself on a chair at the end of the bed. He took a firm grip on the handles of the silver chrome implements and said, 'Okay Louise, push now, push as hard as possible!'

She squeezed Adam's hand so hard that he almost cried out in pain himself. With every fibre of her being she tried to push her baby out, her face turning purple with the effort and tears flowing from her eyes. For a few seconds she pushed with a quiet whimper, then emitted a deep guttural growl, as Dr Shah heaved with all his might, pulling baby Alice from her mother's body and into the arms of the female midwife. Baby Alice's face was screwed up and blue from cyanosis.

Dr Shah said to the midwife, 'The umbilical cord is tightly wrapped around baby's neck, please be careful.'

He stepped forward with surgical scissors and quickly positioned two clamps, before cutting through the umbilical cord between the clamps and unwrapping it from Alice's neck.

Sinking back into the pillow, Louise found she

couldn't rest and repeatedly asked the same question: 'Is Alice all right, is she all right?'

Kissing his wife gently on her brow, Adam said, 'They're cleaning her up now sweetheart. You'll be holding her in a minute.'

Both midwives were standing over Alice, who had been laid down on thick towels. Their actions were being closely monitored by Dr Shah before he gently eased them both out of the way and took control himself.

After two minutes Louise began to become hysterical; they had lifted Alice up, blown on her face, tried ventilating her with a mask, smacked her bottom, rubbed her vigorously with towels, pinched her and now they were pricking the bottom of her feet, but she still didn't respond.

Louise wailed, 'Is my baby dead? Is she dead?'

The female midwife walked over to her, mopped her brow with a cool flannel, 'The doctor's doing all he can. It isn't unusual for a baby not to breath for a couple of minutes. I'm sure she'll be fine in a second.'

Louise reached both arms up to her husband.

'Please God, please let her live, please don't take her from us... please!'

She sobbed her heart out into Adam's chest, while he stared into the pillow over her head, not daring to look towards the medical staff and the frantic work being done on the tiny body.

Memories of the atrocities she had committed flashed through Louise's mind. The same thought kept forcing its way into her head: *This is Karma, this is my punishment for the evil I've done.* Each time the thought appeared she tried to banish it from her mind, but it refused to stay quiet, coming back time after time.

After a further two minutes, they heard Dr Shah say, 'Administering adrenalin now.'

Louise stopped crying and raised herself up on her elbows to see what was happening. She saw Dr Shah glance at the female midwife and give a small shake of his head. He scooped Alice up in his arms and said, 'We need to take your baby to somewhere we can best help her.'

Louise looked up at Adam, who by now had tears flowing freely down his face. The true horror of the situation had suddenly hit home for both of them; they were about to lose their baby, of that there seemed little doubt. Louise fell back into her pillow and screamed at the top of her voice, 'YA ALLAH!'

Adam looked down at his wife in bewilderment, but he hardly had time to think about what he had heard before a wavering 'Waaa' came from baby Alice who was still in the doctors' arms, as if answering her mother's cry.

The medical staff were briefly shocked into silence, then uttered a collective sigh of relief, while the male midwife placed a suction tube inside Alice's mouth. This was followed by a much louder 'Waaa' then an even louder one. Dr Shah continued rubbing Alice's chest as he walked across, smiling, to Louise and Adam. He gently laid Alice on her mother's chest.

'Here's your baby, but I'm afraid you can only hold her for a few seconds. She didn't breathe for a while, so we'll need to run a few tests, but she looks fine.'

The happy parents took turns holding their baby for a minute or so and Adam took a few pictures with his mobile phone, then the midwife gently scooped up Alice and rushed her from the room.

Louise smiled up at Adam, but rather than looking elated at the birth of their second child, he seemed distracted.

'What's the matter darling? Our beautiful little girl's just been born, but you look worried. Aren't you happy?'

He forced a smile, leaned forward and kissed her forehead.

'Of course I'm happy, but when the doctor was about to take Alice from the room, you shouted something strange. It sounded like "Ya Allah". What was all that about?'

A sinking feeling came over her but she couldn't allow that to be shown on her face. In Afghanistan, 'Ya Allah' was often used as an appeal to God. She hadn't realised what she'd shouted; in fact, she hadn't realised she'd shouted anything at all but she now had to think quickly. Luckily, a feasible response came to mind and she feigned laughter.

'Did I? How weird. Sorry darling, that's a throwback to my time in Afghanistan. Whenever there's something horrible going on in their lives, the Afghan women try many different prayers, but when every other prayer has failed, they look up to the heavens and scream "Ya Allah" as loud as they can.'

Adam nodded slowly, a smile beginning to develop at the corners of his mouth.

'I see. I was confused there for a moment. I thought you might be going full Muslim on me.'

She could sense that he was still a little sceptical.

'I suppose I'd seen and heard it so many times that it's lodged somewhere in my subconscious. That's the only explanation I can think of.'

His expression softened and he squeezed her hand.

'Well, that would explain it. Anyway, we should be directing all our thoughts, hopes, and prayers towards our beautiful Alice.'

They stared at one another, sharing that special moment between the parents of a new-born child, a moment which is even more special when the life seemed to be so fragile.

41

Islamic Centre, Royston, Hertfordshire
Thursday 3rd May 2029, 12.45pm

'The Imam will see you now, Mrs Williams.'

The Imam's assistant was a young Pakistani male with a short, neat beard. He held out his arm indicating for the woman, wearing a green hijab and matching trouser suit, to follow him out into the corridor.

Louise had come to realise that she was in urgent need of spiritual guidance and advice and had given a false name for obvious reasons. Ever since that moment over six months ago when she had looked down at her friend Millie dying of wounds she herself had inflicted; her mind had been a mess. She couldn't concentrate on anything properly or think straight, to the extent that it had spoiled her enjoyment of the first few weeks of Alice's life, leading to concerns from friends and family that she might be suffering from post-natal depression.

Her heart was telling her that the acts of violence she had committed in the name of Islam could not be justified, but the brainwashing she'd undergone in Afghanistan wasn't about to be erased that easily, visiting her in dreams and whenever she had a quiet moment, trying again and again to convince her that everything she'd done in the name of Harb Alsheueb had been the right thing and that her past actions would eventually make the world a better place.

She simply had to speak with someone unconnected with her everyday existence, someone who had extensive knowledge of the Islamic religion, and who might be able to make sense of what she was going through. She'd made the appointment with Imam Parvaiz Bashara two weeks previously and had many questions for him. That meeting was about to take place.

Adam was busy all day and Louise had lied that she was going to meet a couple of friends from university in Cambridge. She'd explained that they were desperate to meet Oliver and Alice and that she would be spending the day showing them off.

Having travelled to Royston by a series of trains and the tube, she had arrived at the Mosque thirty minutes early and was pleasantly surprised to find a strikingly attractive building, topped by an amazing emerald green dome, albeit situated between an empty shop and a run-down greasy-spoon cafe. During the journey, she had changed her costume to that of an Islamic woman and was unlikely to be recognised.

She had been shown through to a sparsely furnished room, with a bare wooden table in its centre and half-a-dozen wooden chairs along one wall. She had chosen a seat, settled down and waited. When the young assistant called her, for a moment she forgot her assumed name, then realising her time had come, lifted herself from the chair with Alice strapped to her front in a papoose and pushing Oliver in his buggy.

The door at the far end of the corridor was opened by the assistant, who held out an arm for her to enter. Louise pinned her shoulders back, stood up tall and, pushing the buggy in front of her, entered the room. She was rather surprised to see the assistant remain outside, leaving her alone in the room with the Imam. She closed the door and turned to face him.

'Assalamu Alaikum.'

Imam Bashara responded, 'Wa Alaikum Assalam.'

He was seated behind a large dark-wood desk, on what looked like a black computer chair. Rising to his feet, he placed his right hand against his chest by way of greeting, a gesture which Louise reciprocated.

'I'm very glad to meet you, Mrs Williams. Please take a seat.'

He indicated the basic wooden chair on Louise's side of the desk. She manoeuvred the buggy alongside and sat down, checking that Alice was comfortable as she did so. She was relieved to see that she, like Oliver, was fast asleep.

Looking nervously behind herself towards the door, she looked enquiringly at the Imam, who smiled reassuringly.

'Do not worry, Mrs Williams. It is entirely acceptable for us to be alone together. Imams are frequently required to speak with worshipers in private, be they men or women.'

'Oh, I didn't realise that.'

Looking more closely at him, she guessed he was around sixty, sporting a full beard and moustache, with short salt and pepper hair. He wore a dark grey Thawb, an ankle-length garment, and had round metal-rimmed spectacles. Although not an imposing figure, he radiated a calm confidence.

Bashara raised his eyebrows and inclined his head to one side.

'You sounded keen to meet with me in your email and even more so over the phone. Tell me, Mrs Williams, how can I help you?'

She removed her handbag from her shoulder and

lowered it to the floor. Now the time had come, she had to find the right words to explain her confusion.

'I was in Afghanistan as an aid worker a few years ago and soon realised that I should begin following Islam and the teachings of Allah.' She fidgeted a little, adjusting her headscarf. 'The religion completely gripped me during my time there, and I have since become a devout Muslim.'

The Imam smiled broadly. 'That's wonderful, did you have no belief or faith before you discovered Islam?'

Louise sat forward. 'I was raised as a Christian, and regularly attended Church of England services.'

'I see, please continue.'

Louise understood that she needed to be very careful. She definitely couldn't reveal what had actually happened in Afghanistan, but she needed answers to why she was experiencing such conflicting emotions.

'I became involved with a group who believed in direct action against western governments.'

She paused, trying to assess his reaction, but he remained impassive.

'I refused to allow myself to be taken in, but they were adamant that what they were doing was Allah's will and it's left me confused.'

A knowing look spread across the Imam's face, and he spoke with weariness in his voice. This was something he'd dealt with many times before.

'You want to know if the Quran advocates or permits violence in certain circumstances, don't you Mrs Williams?'

He had got straight to the heart of the problem and she fixed him with a desperate stare.

'Yes... yes, I do.'

Sitting back in his chair and interlinking his fingers, the Imam emitted a heavy sigh.

'This is a problem that's becoming all too common.'

He placed his palms together and pushed the tips of his index fingers onto the point of his nose. He remained silent for a few moments as if to marshal his thoughts then looked into Louise's eyes.

'People who claim that the Quran gives Muslims the right to use violence against others are perverse. They are simply cherry-picking phrases from the holy scriptures to suit their own ends.'

He paused again and drew a deep breath.

'You see, Mrs Williams, if you decide to read the Quran, you are required to read it in full, not just sections of it. If you comply with this instruction, you'll see that the Quran only permits violence in strictly limited situations...'

Louise leaned forward and interrupted, 'Yes, I understand that, but what are those situations?'

Iman Bashara slowly turned his head from side to side, seemingly trying to loosen a stiff neck.

'The situations are mainly when war has been declared against you, or you are under constant attack,' he leaned forward in his chair, 'but even then it is only allowed in self-defence, and that means the defence of people from your community, people of all religions, not just Muslims.'

He tilted his head back and closed his eyes, weighing his words carefully.

'All verses of the Quran relating to fighting are pre-conditioned on clearly outlined rules of self-defence. Those that behave contrary to these rules are, as I said, selectively using phrases to suit their own ends, something which the Quran strictly forbids and describes such people as 'perverse'.'

Louise felt deeply comforted to hear an Imam explain precisely what the Quran taught, not just what had been instilled in her during her time in Afghanistan. She had read this in the Quran for herself many times, but having it confirmed by a person of the standing of Imam Bashara meant a lot.

'So, the Quran doesn't permit violence against innocent people in any circumstances?'

'No, Mrs Williams, not in any circumstances. Those who claim that this is the case are going *against* the teachings of Allah.'

As their discussion continued, the Imam extolled the virtues of the Islamic faith as a loving, caring, and forgiving religion. His words acted as a balm to Louise's troubled mind. The truth was not as she had been instructed by the evil people with warped minds she had been influenced by in Afghanistan, but lay in kindness and love for all persons, irrespective of their religion: the very principles which had drawn her to Islam in the first place.

'Thank you so much for seeing me. I understand what an incredibly busy person you must be.'

A tired smile and the merest of nods were the only recognition of her words.

'I spend much of my time reassuring people like you that the pathway of Islam is a path of peace, not violence. Go in peace, Mrs Williams, and spend the remainder of your life spreading peace and love, not hatred and violence.'

Louise picked up her handbag and slowly rose to her feet.

'Thank you so much.' She bowed her head. 'Assalamu Alaikum.'

He raised his right hand in a gesture of farewell, 'Wa Alaikum Assalam.'.

She wheeled the buggy round and opened the door, to find the assistant still waiting outside. She smiled warmly at him.

'Assalamu Alaikum.'

He returned her smile.

'Wa Alaikum Assalam.'

She thanked him for his assistance and walked out of the Mosque into the busy streets of Royston.

42

One Tree House, Pilgrim's Way, Otford, Kent
Sunday 21st October 2029, 6.50pm

"The bear waved goodbye to his new friends and went back inside his cave. Chloe and Tom walked home to their mummy and daddy and they all lived happily ever after."

Louise closed the storybook and kissed Oliver on the cheek.

'Goodnight, sleep tight, don't let the bed-bugs bite.'

Oliver chuckled happily to himself, sucked his thumb and snuggled down under his small duvet, cuddling his toy bunny. Standing up, she made sure his monitor was switched on at the plug, turned the light off, closed the door quietly and tiptoed from the room.

Before she went back downstairs to re-join Adam, she popped into Alice's room to check that her monitor was also switched on. Leaning over her cot, she gently kissed her on the forehead as she slept then quietly closed the door and walked out onto the landing.

Her latest meeting with Sulayman, which had happened four months previously in June, suddenly entered her mind. He'd told her that Harb Alsheueb were now relying on her relationship with Adam to carry out their greatest attack on any western government since their creation. Hearing their plans had caused her profound dismay.

She knew that her plea to Allah had been answered when he helped Alice to take her first breath. Indeed, Alice's life was a gift she could never hope to repay, but she was determined not to repay him by carrying out the wishes of Harb Alsheueb. Her heart remained true to Allah, but Imam Bashara had shown her that the way of violence was not acceptable. She had heard Sulayman out but had not responded with her usual enthusiasm; in truth, she needed time to work out how to extricate herself from her commitment to Harb Alsheueb, which could prove very tricky.

Walking downstairs into the lounge, she wasn't surprised to see Adam fast asleep in his armchair. He rarely took time off these days and often had to manage with only four or five hours' sleep a night. It had been wonderful to have him home for a whole day, and they'd taken full advantage by enjoying a day out with the children at Knole Park in Sevenoaks, feeding the deer by hand, and Adam had collected a carrier bag full of chestnuts for roasting. Roast chestnuts were a particular favourite of Louise, a memory of her childhood, a fact Adam knew well.

Louise crept upstairs, entered one of the two spare bedrooms and knelt down to pray. One of the first things she had done after moving into their house was find out which way was south-east, the direction of Mecca. In fact, she'd learned that if possible, the prayers should be made in the precise direction of 119 degrees on a compass, something which she had also worked out shortly after they moved in.

She wouldn't normally risk praying when Adam was in the house, but he was sound asleep and she would only be a few minutes. She removed a headscarf from a drawer and placed it on her head, because a Muslim woman's prayer was worthless unless her hair was covered. She'd hidden a hijab in a drawer in both spare bedrooms, ensuring she was well prepared whenever she had the opportunity to pray. They were left over from her time in Afghanistan and had proved extremely useful since she'd returned. Sadly, she'd been unable to purchase her own prayer mat, which would have been too difficult to explain away should it be discovered.

Louise began saying her prayers in her head, starting with 'Allahu Akbar' (God is the greatest). As part of each prayer, she knelt down and laid her torso onto her thighs, elbows tucked in to her sides, hands and head touching the floor.

She loved praying so much; it blessed her with inner peace and made her feel closer to God. In her difficult, duplicitous life, praying had always given her moments of calm and tranquillity.

Suddenly, she heard the door of their bedroom open, and realised with a start that Adam was looking for her. She leapt to her feet, whipped the headscarf off and threw it back into the drawer. Just as she closed it, Adam walked in.

'I woke up and wondered where you'd got to.'

Her mind worked quickly.

'I was looking for the winter duvet. I'm certain it's in one of the drawers, but I can't find the bloody thing anywhere. I've got no idea what I've done with it.'

He chuckled, reached out, and took her by the hand. Leading her into the other spare bedroom, he opened the ottoman, pointing out the winter duvet lying on top of a large pile of linen.

'You've got a memory like a sieve. Don't you remember, we put it here last spring?'

'My God, what's wrong with me?' she said, rolling her eyes, then she lied to him, 'I don't remember that at all.'

'Come on, let's go and watch some telly before bed.' He followed her downstairs, where they snuggled up together on the settee. Adam idly glanced through some work papers.

A couple of hours later, just as Louise's eyes were beginning to droop, the ITV News at Ten opened with some startling news.

'We have breaking news that counter terrorist police have tonight charged four people under the Prevention of Terrorism Act, 2000. Two of those charged are a thirty-one-year-old man from Bristol for the Gloucester bombing on 5th May 2028, and a twenty-four-year-old woman from Stalybridge in Cheshire for the Manchester attack on the same day. Over now to our crime correspondent Abdul Alkham.'

Louise was now wide awake.

'Good evening from outside New Scotland Yard, where fifteen minutes ago, Detective Chief Superintendent Mark Dawes made the following statement.' The reporter began to read from a piece of paper. "At 8.00pm this evening two people were charged with Murder, Possession of an article for Terrorist Purposes, and Membership of a Proscribed Organisation. Thirty-one-year-old Payam Wahab from Bristol has been charged in connection with the Gloucester bombing and twenty-four-year-old Taalia Nour from Stalybridge has been charged in connection with the Manchester bombing."

He paused for a moment while glancing down at his notes, then continued, 'DCS Dawes explained that they have also charged two other men with Conspiracy to Murder, and offences under the Preparation of Terrorism Act, 2006. These men are thought to have been the handlers of the bombers. All four have been charged in connection with the bombings on 5th May 2028. These charges have been brought thanks to the co-operation of a high-ranking member of Harb Alsheueb, who has been in prison for some time.'

Louise could feel a cold hand clutching her heart. This meant that she and Sulayman were now the only remaining pair at large for the 5/5 attacks.

Adam looked up from his paperwork.

'Wow, one of them is grassing, that's fucking brilliant. Only a matter of time before they nail the final two scumbags.'

She forced a smile while controlling her body's urge to shake or stand up and run from the room.

'Yes, it's about time they caught them isn't it?'

Deep down though, she was screaming inside. If they'd received further information from a high-ranking member of Harb Alsheueb, why hadn't she and Sulayman been arrested and charged? This man had firstly given up three bombers and their handlers, and now, many months later, he'd suddenly decided to give up two more pairs. How much more freedom might she be allowed to enjoy before he eventually gave up her and Sulayman? She felt physically sick and faked a yawn.

'Sorry darling, I'm really tired, do you mind if I turn in?'

Adam kissed her on the cheek and whispered, 'Of course I don't mind. Sweet dreams,' then held up his red box and made a sad face. 'I'll be up in a while. Just got a few things to go through first.'

Louise had heard this many times before and knew that he wouldn't be coming to bed anytime soon. She didn't really mind; after all, his job had given their family the wonderful lives they enjoyed. She especially didn't mind on this occasion because she was quaking with fear and felt as if she were about to burst into tears, neither of which she wanted to do in front of him. Smiling, she squeezed his hand, and made her way quickly upstairs to bed.

However, once tucked up under the duvet, the tears wouldn't come. Instead, she lay there, eyes wide open, looking up into the darkness while trying to imagine what her existence would be like banged up in prison for the remainder of her life. Instead of tears and despair, she experienced a bizarre sense of anger; which was ironic, as she was one of the bombers that had caused so much death and mutilation in the first place.

A few months previously, she would have given up her family if that's what Harb Alsheueb had wanted, but now she knew that life without her husband and children would be unbearable. She resolved to do whatever was required to ensure she didn't go to prison.

The same question plagued her mind again and again: why hadn't they arrested her and Sulayman? Could it be possible that the high-ranking member of Harb Alsheueb only knew the details of five handlers and operatives? It seemed unlikely but appeared to be the only rational answer.

Then it came to her, and it was obvious when she thought about it. The grass did know the details of Sulayman and herself, but their value and importance to the organisation was far too great for him to give them up. After all, Adam aspired to, one day, hold one of the great offices of state, perhaps even becoming Prime Minister.

By giving up details of the first three pairs, the informant had assured himself a substantial reduction in prison sentence; then, several months later, by providing details of another two pairs, he could gain himself privileges in prison, while at the same time allowing Harb Alsheueb to retain part of their terrorist capability, by leaving the pair who could do most damage free to carry out an attack. At the same time as cooperating with the authorities, he would be ensuring that he retained a few of Allah's blessings.

This left Louise in a quandary. She really didn't want to meet with Sulayman or carry out any further operations on their behalf, but she needed some kind of reassurance that she wasn't about to be arrested. The next time she was directed to meet Sulayman, she would question him about the arrests of the other operatives and handlers, then find a way to explain that she no longer supported Harb Alsheueb and refuse to carry out their orders. Her mind was made up.

43

St John's Gardens, London
Wednesday 24th April 2030, 8.10am

Sulayman saw Louise approaching along the gravel path and greeted her.

'Assalamu Alaikum.'

'Wa Alaikum Assalam.'

'Hi, how are the kids?'

She regarded him with a quizzical look.

'They're great thanks, how are you?' She practically spat the words at him.

He picked up on her angry tone and raised his hands in a defensive gesture.

'You were told at the very start that contact would be minimal. Please don't be cross with me, Louise. I'm only following orders, same as you.'

Her expression changed from one of bewilderment to one of indifference.

'Sorry. It's just that after the arrests in October some kind of reassurance would have been appreciated. Instead, I got nothing, absolutely nothing, total silence.'

'I know, and believe me I was just as worried.'

'Who the fuck is passing the police information about operatives and handlers?'

'The man who blew the whistle is called Haalim Mahood, a section commander in Harb Alsheueb, the highest-ranking member ever arrested. Unusually, he decided to sing like a canary once he was in custody.'

He wrapped his scarf tighter around his neck.

'The puzzling thing is, he definitely knew about you and me, but said nothing. So the question is... why did he keep schtum?'

'I know all that, but why no contact? I was absolutely terrified.'

'I've been informed that because of the risk involved, the hierarchy weren't prepared to chance contacting either of us. They assumed any contact could leave a trail back to them.'

'Oh, so as long as they're safe everything's fine?'

'We're not here to question our leaders. Believe me, I was shitting myself, too. I was waiting for the police to knock on my door at any time.'

Louise shrugged, not bothering to reply.

Sulayman decided to change the subject.

'How is Adam?'

'He's fine now, but he struggled to understand what was causing me to be so tetchy.'

They walked round one of the paths in an anti-clockwise direction. Sulayman looked at the ground as he walked, breathing in deeply through his nose.

'We've activated an operative who happened to be in the same prison as Mahood. I'm here to pass on good news.'

She looked intrigued. 'What's that?'

'He's no longer a threat to either of us.'

She let out a small yelp of pleasure.

'Oh Sulayman, that's wonderful!' She beamed at him. 'But why hasn't it been on the news?'

He shook his head.

'I've no idea. The security services must have their reasons for keeping it from the public. Anyway, you don't need to worry any more. I'm reliably informed he was stabbed to death in the exercise yard.'

'What about the man who killed him?'

'He was on a life sentence anyway.'

'So, the reason for this meeting was purely to tell me the good news?'

He kicked a couple of loose twigs on the ground.

'No, not just that.' He folded his arms. 'I understand that Adam is the blue-eyed boy of the Labour Party.'

Louise knew where this was going and felt a rising sense of dread.

'Yes, he's doing very well. Nine months ago, he was promoted to Home Secretary in a reshuffle, but you already know that.'

Sulayman pulled his scarf up against the chill wind.

'Yes, I heard. He's climbing the ladder, but he's still only forty-two, isn't he?'

'Yes, his birthday was a few weeks ago. What's his age got to do with anything?'

He ignored her question.

'Does he have aspirations to become Prime Minister?'

Narrowing her eyes, she answered warily, 'Yes, he does. In fact, he's almost certain he's got sufficient support to stand as a candidate for the leadership right now, and he thinks he could be successful.'

'Isn't he rather young to be PM?'

'Not really. Blair and Cameron were both forty-three when they got the job.'

'If Adam became Prime Minister, it would give us the platform we've been looking for. It would be better than Harb Alsheueb could ever have hoped for.'

She lifted her eyes in resignation.

'You want to use Adam's position to strike at the government again, don't you?'

He nodded and shrugged. 'What else would you expect?'

'Nothing I suppose.'

'Complete this mission, and when the day of your death arrives, your position alongside Allah in paradise will be assured. That's got to be worth what we're asking, isn't it?'

Louise could no longer control herself.

'I'm not buying that rubbish anymore, Sulayman, and I won't do it. I've been learning about Islam, the real Islam, not your version of it.'

'And what would that be?'

'I've been to see an Imam and he explained that violence other than in self-defence is not permitted.'

Sulayman laughed. 'So now you think you know better than us? How naive!'

He looked down at her sternly and continued, 'Our bosses anticipated that, at some point, you might get cold feet. They've asked me to advise you to think carefully. They wouldn't want your children to suffer.'

She grabbed his arm and span him round, an act forbidden between a man and woman who were not related or married, but she didn't care. He couldn't meet her gaze.

'Those bastards! After all I've done, they'd threaten my children?'

Still unable to meet her gaze he said, 'Sorry, Louise. They're insisting you carry out one final operation. Please understand this is not my decision, it's not my wish.'

Her face contorted with fury and she had to stop herself from hitting him and screaming. Her mind worked quickly. Realising that she couldn't allow her children to suffer for a situation of her own making, she brought herself under control.

'You listen to me, Sulayman, I will not endanger my husband or children. I'll do whatever I'm required to do, but I no longer believe in their sick methods. I'm not stupid, I understand that I'm in too deep to refuse.' She was breathless with anger. 'But this is absolutely the last thing I'll do for them. I hope I've made myself clear?' She glared fiercely at him then let go of his arm.

Sulayman gave her a withering look.

'I'll be straight with you. Their goal is to detonate a device at 10 Downing Street, so the operative *must* be you. Of course, this all depends on Adam becoming Prime Minister and you living there.'

She nodded. 'I thought that might be the plan.' She looked at her watch. 'I'm expected at work soon. I'll anticipate your contact if Adam ever becomes PM. As long as they understand that it might never happen.'

'I knew you'd see sense, and I can promise you that if you complete this one final operation, you'll be free to live your life without further contact from Harb Alsheueb.'

She didn't reply, just shook her head.

'I'll see you in a year or two, hopefully when Adam is Prime Minister.' He raised his right hand to say goodbye, 'Assalamu Alaikum.'

She didn't respond or return the gesture, aware of how rude that was. Instead, she turned and walked swiftly through a nearby gate and out of the park.

On her way to the office she fought back the tears, hating the predicament she now found herself in. How could she have been so stupid? Why had she let herself be seduced by such an evil organisation? How could she possibly consider killing more innocent people in the name of Islam? The simple answer to all those questions was that Louise would do anything to protect her family.

She was no longer fooling herself that she was carrying out the wishes of Allah, but she would reluctantly carry out the wishes of Harb Alsheueb and see innocent people die, if that were the only way to ensure that her children lived.

44

SO15 Headquarters, Edgware Road, London
Monday 6th May 2030, 2.00pm

DCI Barney Briscow raised his hands to bring silence to the briefing room, then nodded to an officer sitting to one side. The officer pressed a button on his laptop, causing the images of five bombers and five handlers to flash up on the screen above his head.

'Ladies and gents, yesterday was the second anniversary of the shop bombings which rocked the UK and brought this country to a standstill. Two years have passed, yet we're still searching for the Clothes Bazaar bomber and her handler. Dozens of suspects were suggested by the public at the time and from that huge response eight suspects were arrested and interviewed but all of them had cast-iron alibis.'

He paced restlessly from one side of the briefing room to the other and used a pointer pen to indicate images of the bombers and handlers who had already been convicted and sentenced for the five other attacks. He allowed the bright red dot to linger on each of their faces for a couple of seconds.

'These fuckers are now serving thirty-year-plus sentences,' he nodded to the officer at the laptop and the image changed to one of Louise in her disguise, 'but this bitch is still out there, living her life just as before, unhindered by the attentions of the police or security services. Together with her handler she is free to carry out another attack whenever required.'

A female detective sergeant raised her hand.

Pointing at the officer he said, 'Yes?'

'She'll have fled the country by now wouldn't she?'

Briscow shrugged and raised his eyebrows.

'That has to be a possibility, it might even be considered a probability, but for the moment we need to assume she's still here in the UK. My purpose for calling you in today is to re-focus our efforts on tracing her, because we now have reasons to believe that the woman involved in the abduction of Sarah Cairn, and this woman, are the same person.'

His words brought small gasps from the officers around the room; they began straining to look more closely at the dual images on the screen.

'Although the woman on the Regent Street attack did a great job of keeping her hijab well forward to hide her face, our boffins have been analysing the movements of both women, especially the way they walk, and they're almost certain this is the same person. That doesn't necessarily help with identification, but it certainly gives us more to work on, and hopefully we'll be able to narrow down the field of suspects who could have carried out these crimes.'

He looked down at his notes.

'The CCTV checks of people leaving Green Park after the attack have proved inconclusive as there are simply too many people who changed appearance once the rain started. We've somehow managed to trace images of nineteen different women who are seen leaving the park, but we've been unable to find them entering, so that's a non-runner. Even if we were to successfully identify her, which is highly unlikely, it would never stand up in court.

'On today's early evening news, they will be repeating the original reports from the day of the attacks, passing on to the public the information I've just given you, and re-showing the images of this woman. I'm convinced that someone, somewhere, must have recognised something about her, so let's jog their memories. It could be the way she walked or maybe another mannerism. There is even the possibility that someone knows who she is, but is not prepared to report her to police because they're struggling with divided loyalties.'

Commander Mark Dawes, who had been recently promoted, entered the room but said nothing, taking a seat behind everyone at the back. Briscow nodded in his direction, acknowledging his presence.

'I want all DI's to task officers under their command with reviewing every piece of information received in the weeks following the attack. That means every CCTV, every witness statement, every victim statement, every interview with suspects for each and every attack, whether they ended up being charged or released. That includes every known associate of the suspects and every electronic communication suspected to have come from Harb Alsheueb in the lead up to the attacks.'

Thirty minutes later, while Briscow was still in full flow, passing on the latest information about the investigation, Commander Dawes climbed to his feet and moved slowly around the side of the room to join him; Briscow held out his hand to indicate that the stage was his. Dawes rubbed his hands together, then opened his palms and stared intently at them before raising his eyes.

'Following the 5/5 bombings we got really lucky.

Haalim Mahood was the highest-ranking whistle-blower from a terrorist organisation we've ever managed to obtain information from. His testimony helped with the arrest, charging, and conviction of operatives and handlers for five of the attacks but the public still look upon us as failures, because that fucking woman,' he pointed angrily up at the screen, 'has made monkeys out of us all.'

He was blatantly working hard to remain calm and professional.

'Unfortunately, we weren't able to protect Mahood as we'd promised and now he's dead. Apart from anything else, that means he will never be able to divulge the identity of the final bomber.

'Yesterday was the second anniversary, and I know how hard you've all worked, especially those who've been retained on this investigation throughout that time. However, until further notice, and certainly for at least the next two weeks, everyone working on other enquiries will be re-deployed onto the 5/5 investigation.' He looked up at the image on the screen. 'It's time that bitch got her come-uppance.'

He'd said his piece and stepped to one side. Barney Briscow moved forward and positioned himself directly underneath the screen. He reached up with his right hand and rubbed his right ear between forefinger and thumb.

'This woman is not believed to be Arabic or Asian. She appears to have white skin tone, so could well be Northern European, possibly even British.'

He took two paces forward. 'Now there's a thought - she could be *British*; she could even be living right here in the centre of London. If that is the case, there's every likelihood she's someone who's continued living a normal life, someone well known and well loved, so don't discount anyone.'

He stared blankly.

'That's enough for now. We need to get out there and fucking find her. Thank you for coming and good hunting everyone.'

45

Outside 10 Downing Street, London
Thursday 22nd August 2030, 2.00pm

The Prime Minister walked briskly out of the famous door into the cold drizzle and approached the lectern. An aide walked alongside, holding an umbrella over her. She was followed out by her husband, who moved to one side and wore a solemn expression, ten paces to her left; he had no umbrella and stood stoically still, slowly getting wet.

Standing with a hand resting on either side of the lectern, Caroline Farrell faced the mass of cameras and reporters on the opposite side of the road. She cast her gaze from left to right then looked down at her notes before speaking.

'Thank you for coming out in this awful weather. I won't keep you too long.'

Her voice faltered. Sucking in a deep breath, and regaining control, she continued, 'I have enjoyed three wonderful years as Prime Minister and served our great nation to the very best of my abilities. Sadly, some of my colleagues within the Parliamentary Labour Party feel that my best hasn't been good enough.'

She looked down at her feet before lifting her head

and carrying on.

'Therefore, I am standing down as leader of the Labour Party and as Prime Minister. I will remain leader and Prime Minister while the party conducts a leadership contest over the next few weeks. I can assure you that whoever takes over from me will have my full support, to enable this wonderful country of ours to drive forward and prosper. Thank you.'

Her last few words were spoken with her chin quivering and tears in her eyes. After completing her statement, she reached for her husband's hand and walked with him to the door, where they stood waving goodbye, before turning their backs on the cameras and disappearing inside number 10.

46

Labour Party Head Office, London
Monday 30th September 2030, 10.00am

Labour Party Chairman William Head received the numbers of votes cast from the three tellers and checked the figures with each of them before rising to his feet.

'Members, the process for electing our new leader and therefore our Prime Minister is at an end. It began six weeks ago when seven members entered the race. This was reduced to five after the first vote, three after the second, and finally down to the last two - Adam Greenacre and Andrew Sheen.' He paused and looked around at the Labour members of parliament gathered in front of him.

'The total number of votes cast was 332 and there were no spoiled papers. The result, which has been checked and verified, is as follows. Andrew Sheen, 157, Adam Greenacre 175, and I hereby declare that Adam Greenacre has been duly elected as leader of the Labour Party and therefore Prime Minister of the United Kingdom.'

Spontaneous applause and cheering filled the room. Andrew Sheen, although bitterly disappointed with his narrow defeat, forced a smile and warmly shook Adam's hand in congratulation. He leaned forward and spoke directly into Adam's ear.

'Well done, Adam, you'll make a great Prime Minister. Be assured you'll receive the full support of myself and my team.'

'Thanks Andrew, and thanks for a clean campaign. It was the first decent contest for years.'

Twenty minutes later Adam received an enthusiastic ovation from his parliamentary colleagues after concluding his acceptance speech. He left the hall after shaking countless hands and stepped outside, where he found the Prime Ministerial Car and a team of police protection officers waiting for him. This was what he had striven for his whole political career, but he knew that his life was never going to be the same again.

Five minutes later, Adam arrived outside Number 10 and smiled to himself as his car door was opened by his personal protection officer, Claire. He nodded his appreciation but she didn't make eye contact as she said, 'Congratulations, Prime Minister.' She was a consummate professional and her eyes were fixed on the press gathered on the opposite side of the street, searching for any threat of danger.

Waiting on the doorstep of Number 10 were Louise, Oliver, and Alice. After waving to the cameras, Adam walked over to his beaming wife, kissed her on the cheek then crouched down and hugged his children, who both seemed somewhat overwhelmed by the crowds of shouting journalists.

As he stood up, Louise whispered excitedly, 'I can't believe this, I'm the wife of the Prime minister!' She was enjoying the moment so much that all thoughts of the implications of Adam's success had been temporarily banished from her mind.

'Got to make my speech now darling. Back in a

minute.'

Adam stepped forward to the lectern and began to speak. Ten minutes later, following a speech during which he stressed that one of his top priorities would be dealing robustly with the threat from terrorism, he gathered Louise and the children together for the usual family photo shoot in front of the famous door.

Once the photographers were satisfied, the door slowly opened and the family were encouraged to step inside by aides. Staff lined the corridors and up the staircase, politely applauding and cheering as their new charges were shown around the building and the family were taken upstairs to the living quarters, which would be their home for the foreseeable future. Louise smiled at everyone, slightly overawed, and marvelled at the portraits of Adam's predecessors covering the walls. Adam had seen them many times before, but seeing them again today somehow reinforced the responsibility and gravity of his new role.

An unwelcome thought briefly entered Louise's head. *How the hell am I going to get a device in here?* For the first time, she felt pangs of regret at Adam's rise to power.

Having entered their apartment, Louise and the children looked around, astounded at the size of the rooms and the grandeur of their new surroundings. Gradually, the private secretaries and aides backed away and the door into their private quarters was closed; the family were alone at last.

Adam gathered them together in a group hug.

'We'll sleep at Otford tonight. The removal company will arrive in the morning and tomorrow night we'll be sleeping here, in Number 10 Downing Street! We are now officially the United Kingdom's number one family!'

Louise knew that for her, the change would be

immense; she would be the wife of the Prime Minister and at some stage in the future, she would be required to plant a bomb right there in their new home!

After lunch, Adam got down to business. He needed to construct his cabinet, which meant sacking people he didn't like or who disagreed with him and appointing new members to the cabinet who shared his vision for the country; making a statement to parliament about how he saw the way forward and finally driving to Buckingham Palace, where the Queen would symbolically appoint him as her new Prime Minister.

The journey from Number 10 back to their home in Kent felt surreal. Stepping outside onto Downing Street, Louise and the children were greeted by the flashes of countless cameras and journalists shouting inane questions like, 'What's it like to be the wife of the Prime Minister, Louise?'

They were ushered into an unmarked Jaguar by plain-clothed protection officers and when the vehicle pulled away, Louise glanced behind, to see they were being followed by a similarly unmarked Range Rover containing three armed officers. Their lives had changed, certainly for the moment, but probably forever.

She held the hands of Oliver and Alice tightly.

'Well, what did you think of today. Did you enjoy it?'

They both excitedly said, 'Yes, yes, yes!' although Alice clearly didn't know what she was excited about; 'yes' was one of only four words she could say.

Oliver spoke over his younger sister. 'Is Daddy clever now, Mummy?'

Louise smiled, 'Yes, he is. He was already clever, and now your Daddy is the cleverest person in the country. He's one of the cleverest people in the world.'

That night, Adam didn't arrive home until after midnight. He crept into the bedroom, undressed and slid into bed alongside Louise. He was tired but his mind was buzzing. Suddenly Louise said something unexpected.

'So, Prime Minister, are you as horny as me...?'

She slid over to his side of the bed and placed her left hand on his chest. He responded by pulling her to him, wrapping an arm around her and kissing her.

'It's after midnight. Why aren't you asleep?'

She whispered, 'Because I'm looking forward to having sex with the Prime Minister. What could be more of a turn on than that?'

She climbed on top of him. 'You may be Prime Minister, but you were my husband first and I'm going to make sure you don't forget it.'

Twenty-five minutes later, they lay in each-other's arms after the best sex they'd had for months.

'Wow! If that's what making love is like as Prime Minister, I hope I get at least three terms.' He chuckled at his own joke, kissing Louise on the forehead as he did so.

She lay quietly then said sadly, 'We aren't going to see much of you from now on, are we?'

He ran his fingers through her hair.

'I can't lie, Lulu, I'm going to be much busier than before and I'll be away a lot.'

He turned onto his side and lifted himself up on one elbow, looking directly into her eyes.

'But my family will always come first. I'll be home as often as the job allows, and if there's a problem I'll drop whatever I'm dealing with, no matter how important.'

His words reassured her. They kissed, snuggled down and fell asleep in each other's arms.

47

St James's Park, London
Tuesday 29th October 2030, 11.00am

The leaves were falling gently around her on a warm, glowing autumn day. Louise sat on a bench overlooking the now familiar lake, watching the water birds going about their business. The scene was tranquil, but inside her head was a ball of anxiety and confusion caused by the hideous position she now found herself in. She had needed to escape to the park to get away from the confines of Number 10; she needed time on her own to think.

Her dark sunglasses and wide-brimmed hat completely hid her identity, meaning members of the public and tourists would have been unaware they were walking past the wife of the Prime Minister. The protection officers were unhappy that she insisted on going out alone, but were unable to stop her.

The previous day she had met Sulayman in the deserted Archbishop's Park behind Lambeth Palace, just over the River Thames from the Houses of Parliament. The rendezvous followed an email from Haasim she had been dreading. It simply didn't seem fair, coming so soon after Adam had taken up his post.

She had pleaded with Sulayman but her entreaties had fallen on deaf ears. Eventually, he became exasperated with her refusal to comply and lost his temper, shouting that she'd be carrying out their instructions, whether she liked it or not, otherwise she would face the terrible consequences. Her despair had cut no ice with Sulayman, who'd explained angrily that members of his own family would be killed, too, if he failed to force her to continue with the operation.

Finally, she had conceded, agreeing to plant the device, while questioning whether smuggling it into Number 10 without being detected was even possible. It was, after all, one of the most secure buildings in the country.

Then he dropped a bombshell, something that shook her to the core. They wanted the device planted inside somewhere specific, the Cabinet Room; and they wanted the explosion to take place when the Cabinet was sitting.

Louise had questioned repeatedly how she was supposed to ensure Adam wasn't there. He was the Prime Minister and normally chaired cabinet meetings. Where was she going to send the children, who would be at home with their nanny, Sandra? And how was she supposed to gain access to the Cabinet Room?

Sulayman had looked anxiously around, fearful that their conversation, which had become heated, might be overheard, but the park was almost empty. He'd insisted that it must happen, whatever the difficulties, and that she must ensure it happened on a Thursday, when the Cabinet were sitting. He was unconcerned about Adam and the children; it was her problem how she protected her own family.

The device would be the same as the one at Adam's department, on a nine-day timer. They wanted the explosion timed for maximum effect, in December, just before the Christmas recess. He had left her with instructions that they would be in contact again in late November, deaf to the volley of insults directed at him.

A day later, sitting quietly on the bench in St James's Park, she racked her brains to think of a way to carry out the operation. She knew that Adam occasionally missed a cabinet meeting due to other commitments, and that there were three Thursday meetings in December before they broke up for recess, on the 5th, 12th, and 19th. She needed to check through Adam's diary for December; there was a chance he might miss one of those meetings for some reason and if he did, that was the Thursday she'd choose.

The children were less of a problem. They only went to nursery on Tuesdays and Fridays, so they'd normally be with Sandra inside the apartment, but she would speak to her and arrange for her to take them out for the day. She would think of something suitable for them to do; there was no rush at the moment, she had plenty of time.

Getting the device inside Number 10 would be the most difficult issue, not to mention getting past the increased security, which had been installed at the cost of a million pounds two years earlier in November 2028. Her only hope would be to carry it into the building with Adam alongside her, thereby allowing her to go straight through security without any of the usual checks.

Louise's head had slowly started to clear; she was beginning to see a way forward, a light at the end of the tunnel. It was fraught with problems and potential pitfalls, but it was a way forward nonetheless and concentrating on the practical difficulties somehow distracted her from facing up to the awful significance of what she had agreed to do.

48

Archbishop's Park, London
Tuesday 3rd December 2030, 12.45pm

Louise's umbrella was failing to provide any real shelter from the driving wind and freezing rain, the weather perfectly matching her mood as she watched Sulayman battling to control his own brolly. Louise had moved close to a tall, ivy-clad wall, where she was on the leeward side of the wind, providing her some protection from the weather.

A brief email exchange at the end of November had ended when Louise chose the date for the device to explode – Thursday December 19th. After the animosity at the end of their last meeting, Sulayman dispensed with any pleasantries as he approached her.

'Hello, Louise. The device is identical to the previous ones, so it should be easy to conceal. Incidentally, why have you chosen the 19th. Why not sooner, on the 5th or 12th?'

Louise's face remained expressionless. Pushing strands of wind-blown hair away from her face, she just wanted to get down to business.

'Because on the 19th Adam will be giving a speech to the TUC at Congress House, meaning the Deputy PM will be chairing the Cabinet. I've also checked Adam's diary around the next couple of weeks, and on the 10th he has a gap, so I've arranged to meet him for brunch.'

'What does that have to do with anything?' Sulayman said, impatiently.

'Well, I assume I will be receiving the...' she paused, 'package, nine days in advance, which would be next Tuesday, the 10th. On that day, I'll be arriving back at Number 10 with Adam in his Prime Ministerial car. It's worked out rather well, because otherwise I'd have needed to hide it somewhere until I enter Number 10 with Adam.'

'How does that help? What happens when you get there?'

'I'll simply walk in alongside him and go straight through internal security without being checked.'

'Won't it be awkward if he's with you?'

'Not really. He always has people he needs to speak with before he comes upstairs so that should give me plenty of time to hide it somewhere in the apartment temporarily.'

'Have you thought of somewhere?'

'Yes, it's all in hand.'

Their umbrellas were now overlapping, and between them they formed a much better barrier against the elements. The wind suddenly rose in strength and Sulayman had to raise his voice to be heard over the noise of the tree branches crashing overhead.

'Very well. Be at the same bench in St James' Park as before, at exactly 9.45. The same woman will deliver the device. Once you've taken possession of it, the deployment is entirely up to you, as long as it's in position for Thursday 19th at 10.30.' A wicked smile swept across his features. 'They're going to have a cabinet meeting that the whole world will hear about!'

Louise pulled back in horror, but she knew she had no choice. She had concerns though and wanted answers.

'I've got a couple of questions.'

He struggled to hold onto his umbrella against a particularly strong gust.

'Okay, shoot.'

She shouted against the wind, 'What if I can't find a suitable hiding place in the Cabinet Room?'

'Haven't you done any research? You've had weeks to think about this!'

'Yes,' she spat back at him, 'I've done plenty of fucking research. The Cabinet Room is off limits if you're not a member of the Cabinet, and that includes the PM's wife.'

'For fuck's sake! You're telling me this now?'

Sulayman stared at her furiously. Louise returned his stare with interest, then fought to calm herself down.

'There is one other option which might just work, but would point the finger strongly at me, or a member of our staff.'

'Go on.'

'Our bedroom is directly above the cabinet room. If I could pull up the carpet and raise a floorboard, I could plant the device directly above, in the space between the ceiling and floorboards. That would probably work just as well as having a device inside the room.' She could see by his face that Sulayman was considering it. 'What do you think?'

He wiped rain from his face.

'It sounds feasible and, let's face it, they're bound to suspect one of the staff rather than the Prime Minister or his wife. How easy would it be to lift the carpet and replace it neatly?'

'No problem. We have a small settee in the corner of our bedroom. It's on casters, so I could slide it out of the way while Adam's out, pull up the carpet, unscrew a floorboard, place the device and return everything exactly as it was.'

'Sounds perfect. Now what was your other question?'

Strands of her hair once again escaped from her hood and blew into her mouth; she pushed them away in irritation.

'They sometimes send in sniffer dogs to check the whole building. Apparently, they can detect the tiniest amounts of explosives, so what if they visit between the 10th and 19th?'

Sulayman laughed.

'We're way ahead of the police and their search methods, Louise. The device will be fully taped and sealed, including masking material to kill any scent. The dogs won't be able to detect a thing.'

She looked doubtful.

'I'll have to take your word for that. Okay, that's all.'

Louise span round as if to walk away, then turned and looked at Sulayman sadly through the pouring rain.

'It's a shame it ended like this between us. I used to like you and I shared your values. But now I see the organisation for what it is, and I despise it and everyone involved in it.' She could see the irony in her statement and continued before he could interrupt, 'I know, I was one of them and, believe me, I despise myself most of all. I am about to carry out another evil action, and I will never be able to forgive myself for it.

'Now, are we done here Sulayman?' she was shivering. 'I need to get back to Number 10. There will be questions asked if I'm away too long.'

The rain was getting steadily more uncomfortable. Fighting with his umbrella and stamping his feet against the cold, Sulayman said, 'Yes, we're done.' He moved closer to her. 'Goodbye Louise, you've been a good soldier. Assalamu Alaikum.'

She turned her head away.

He shrugged, turned on his heels and walked towards the exit, Louise following him at a distance. Once outside the park, they joined the path on Carlisle Lane. Sulayman turned left, Louise turned right; they would never meet again.

49

Outside St James' Park Café, London
Tuesday 10th December 2030, 9.40am

The icy drizzle had deterred most people from bothering with a walk in St James' Park on a cold and damp Tuesday morning. Louise was the only person anywhere near the benches outside the café, which was closed until ten. She was carrying the biggest handbag she owned, large enough to easily hold the device and conceal it underneath her other possessions.

Adam had left Downing Street for Parliament at 8.30, where he was due to be answering questions from an all-party committee about the current terrorist threat until ten. After that, he had a window in his schedule until he was due to visit a primary school in Battersea at 1PM. He'd agreed to meet Louise for brunch at 10.15, returning to the café where they'd first met. After that, he needed to get back to Number 10 to change into casual clothes before setting off for the primary school. His change of clothing was something Louise hadn't bargained for.

She had reassured the protection officers that she would be fine walking on her own. This was something they were unhappy with, but over the past few weeks they'd learned there was little point in arguing about it. She was a very single-minded lady and each time she went out, she disguised herself well enough to stop members of the public recognising or bothering her. Today she was wearing the hood up on her jacket, perfectly concealing her identity.

Louise had been standing by the bench, which was far too wet to sit on, and there was nobody else within fifty metres. Less than a minute after she arrived, the same woman who had delivered the device for Adam's department walked up to her, this time dressed in black waterproof trousers and a dark green cagoule with the hood up. They nodded at each other, then both checked the surrounding area, to confirm nobody was near enough to witness their exchange. The Asian woman lifted the small package from her handbag and placed it straight into Louise's. The women exchanged the briefest of glances before the Asian woman said quietly, 'Good luck,' before walking swiftly away.

Louise's whole body was quaking with fear, something which she knew from previous experience would slowly subside and could be put down to the miserable weather. It was hardly surprising; after all she was now carrying an explosive device in her handbag, which would change the UK's history for ever if she managed to successfully deploy it.

She headed off alongside the lake towards Buckingham Palace, crossed the bridge spanning its centre, left the park and crossed Birdcage Walk. Within two minutes she arrived at the café, just after ten.

She entered and removed her soaking wet jacket, smiling at the 'reserved' label on the table where they'd enjoyed their first date. In the centre of the table was a vase containing a single red rose. The only other customers were four female office workers, and a couple holding hands across a table. She pulled back her hair into a neat ponytail and walked to the counter, where she was instantly recognised.

'Hello, I'm the manager. Please call me Rosemary,' said a slight, mousey-haired woman in her early thirties. Her voice quivered a little with excitement. She lifted a flap in the counter and stepped through.

'We're honoured you've chosen our cafe. Hopefully, we've reserved the correct table.'

Louise smiled and nodded. 'Thank you, Rosemary. Yes, that's the one, just as I remember it.'

She was struggling to disguise the crippling terror she was experiencing; her right hand was shaking so much she had to put it inside her coat pocket until it stopped. As the manager smiled at her, Louise wondered what Rosemary would think if she discovered she was carrying a package that could blow her café into a million pieces.

'Can I get you a drink?' asked Rosemary.

'No, thanks, I'll wait for my husband.' Her voice sounded strained inside her own head, something which she hoped hadn't been detected by the staff or customers.

Rosemary grinned and went back behind the counter.

By now, some of the other customers had recognised Louise. The office workers were leaning forward across their table, talking excitedly in hushed tones while sneaking glances in her direction.

Louise chose the same seat she'd taken on their first meeting, facing away from the counter. Suddenly, flashing blue lights outside the café announced the arrival of Adam's convoy. Thirty seconds later, he opened the door and grinned when he saw Louise sitting at the table where they'd fallen in love.

Two plain-clothed officers, one of them a woman Louise knew to be Claire, Adam's Personal Protection Officer, and another who she assumed was also from his protection team, entered immediately behind him and discreetly sat at a table near the door. They scrutinized every customer in the café, as well as the staff working behind the counter then checked through the windows to make sure all was well outside.

Those same customers were caught between trying not to draw the attention of the security personnel to them, while craning their necks to get a better look at the famous couple.

Adam made his way between the tables, bent down, and kissed her forehead.

'Hello beautiful.'

Controlling her terror, she smiled back at him.

'Hello yourself. Had a busy morning?' One of her legs twitched involuntarily with nerves and she had to place a hand on her thigh to suppress it.

He sat down and his smile faded as he spoke in a low tone to prevent them being overheard.

'Same shit, different shovel. I spent an hour and twenty minutes answering questions about the current threat level. Some of those Tories are such wankers. All they're interested in is political point-scoring, not keeping the country safe.'

His words were a stark reminder of Adam's position as the man leading the UK's fight against terrorism. Yet here he was, sitting in a café in the heart of London holding hands with his wife, a woman whose actions had already caused the deaths of ten people, not to mention all those she'd maimed and injured.

'And how is the threat level?' she asked calmly, desperately hoping he couldn't detect her inner turmoil.

'We've just reduced it from 'severe' to 'substantial'.'

'Why has it been reduced?'

'There hasn't been an attack for a while and there appears to be nothing in the pipeline. The security services assure me there's nothing to cause concern.'

Suddenly, she could no longer bear this line of conversation, and gripped his hand tightly.

'Let's not talk about your work! Let's just reminisce about when we met and enjoy our brunch.'

He wrinkled his nose and returned her gaze. Rosemary arrived to take their order, but they'd been so engrossed in conversation they'd completely forgotten to look at the menu. Apologising, they asked for a few more minutes to make their choices.

Out of the blue, a horrific thought came into Louise's head, leaving her cold with fear. She found herself fighting the urge to grab Adam's hand, leave the handbag containing the device in the café, and run.

The thought that Harb Alsheueb might have lied to her and set a short delay on the timer suddenly became glaringly obvious. After all, they were aware of her reluctance to carry out this deployment; they were aware she was meeting Adam shortly after collecting the device and that she would be with him for at least an hour. Having recently become a problem for Harb Alsheueb, this would be the perfect opportunity to dispose of her, while at the same time killing the Prime Minister. *Of course, that's what they're up to. They could take out Adam and me in one explosion.* She masked her rising sense of dread by looking down intently at the menu.

Glancing up, Adam saw the colour drain from his wife's face.

'Are you okay? You look like someone's just walked over your grave.'

She needed to think swiftly but for a moment could think of nothing remotely believable. The feeling of panic was overwhelming. The problem with panic is that irrational thoughts suddenly invade your head, making it even worse. She needed to get a grip and take command of herself, right now.

'Sorry sweetheart, I don't know what came over me. I suddenly felt really uneasy. Whatever it was, it's gone now.'

Adam sat back in his chair, smiling.

'You want to try walking in my shoes. Since I've been Prime Minister, I get that feeling every day. Perhaps it's catching.'

Louise began to relax, convincing herself that Harb Alsheueb wouldn't want their attack to take place outside Number 10, even if it did mean killing the Prime Minister. No, they wanted to make a significant statement; they wanted to show the British people that nowhere was safe from them. That's why the attack had to take place inside one of the most secure locations in the UK and why they'd decided to attack the Cabinet Room; it was symbolic. The panic slowly subsided, leaving Louise glad she hadn't done anything rash.

Rosemary came over to their table and took their orders and from that moment on, they thoroughly enjoyed their stolen hour together. Louise was still finding it difficult to completely relax but she played her part to perfection.

However, when the time came for them to leave, the fear returned. She was now faced with the task of smuggling the device into Number 10, knowing that if it were found in her possession it would mean losing her husband, her children, and her freedom.

50

The Prime Ministerial motorcade swept through Downing Street's security gates. There had been a time, many years ago, when the public were permitted to enter and take pictures outside the front of Number 10; a few elderly people still have photos in an album showing family members standing on the doorstep, posing outside the famous door. Those days were long gone.

Their car pulled up and Adam said, 'That was great. Thanks.' He squeezed Louise's hand.

She pecked him on the cheek.

'My pleasure.'

All the while she was fighting the need to tremble, convinced she would be found out. Holding herself together was taking every ounce of willpower she possessed.

A protection officer opened her door. She brushed herself down, took a deep breath and stepped from the car. She smiled and thanked the officer, waited until Adam walked around to her side of the car and took his hand to walk into Number 10 alongside him.

The doorman greeted them cheerfully.

'Good morning, Sir. Good morning, Madam.'

Adam nodded. 'Morning, Dave. Everything all right?'

'Yes, thank you, Sir.'

Staff stood to one side, allowing them to bypass security, but instead of heading for his office, Adam walked with Louise straight up to the apartment. This was not part of her plan. She'd assumed he would firstly speak with advisors to discuss the day's schedule. Whatever his reason was for coming upstairs, she needed to remain calm.

Forcing herself to behave as naturally as possible, she did exactly what she always did and casually put her handbag down on a chair in the lounge, walked into the kitchen and put the kettle on. Adam hurried straight through to the dressing room, shouting that he needed to get changed.

'Do you fancy a cup of something?' she asked.

'No thanks, love. I'll be heading straight out.'

His reply didn't surprise her as they'd had plenty of hot drinks and cakes at the cafe. What's more, she'd learned over the past ten weeks that a Prime Minister's timetable is like a military operation, leaving very little time to spare between engagements. He could only ever allow himself a brief break. He'd been off-schedule for their meeting in the café but was now back on-schedule and couldn't spare time for a coffee, even if he'd wanted one.

'Sorry love, got to go. I've nothing on tonight, so should be home by six.' He gave her a quick hug then he was gone.

Louise breathed a sigh of relief as the door closed, then walked through to the lounge and flopped down onto the settee. Phase one was complete. She'd managed to smuggle the device in, and now had the tricky task of placing it under the floorboards and onto the ceiling of the Cabinet Room, which lay directly beneath.

She needed to be certain Adam wouldn't suddenly

return, so fifteen minutes later she innocently went downstairs, pretending she needed to speak with him before he left.

Dave said, 'Sorry Ma'am, his car left ten minutes ago.'

She made a disappointed expression.

'Never mind, it wasn't important. I'll speak to him this evening. Have a good day, Dave.'

'Thank you, Ma'am. You too.'

Back upstairs, she weighed up when would be the best time to plant the device, swiftly deciding that her best opportunity was right there and then. The cleaners had finished, the children were at nursery, and Adam was out until six. Locking the front door, she removed the device from her handbag and took it through to their bedroom. The parcel looked deceptively innocent, the shiny covering concealing its lethal contents.

The master bedroom was large and had been redecorated to Louise and Adam's taste. There was a deep burgundy carpet, thick grey curtains, and the king-sized bed had duvet and pillows to match. In one corner, to the left of the door as you entered, was a small armchair with pale grey upholstery and in the opposite corner, to the right of the door, was a matching two-seater settee.

Louise carefully placed the parcel on their bed then pulled the settee away from the corner. The dust behind the settee showed her that the cleaners rarely pulled it out and cleaned behind. This was very good news, as any minor damage she made would almost certainly remain unseen until the device detonated.

Returning to the kitchen, she removed several pots and pans from a drawer and reached to the very back of the cupboard, where several days ago she'd concealed two large screwdrivers and a claw-hammer. Back in the bedroom she crouched down and used the flat-headed screwdriver to lift the carpet from the gripper-rods, which turned out to be far harder than she'd imagined.

After five minutes of effort she feared she might need to change her plan and look for another place to plant it. Eventually however, it gave way, and she lifted the carpet and underlay for a few feet in each direction from the corner, allowing her access to the floorboards beneath.

Brushing the dust from the boards, she could see they had been secured to the joists by flat headed screws. This was more good news; she'd dreaded finding that they'd been secured with nails which would have required extra effort and created suspicious noise as they were prised out.

She chose a board where two screws were slightly proud of the wood and started unscrewing them. The first came out easily but the second one proved far more difficult. A mixture of fear of being discovered, terror of the device detonating, and the physical effort of removing the stubborn screw, left Louise moist with perspiration by the time it finally submitted to her efforts.

Forcing the screwdriver into a crack between the boards, she managed to lift one board enough to get the claw of the hammer into the gap and raise it. With the hammer in position, she collected the device and placed it gently on the floor next to where she was working. With her left hand she lifted the board using the hammer which allowed her to get the fingers of her right hand under the board, which she heaved upwards with all her might, making it bend into an arc. Once she had a gap of around fifteen centimetres, she reached over with her left hand and picked up the device. Then, something totally unexpected happened.

A loud knocking on the front door of their

apartment caused Louise to freeze with fear. If she was discovered at this stage, it was game over. She remained silent, hardly breathing, hoping whoever it was would go away, but the knocking came again. *Fuck,* she thought, *what if Adam's forgotten something?* The thought that he might have returned home to find the door locked, made her feel physically sick.

She released the board, quickly wiped beads of sweat from her forehead, brushed her hair tidy, and placed the device back in her handbag. There was no option; she had to discover who was at the door. Walking swiftly through to the hallway, she stood listening for voices on the other side, terrified that it might be Adam. She had no idea how to react if it was him. When she heard nothing, she called out, 'Hello, who is it?'

A voice she knew well answered.

'It's Tala. Can I come in please?'

Tala was a Filipino cleaner who'd been cleaning the private apartments in Downing Street for several years and had served under three different Prime Ministers.

Louise stifled her irritation at being bothered at a moment like this by one of her staff, and said, 'I'm sorry, it's not really convenient. Could you come back later?'

Tala however persisted.

'Sorry Ma'am, I've left my mobile in the apartment. My sister is travelling down to London by coach and I'm supposed to be meeting her at Victoria this afternoon. I need my phone for her arrival details, otherwise I might miss her.'

Making Tala wait outside while she searched for the phone would look extremely odd, but she couldn't allow her near the bedroom, so Louise opened the door, an artificial smile on her face.

'I'm afraid I'm busy in our bedroom at the moment, wrapping Christmas gifts, so you check the rest of the apartment and I'll check our bedroom.'

She retreated to the master bedroom, ensuring that Tala was unable to see anything incriminating. After a cursory look, Louise was satisfied that Tala's phone wasn't in their bedroom, en suite, or dressing room. She returned to the lounge just as Tala came out of Alice's room, proudly holding her phone aloft.

'Got it!'

'That's great,' said Louise. 'Isn't it awful how much we depend on our phones? I'd be lost without mine.'

'Thank you,' said Tala. 'I know you're busy and I'm really sorry for bothering you. It won't happen again.'

Showing her out, Louise said, 'Don't be silly. Anytime I'm here you're very welcome. See you tomorrow.'

Tala smiled broadly and left.

Closing the door and re-locking it, Louise could feel her jitters subsiding. Still shaking slightly, she removed the device from her handbag, resumed her position by the floorboards and placed it close to her side. She lifted the floorboard again and managed to force a gap of around fifteen centimetres. Reaching over, she lifted the device with her left hand and moved it carefully across to the gap. Contorting her body forwards, she lifted the floorboard as high as possible then with infinite care placed the parcel underneath, on the plasterboard that formed the ceiling below. She slowly withdrew her hand and picked up the claw hammer, using it to take the strain of the board, which was trying its best to drop back into position. Slowly releasing the tension on the hammer, she lowered the board back down, and when she removed the claw from the joint between the boards, it dropped back into place with a dull thud which made her heart race for a moment.

She quickly tightened the screws, replaced the carpet

and reattached it to the gripper-rods. A metal spatula from the kitchen drawer proved to be the perfect tool for neatly prodding the carpet's edges down. She stood back and examined her handiwork; it wasn't perfect, but it was hardly noticeable that she'd been there at all.

Sliding the settee carefully back into place, she checked it from various angles until satisfied that nobody would suspect it had been moved. Louise vacuumed the area around the settee to collect any mess caused during her work, and to iron out the track marks made by the settee's casters, which might give the game away.

When she'd finished, Louise released the lock on the front door, walked to the bathroom and ran herself a deep, hot bath. She was dusty, sweaty and desperately miserable; she'd fought against it as hard as she could, but in the end she'd had to give in to Harb Alsheueb's demands. Whatever the terrible outcome of her actions, she would eventually be able to resume some semblance of normality and she convinced herself that the pleasure of spending the remainder of her life with Adam, Oliver, and Alice would make everything worthwhile.

51

SO15 Headquarters, London
Monday 16th December 2030, 11.00am

Once again, Commander Dawes stood at the front of the briefing room as it slowly filled with senior officers, none of whom were below the rank of Inspector. His grim expression betrayed the fact that he had serious news to impart. Once the final officer had taken their seat and silenced their mobile phone, he began.

'Thank you all for attending at such short notice. The reason for calling you here this morning is that we've received information of a threat to Number 10 Downing Street.'

An image of a bearded Arabic-looking man appeared on the screen above his head.

'This is Mohammed Al Barook, a Somali national and high-ranking official in Harb Alsheueb. He has been here for four days, having been extradited from Kenya at our request. A mobile phone and laptop found in the apartment where he was arrested were examined and messages recovered from both of them indicate the possibility of an imminent attack on Number 10.'

His words caused a murmur of dismay around the room.

'Three days of interviews have failed to drag anything further from him. He knows we've found the emails and messages; he knows we've decoded them, yet he's remaining resolutely silent.' He took a sip of water from a glass on the table in front of him. 'We don't have a date for the attack, how it will be carried out, or who will be carrying it out, but judging by the excited tone of exchanges between the organisation's top brass, there's one thing we do know. The attack is imminent and we have to move fast.'

DCI Briscow raised his hand.

'Why don't we simply surround Downing Street with extra security measures and cordons, carry out extensive searches for explosives inside Number 10, and arrest anyone suspected to be involved with Harb Alsheueb? That way we'll be landing a pre-emptive strike against their plans.'

Dawes laughed out loud.

'Did you hear that ladies and gentlemen? That's why he's a highly respected Detective Chief Inspector! DCI Briscow has hit the nail on the head. What he's just suggested is exactly the plan of action we're adopting. The Prime Minister has been made aware of the threat, together with the approach we're adopting, and he is in full agreement with our measures.'

Al Barook's face disappeared from the screen, to be replaced with a detailed map of Downing Street and the surrounding area. A black circle had been drawn on the map with Number 10 at its centre; where the line crossed roads or footpaths, firm lines of red were drawn across. The circle was 150 metres from Number 10 and Dawes indicated what was planned with the help of a laser pointer.

'We're banning all vehicular and pedestrian movements within this area.' He turned to the room.

'Any questions?'

There was a deafening silence.

The next slide showed a plan of Downing Street's interior, with detailed plans of its four floors.

'The plan is to have four PolSA (Police Search Advisor) teams comprising an Inspector, a Sergeant, and six Constables, one for each floor. In addition, there will be two explosives search dogs working two floors each.' He turned to the officer working the computer images. 'Kill the slideshow please.'

The images disappeared. Dawes looked stressed, shifting uneasily from foot to foot.

'The cordons will be in place within the next hour and during the following hour the area will be cleared of vehicles and pedestrians. Our traffic section will re-route vehicle and pedestrian traffic to minimise disruption.' He cleared his throat then took a drink of water.

'At 2pm, the search teams will deploy into Number 10. Any questions?'

A female Detective Inspector raised a hand and asked, 'What about the Prime Minister and his family?'

'They're being moved to places of safety. Any other questions?'

The room remained silent. Dawes banged his fist angrily on the table to ensure he had everyone's full attention.

'I can't help wondering whether the person who carried out the abduction of Sarah Cairn, and the 5/5 attack in Regent Street has been re-activated.' The veins stood out on his forehead. 'If that bloody woman is involved again, she mustn't get away with bombing the home of our Prime Minister. This time we must fucking catch her!'

His anger and passion were reciprocated by his audience, who responded with supportive muted 'hear hears'. Once the noise had died down, Dawes handed over to Detective Superintendent Morris, who handed out individual responsibilities to several officers.

Dawes then closed the briefing with worried words.

'If she has been re-activated, the next couple of days will determine whether we've captured the bitch once and for all, or whether we have a great deal of explaining to do. Please pass this information to your respective teams as soon as possible. I fear we don't have much time.'

52

Private Quarters, 10 Downing Street

Louise was busy in the lounge, wrapping Christmas presents, when she heard a key turning in the front door. It was 10.45, the cleaners had finished an hour ago and Adam wasn't due home until the evening. She looked up and stared over at the door from the hallway, an uneasy feeling creeping up her spine.

A familiar voice called from the hallway, 'Hi love, it's me.'

This was most unusual; Adam always stuck rigidly to his schedule and was never home earlier than expected.

'Adam? What's happened? I thought you were busy all day.'

He walked into the lounge without smiling, his right hand in his trouser pocket, ruffling his hair with his left. Something serious had obviously happened.

'I need to talk to you about something. Sit down.'

'What's the matter?'

Louise sat slowly on the settee and looked up at her husband with anxious eyes.

'I've cancelled an appointment with the CBI to come home and see you.'

She started to feel as if an ice cube had been

dropped down her back.

'It's the children isn't it? Something's happened to one of the children.' Her voice was starting to sound hysterical.

'No, it's not the children, they're both fine.'

She fell back against the cushions with a huge sigh of relief then a sinking feeling enveloped her: had he learned she was about to betray him?

'What is it then?'

Adam breathed in deeply, before continuing in a calm voice, 'The security services have arrested a man called Mohammed Al Barook. He was detained in Kenya and extradited here on an international arrest warrant. He's a high-ranking member of Harb Alsheueb and searches of his mobile phone and computer have unearthed plans for an attack on 10 Downing Street.'

Louise was appalled; her two worlds were about to come crashing together and her anonymity and liberty could be blown wide apart. She had no way of knowing whether her name had been mentioned and knew that her reactions in the next few minutes had to be carefully choreographed. She feigned surprise, something she had become increasingly good at.

'Oh my God! What are we going to do?'

Adam dropped to his knees in front of her and held her forearms.

'Don't worry, they have everything under control. Start packing things for yourself and the kids immediately. You're going to be living at One Tree House until the all clear's been given. The whole building will be cleared shortly.'

Louise opened her mouth to speak but he cut her off.

'A 150-metre cordon around Number 10 will be imposed in an hour's time. At 2 O'clock, four police search teams and two explosives dogs will arrive and I'm told that they'll thoroughly check every inch of the place.' He kissed her forehead. 'They don't know exactly what form the attack will take but rest assured, if there's been a device planted here, they'll find it.'

Louise nodded dumbly but could feel herself trembling; not, as Adam would assume, through fear of the possible attack, but through fear of discovery. If the device were to be found and defused, it would be checked for DNA and fingerprints, and hers were all over it! She silently cursed herself for not wearing gloves or using her sleeves when handling it, as she'd done with the other devices. She hadn't bothered this time, assuming there was no chance of it being discovered underneath the floorboards and that any evidence linking her to it would be vaporised in the explosion. Steeling herself against her anxiety she nodded.

'Okay, I'll get packing. How much will we need?'

'Enough for three or four days. We should have the all clear by then.'

'What about the children? They're at nursery until five.'

He was one step ahead of Louise and reassured her.

'They're being taken straight to Otford from nursery. All you need to worry about is packing their things.'

Louise knew that, whatever happened, her world could soon collapse around her ears and started to shake uncontrollably.

'Hey, hey, it's all right,' said Adam. He walked swiftly over to sit with her. 'You're shaking! Don't worry, you'll be perfectly safe.'

Through tear-filled eyes she said, 'Will you be coming to Otford with us?'

'No. I'm being housed at a secret location. It's a bolt hole for when the Prime Minister is under threat. I don't know where it is myself yet.'

'Will I be allowed to contact you?'

'Yes. Other than living apart for a few days, life will go on as normal. My staff are being moved there this afternoon.' He gave a grim laugh. 'Governing the country must continue as usual.'

Looking downcast she said, 'So, we'll be living apart?'

'Sorry love, yes we will.'

'I suppose that's understandable. How will I get to Otford?'

'A car will collect you at twelve. It's all arranged.'

He rose and walked over to the window and stood staring into the rear garden, where sleety rain had started to fall.

Louise knew that if the device were found, this could be the last time that Adam would think about her with love and affection. Once she'd been unmasked as a terrorist sleeper, his love for her would turn to loathing. She would never again enjoy a normal, happy family life and the best she could expect would be to see her children once a month, on organised prison visits. The urge to scream was overwhelming. It seemed so unfair; she'd hated placing the bomb as much as Adam would hate her for planting it.

He looked over his shoulder.

'Don't worry darling,' he said reassuringly, 'it goes with the territory. Everything will be back to normal as soon as we're back inside Number 10. It'll be over before you know it.'

He walked across to her, pulled her tightly to him, and kissed the top of her head.

She lifted her face to look at him, placed her left hand around the back of his head and kissed him firmly.

'I love you so much and I always will. Whatever

happens, never forget that.'

Adam was struck by Louise's words and her almost desperate tone.

'I love you too, darling. Look, I'm really sorry, I need to get going.' He smiled broadly. 'I've got a country to run.'

Louise gulped and forced a smile.

'Of course, you get going. I'm so proud of you Adam. I'll see you soon. Love you.'

53

By 11.50 Louise had moved two large suitcases containing clothing and toiletries for herself and the children into the hallway where she waited with the doorman, watching the CCTV screen of the road outside. Her car arrived on the dot at twelve and the doorman opened the door as the rather portly, bald driver approached. He collected the cases, placing them carefully into the boot, while Louise made a dash through the freezing rain to the car.

As the car pulled out of Downing Street, a marked police Range Rover moved smoothly in behind. She noticed the cordons on Whitehall and lines of yellow-vested police officers moving across the footpaths, sweeping pedestrians to the far side of the tape. An hour and twenty minutes later they arrived at One Tree House, the home where they'd raised their children and where they one day hoped to return and live out their lives in happiness.

The marked police Range Rover had stayed unusually close to their vehicle as it followed them to Kent, which meant they were taking the threat very seriously. Louise knew better than anyone just how wise that was.

After they'd pulled onto the driveway, the driver

quickly jumped out and opened her car door. Louise climbed out and thanked him, then walked over to the marked police vehicle which had pulled in behind them. Although the rain had eased, it was extremely chilly and she was shivering against the cold, buttoning her coat up around her neck. The driver wound down the window to see what Louise wanted.

'Thank you so much for looking after me. It's very much appreciated.'

'No problem Ma'am. We'll be here until two then we'll be relieved by the late-turn unit. There are officers covering the rear of the property as well. Your family will be well protected here until you return to Downing Street.'

She noticed that the other two officers were carrying what looked like machine-guns.

'Well, thank you anyway. Would you like some hot drinks?'

'No thank you ma'am, we've got everything we need.'

'Fair enough. Goodbye then.'

She walked to the front door, where her driver had left the suitcases in the porch. She hoisted them inside then glanced at her watch. It was almost half past one; she had a few hours before the children arrived home and couldn't wait to see them. That was assuming she hadn't been arrested by then.

Inside the house she felt an urgent need to pray; whenever she was down, it helped her to feel at one with God, to know that there was someone apart from her family who loved her unconditionally.

Once Adam's political career had ended, she fully intended to explain to him her feelings towards Islam. It would be difficult, but she felt sure that, given enough time, he would eventually accept it was something she desperately needed. The thing she wanted more than anything was to be able to pray with Adam. It was something that every Muslim woman longed for, to pray with their husband but Louise knew Adam's views and realised with a heavy heart it was extremely unlikely it would ever become a reality for her.

After praying, she walked back downstairs and wandered sadly through to the lounge, lay down on the settee and wept until there were no tears left, until she'd become numb with misery. In the next day or so, she would very probably lose everything, and there was not a thing she could do about it.

54

Shortly after 2 O'clock, four marked police carriers swept down Whitehall from Trafalgar Square, the barriers forming the 150-metre cordon opening to allow them through. They drove further down Whitehall before turning right through the large metal security gates and into Downing Street. Each carrier contained a full PolSA search team, one for every floor; each officer was a highly trained search specialist and they would leave nowhere within Number 10 unchecked. The team assigned to the first floor, including the Prime Minister's private apartment, was Team 2; its officers were the least experienced of the four, so they'd been tasked to search the floor where it was believed the device was least likely to be located.

Inspector Stephen Waters had been in charge of his team for three years. He was a strict boss but well respected and a good send-off was planned for his retirement in a month's time. Many years ago, as a sergeant, he'd been great friends with a young inspector called Mark Dawes.

His second-in-command was Sergeant Lucy Handel, a young, ambitious officer with only eight years' service. She'd joined the team less than a year ago and was popular with the PC's, but less so with her inspector. Her presence on the team rankled with Waters, who thought she should still be learning how to supervise constables on core relief duties at the sharp end of policing, not employed on a specialist unit.

Lucy, however, was confident and assured, frequently challenging Waters' decisions; the fact that she would do this in front of the constables only compounded his dislike of her.

Their first day of searching was entirely taken up with checking offices, toilets, side rooms, hallways, and the first-floor dining room. Nothing untoward was found and the remaining search teams reported the same result. Once searches for the day were concluded, all four carriers left Downing Street at 8.30 in the evening. The Superintendent overseeing the searches contacted Commander Dawes with the negative results.

Five minutes later a police dog unit containing two eager explosives search dogs arrived and were set to work immediately. 'Suzie' was assigned with handler, Derek, to search the ground and 1st floors, including the Prime Minister's private family apartment, while 'Chester' was assigned with handler, Claire, to search the second and third floors.

Two hours later the dogs were returned to the dog van, their searches having also proved negative. The handlers passed the results directly to Commander Dawes, who called the Prime Minister and updated him on progress. So far it was looking like a false alarm.

55

By the time the children arrived at One Tree House early that evening, Louise had pulled herself together and welcomed them with hugs and kisses. They were excited but confused, so she explained to Oliver that there was a problem with the building at Number 10 and they would be staying in their old house for a few days. Alice was far too young to have any understanding of what was happening and didn't seem too bothered. Oliver's excitement mounted when his mum told them they wouldn't be returning to nursery until the problem was fixed.

Louise cooked an evening meal of Chicken Nuggets, chips, and vegetables for herself and the children. She listened to them chattering about their day at nursery, while trying to keep her mind from drifting back to Number 10 and what might be happening there.

By 8 o'clock the children had been read their bedtime stories and were tucked up in bed. Kissing them both goodnight, she found herself suddenly gripped by despair, wondering whether she would be putting her children to bed the following night, or sitting in a cell somewhere.

The dishwasher was loaded and running when Louise finally flopped into an armchair, mentally drained.

Again and again, the same thought tormented her. *How the fuck did I fall for the lies of Harb Alsheueb?* Her eyes were sore, her head throbbed and she stared hopelessly at a blank space on the wall. Outside the house, the rain had begun to pour down again and the wind howled in shuddering gusts against the window.

Her misery was interrupted by the ringing of her mobile phone. It was Adam - the only person she wanted to speak to at that moment. She snatched up her phone and tried sounding as natural as possible.

'Hi, I've been hoping you'd call. I guess you've had a busy one.'

He sighed. 'To be honest, there's no other type when you're PM. I've only been in the job for three months, but I can't explain how much harder it is than being a member of the cabinet and being a back-bencher was a breeze!'

'I'm sure you can handle it.'

'I'm glad you think so. How are the kids?'

'They're fine. Oliver's a little confused but delighted there's no nursery for a few days.'

There was a slightly awkward silence, before Louise filled the void.

'How are the searches going?'

Her tone was neutral; she was working hard to disguise her nervousness.

'Commander Dawes called me half-an-hour ago. The first day's searches were negative but they've got another full day tomorrow.'

'Have they searched the first floor yet?'

'Yes, they've got one search team for each floor.'

Louise could feel her spirits lift; could this mean the device had been missed?

'So, can we move back in soon?'

Adam coughed then his response brought her

crashing down to earth.

'No, we can't. If there's a bomb hidden somewhere, it could be anywhere in the building so we won't be allowed back until they're certain everywhere is safe. Anyway, they haven't fully checked our apartment yet. It's being done tomorrow afternoon. Hopefully, we'll receive the all-clear by tomorrow evening.'

He coughed again and when he spoke his voice was hoarse.

'Sorry, got a throat tickle. Think I might have a cold coming.'

Louise struggled to speak and when she did, there was a noticeable quaver in her voice.

'Oh, I thought they might have checked our apartment today.'

Hearing his wife's clear distress, Adam was concerned.

'Are you OK? You sound like you're about to burst into tears.'

'Sorry, I just hate the thought of our home possibly being targeted like this. Imagine if there had been an explosion while Oliver and Alice had been there.'

'Let's just thank our lucky stars the security services unearthed their plans.'

She ran her fingers through her hair.

'You're right, let's see what happens tomorrow.' She desperately needed to change the subject. 'Where are you speaking from?'

'I'm at a house near Notting Hill. I'm not allowed to disclose the exact location to anyone, particularly over the phone, so don't ask.'

Louise heard muffled sounds, as if Adam had covered the receiver and was talking to someone in his room.

'Sorry darling, I've really got to go, I've got a

conference call with three members of my cabinet in a few minutes. It's boring stuff, discussing how much we should release to the press about this threat; got to be done though.'

Smiling sadly to herself, Louise nodded then remembered he couldn't see her.

'I understand. You get going, and remember, I'm missing you.'

'Thanks sweetheart, missing you, too. My evening should be clear tomorrow so maybe we'll have a longer chat then. Love you, night, night. Kiss the kids for me.'

She could hear the urgency in his voice and realised he needed to hang up. Her chest tightened.

'I love you too, Adam, more than you'll ever know. Sleep well darling. Bye.'

As she ended the call, silent tears rolled down each cheek. She would have to endure a further twenty-four hours of mental agony before she knew whether she was still a free woman or would face a lifetime in prison. Twenty-four hours that would decide whether she could continue her life as wife and mother, or would bring disgrace on her family and loathing from everyone who had ever loved her.

56

Downing Street, London
Tuesday 17th December 2030, 9.00am

The storm of the previous day had passed and the weather in London was cold but bright as PolSA Team 2's carrier pulled up outside Number 10. Twenty minutes later the team had resumed their search of rooms on the first floor; they would start with three offices which hadn't been completed the previous day, move on to two large equipment cupboards and finish their search in the most unlikely place for a device to be found, the Prime Minister's private apartment.

By lunchtime, their searches had proved negative and in the early afternoon they moved into the apartment, where Inspector Waters handed out individual postings. He assigned one PC for each of the children's bedrooms, one for the kitchen and hallway, one for the lounge, one for the spare bedroom and family bathroom, and one PC was assigned to the walk-in dressing room and en-suite bathroom; this officer was also the designated exhibits officer, should any items of interest be found during the search. Sergeant Lucy Handel was assigned to the master bedroom. Inspector Waters would assist his officers wherever needed and oversee the operation.

Before the manual searches commenced, one of the PC's checked the whole apartment with a new piece of technology called a GEN-38-NAS, an ultra-sensitive electronic wand for detecting explosive materials. The wand failed to trace anything and shortly afterwards the teams moved in.

Waters gave everyone a brief pep talk, reminding them of the seriousness of the threat, the implications if a device were to detonate in an area they'd searched, and the kudos for their unit if they traced a concealed device.

After two hours and ten minutes, Sergeant Lucy Handel had meticulously searched the bed, including its built-in drawers, the dressing table, a tall cupboard containing an immersion heater, spare towels and spare bedding, and a large wardrobe which was separate to the walk-in dressing room. All that remained for her attention were the small armchair and matching two-seater settee on either side of the bedroom door.

She first pulled the armchair away from the corner of the room, allowing her to check thoroughly behind it, then removed the seat cushion and back cushion, checking the fabric for signs that it had been opened and re-sewn, anywhere in fact that someone could conceal an explosive device. Lucy was well aware that an IED could be as small as a matchbox and that even something that small would still be capable of doing plenty of damage if ignited in the right area.

Having found nothing suspicious, she concentrated on squashing every part of the two cushions, making sure that nothing solid had been concealed inside, then did the same with the upholstery on the frame of the chair. Satisfied that all was clear, she put everything back into place, returning it to exactly the same location as before.

She then moved to the opposite corner and the two-seater settee, which she pulled away from the wall, and carried out the same checking procedure as with the chair. Once satisfied that all was well, she went to slide the settee back into its original position but something caught her eye. She dropped to her knees to take a closer look, then searched the apartment for Inspector Waters, eventually finding him speaking with a constable in the bedroom with a colourful sign saying 'Alice' hanging on the door.

Waters saw her in the doorway.

'What's up, Lucy?'

'Sorry to interrupt, Sir. Could I show you something in the master bedroom please? I'd value your opinion.'

Waters stared in disbelief. Since when did she value his opinion? All she'd done since joining the team was challenge him.

'Okay,' he said, 'I'll be finished here soon. I'll be there in a minute.'

'Thank you, Sir.' Lucy returned to the bedroom,

Five minutes later, Waters opened the door into the master bedroom and jokingly said, 'Right, what's so important that could possibly make you value my opinion?'

Ignoring the sarcasm, she said, 'The settee's clear, Sir...'

'I hope you've not called me in here to tell me that!'

She raised an eyebrow.

'You didn't let me finish. What I was trying to say is, the settee is clear, but what about the state of that carpet?' Crouching down on her haunches, she ran her fingers along the carpet's edges, along both walls and into the corner. 'It looks like this corner has been taken up and re-laid recently. What do you think?'

Standing up, she moved aside to allow him access. Dropping to his knees, Waters peered closely at the area

Lucy had indicated. It was neat enough, perhaps not quite as professionally finished as the rest of the room, but neat, nonetheless.

'Sorry, Lucy, I don't think there's a problem.'

She looked aghast.

'Well I think you're wrong,' she replied, the contempt evident in her voice. 'There's a distinct possibility, in fact I'd say a probability, that this carpet has been lifted and replaced. I really think we should have this corner up and lift the floorboards.'

She was mounting another direct challenge to his authority, and he knew it.

The anger had been building inside him since she'd joined the team eight months previously and this display of insubordination was the final straw. This was the perfect time for him to assert his authority once and for all.

He shouted to the PC checking the dressing room, instructing him to take a fifteen-minute break in the carrier, something he was more than happy to do. As he walked out, Waters closed the bedroom door and stood facing it for a few seconds, before slowly turning around to Lucy, his face furious.

'Right, miss, you listen to me. You need to learn your position, learn some manners, learn that I'm your Inspector, and learn when to button it.'

That word 'miss' confirmed what Lucy already knew, that Waters' real issue with her was with having a woman challenge his authority; but she didn't back down.

'You don't like it because you know I'm right. That carpet looks like it's been lifted and anything could be under those floorboards. As you said... '

Waters' face was going an unhealthy shade of puce and his voice was rising to a shout.

'For fuck's sake Lucy, have you ever laid a carpet?

No, you haven't. Do you understand anything about laying a carpet? No, you don't.'

She frowned.

'So I've never laid a carpet, what's that got to do with anything? That doesn't stop me seeing that it's not sitting right in this corner of the room.'

Waters shook his head.

'Well I have laid carpets, Lucy, and the most difficult area is always the final corner. There's always a crease that won't disappear, a fold that won't flatten, an edge that won't sit right.'

He could see the doubt appearing on her face. His anger abated slightly and his voice softened.

'All that's happened here is that this was where the carpet fitter finished the job.'

He placed a fatherly hand on her shoulder.

'Blimey, Lucy, I know we don't get on, but let's be professional. The wand failed to detect anything. I personally supervised every minute of its deployment. I saw Mikey waving it over the carpet in this corner and it was negative, Lucy. If there had been anything under the floorboards, the wand would have detected it. There's no issue here. Imagine how we'd look if we pulled up the carpet and lifted the floorboards because of slightly sub-standard carpet fitting.'

Lucy bowed her head, leaving Waters content he'd convinced her he was right, and that he'd won the day.

'Sorry, Sir. I don't mean to be disrespectful, and I don't mean to undermine your authority, I just like things being done correctly.'

He gave her an understanding smile.

'That's okay.' He looked around the room. 'Other than not being happy with the carpet, are you done here?'

Looking down at the floor, she said quietly, 'Once the settee's back in place, yes, Sir, all done.'

Between them they slid the settee back into position, making sure the castors were placed exactly on the indents left in the carpet from before.

Once everywhere had been thoroughly searched, Waters got an officer to vacuum the carpets in every room then walked through the apartment making one final check. He was satisfied with what he saw, confident it would seem to the Prime Minister and his family that they'd never been there.

An hour later, at 5.30pm, the PolSA teams had finished, the all-clear was given and the carriers departed, allowing normality to return to Downing Street.

57

Louise had endured what felt like the longest day of her life. She jumped at every noise outside the house and nearly screamed when the phone rang with the usual cold calls. She imagined being informed that a device had been found underneath the floor in their bedroom and every time, her stomach lurched as she thought of evidence to condemn her being recovered from the black taped exterior. She imagined officers at the door, taking her away to provide DNA and fingerprints for comparison. She would be unable to refuse, even though providing them would undoubtedly seal her fate.

As a distraction, she'd taken the children to Knole Park in Sevenoaks again, where Oliver and Alice had a great time feeding the deer and enjoyed lunch in the café. Louise did her best to enjoy the precious time with her children but her true feelings must have been obvious, leading Oliver to ask on one occasion, 'What's wrong mummy, you look sad?'

That evening, the children were in the lounge watching 'Bedknobs and Broomsticks' for the umpteenth time and Louise was tidying the dining room and kitchen after their evening meal. She'd just finished wiping down the surfaces when her phone rang. It was a video call. Picking up her mobile, she saw it was from Adam and immediately felt a rush of mixed emotions. She was frankly terrified of the news he might have for her but also longed to hear his voice. She brought her emotions under control and swiped the screen; Adam's face appeared and she could see he was smiling.

'Hello darling, how was today?'

'Not too bad. You know, same shit, different shovel.'

She'd heard that phrase so many times before, but somehow it always made her laugh. Unsurprisingly, she didn't feel like laughing on this occasion and decided to jump straight in with the question she was desperate to know the answer to.

'Any news on the searches?'

'Yes, it's all clear. They're now concentrating on the likelihood that the attack would be either a suicide bomber on foot, a car bomb driven towards Downing Street's gates, or terrorists on foot with weapons.'

She hadn't heard much after 'Yes, it's all clear'. The feeling of relief and elation was so wonderful that her heart had almost leapt out of her chest. The emotion sounded clearly in her voice when she finally managed to get the words out.

'Oh, that's great news! I can't wait for us to all be together again and for things to get back to normal.'

In reality, she knew that any normality would be impossible for a few weeks at the very least; the bomb exploding would see to that.

'Sorry, Lulu, you can't return just yet.'

'Why not? You said they've given the all clear.'

'It's Number 10 that's got the all clear, not us. We're still considered to be targets. Apparently, they've arrested seven suspects on the watch list and they're making life very difficult for known sympathisers. Commander Dawes says it should be safe for everyone to return by

Friday.'

This was even better news. It now seemed likely the bomb would explode in an almost empty building. Certainly, the private apartment and cabinet room would be empty, so serious casualties were unlikely. She was elated but tried to sound casual.

'Oh well, Friday or Saturday is fine by me. I'm just happy that we'll soon be getting back to normal.'

A sudden wave of guilt swept over her. She hated deceiving Adam but told herself that very shortly she would be able to forget about being a sleeper, forget about Harb Alsheueb, forget about the constant fear and worry.

Adam changed the subject.

'How are the kids?'

'Good. They're in the lounge watching 'Bedknobs and Broomsticks' – again!'

'Can I have a word with them?'

'Hang on, I'll get them. They'll be thrilled Daddy's on the phone.'

Oliver chatted with Adam for about five minutes, during which time Alice joined in, pushing her face close to the screen and shouting the odd word into the phone. They were desperate to get back to their film and said goodbye to their daddy before Oliver handed the phone back to mum.

Louise chatted with Adam for over half an hour, and once they'd said goodnight and blown kisses to each other, she ended the call and released a huge sigh of relief. All she had to do was wait for the explosion on Thursday to happen, help Adam through the aftermath, then life would be sweet again.

58

One Tree House, Pilgrim's Way, Otford, Kent
Wednesday 18th December 2030, 11.15am

Louise was in the conservatory when the house phone rang.

'Hi, darling.' It was Adam. 'Good news. They've just given a full stand-down. They're removing cordons, opening up the roads, and all staff are being contacted to return to work. It's apparently safe for us to go back and Number 10 will be fully operational again by three this afternoon. Isn't that great?'

She didn't know whether to laugh or cry.

'Adam, that's a lot quicker than we were led to believe last night. Are they sure it's okay?'

Louise had immediately realised there would now be significant casualties, especially if the cabinet *were* sitting on Thursday morning. At least Adam would be safe at Congress House and the children would be out with Sandra, so she only had herself to worry about. She didn't want to be anywhere near Downing Street when the bomb exploded.

Adam of course was oblivious to these concerns and couldn't hide his excitement.

'It seems so. It will be chaos for a few hours as

everything gets up and running again, so keep the kids there until this evening. I'll arrange for a car to collect you at six. You'll be back in time to give them a late supper before bed.'

Louise thought on her feet.

'Why don't we stay here for another day or so? The kids are loving it.'

'Because I want to be with my family! Come on, darling - I haven't seen the kids for ages.'

Louise knew that when Adam dug his heels in, there was no budging him.

'Yes, of course. I guess it would be good for the kids to get back to normal.'

'Exactly. I've phoned Sandra to come in as usual and look after them from nine. You'll be able to have a break from them and get everything straight. I told her to keep them home and have a quiet day.'

A shiver ran down her spine. Adam's decision would mean Oliver and Alice would be in Number 10 when the device detonated. However, she feared that arguing with him would be both suspicious and pointless.

'Adam, they'd have been fine staying here instead of bothering Sandra. It's not as though we need to be back for anything urgent.'

'Sorry, I should have discussed it with you first, but I thought – what with the weather, it might be the best thing to do. The main thing is we're all safe. They've gone through everything at Number 10 with a fine-toothed comb. There's nothing that can harm us.'

Oh my God, if you only knew, she thought to herself, but instead she said the words he wanted to hear:

'You're right. Would you like to talk with the kids?'

While they chatted, Louise turned her thoughts to ways of ensuring her family, including herself, were well away from Downing Street at 10.30 the following morning. She knew Adam would be okay; he was giving his speech to the TUC at 9.30 in the morning and wouldn't be back until lunchtime. The children, however, would be in appalling danger, so Louise had to work out a plan that would see them well away from Downing Street between 9.30 and lunchtime. Sandra would just have to take them out, despite what Adam had arranged. She doubted whether he would be bothered about the change of plan once the bomb had exploded; he'd be far too busy with the press and in any case, would never for a moment suspect her involvement.

Following the first explosion at the Department for International Trade, Adam had told her that the police report showed the time of the explosion to be 10.31, only one minute out on a nine-day timer - impressive! This made her reasonably confident that if the device detonator had been set once again for 10.30, it would explode more or less on time.

The children had finished speaking with Adam and Oliver practically threw the phone into his mother's hands, both children keen to return to their toys.

Louise had gained a couple of minutes' thinking time and had what she considered to be a viable plan. With her mind reasonably settled, she chatted with Adam about happier topics.

'I'm looking forward to bedtime tomorrow night. I hope you're not too tired!'

They both laughed.

'How's One Tree House? I've really missed it since we've been at Downing Street.'

'It's lovely. I suppose missing things you love comes with the territory in your job. Give it everything while you're in post Adam. It'll be over soon enough then we can enjoy our house together again.'

They chatted for ten more minutes before the call

ended. Louise was confident she knew how to keep herself and her children safe, and that was all that mattered.

59

Flat C, 38 Boundary Way, Brockley, London
Wednesday 18th December 2030, 2.35pm

Sergeant Lucy Handel paced uneasily to and fro, wearing tracks in her beige lounge carpet. Her loyalty to her team, and in particular the Inspector, were being severely tested. She'd finished duty at six on Tuesday, saddened and bitterly disappointed that her boss had ignored her suggestion of searching underneath the floorboards in the Prime Minister's bedroom.

Although she knew the electronic wand had failed to detect anything, wands weren't infallible, and as they had been told again and again during her PolSA training, 'nothing can replace a fingertip search.'

Her sleep had been interrupted by thoughts of an explosion taking place in the area she'd declared all clear. She was angry with herself because she hadn't followed her instincts and realised now that she should have reported her fears to someone other than Waters. After waking early, she spent the morning plagued with worries and niggles; they hadn't cleared from her head by lunchtime and now the afternoon had arrived, they were nagging like never before.

Staring out of the window of her neat and tidy third

floor flat at the small area of parkland below, Lucy had come to a decision. She needed to speak with someone of higher rank than Waters and pass on her concerns. If she phoned SO15 Counter Terrorism Command and asked to speak with a senior officer, they would have to listen to her, wouldn't they? After all, the safety of the Prime Minister, not to mention everyone else in Downing Street, was at stake. If she turned out to be mistaken, so be it, she would accept whatever criticism came her way.

One of the many phones in the incident room at SO15 had been ringing for thirty seconds without being answered. Lucy was about to hang up when Detective Constable Alan Mount picked up the receiver.

'SO15 Incident Room. DC Mount speaking.'

'Hello, it's Sergeant Lucy Handel from Belgravia Police Station. I was one of the PolSA officers involved in the search of 10 Downing Street on Monday and Tuesday.'

'Hiya Sarge, how can we help?'

Lucy hesitated, unsure whether this was the right thing to do after all.

'Hello... Sarge... are you there?'

Shaking herself, Lucy managed to get the words out.

'Yes... sorry... umm, could I speak with a senior officer about our search on Tuesday please?'

'Sorry Sarge, it doesn't work like that. Tell me what's happened and I'll pass it on. The bosses are mega-busy at the moment, but if they think it's worthy of their time, they'll contact you.'

She thought for a moment. This could be her one and only chance to prevent a disaster and there could be no time to lose; she had to stick to her guns.

'No, I need a senior officer now. I don't wish to appear rude, but it's not for someone of your rank. This is quite possibly of national importance.'

Alan Mount was taken aback by the urgency in her voice and decided to pass the call on.

'Hold the line Sarge. I'll pass on your request right away but I'm not convinced it will do much good.'

Mount put the phone on hold, walked swiftly to DCI Briscow's office and knocked on the glass door.

'Come in.'

Inside Briscow's office he was surprised to see two other senior officers in conference with him: Commander Dawes and Detective Superintendent Karl Morris.

'Sorry sir, I didn't realise you had company. I'll come back later.' He turned to leave and started to pull the door closed.

'Alan!' barked Briscow.

'Sir?'

'It was important enough for you to knock in the first place, so what's up?'

Dawes and Morris smiled at each other, Mount's obvious discomfort bringing back memories of their own early days as young detectives. They vividly recalled how intimidating senior officers could appear.

Mount walked back in and closed the door.

'There's a Sergeant Lucy Handel on the phone, Sir. She was deployed as a PolSA officer in Downing Street on Monday and Tuesday. She wants to speak with a senior officer, says it could be of national importance.'

Briscow glanced at Dawes and Morris, both of whom leaned forward in their chairs. Dawes broke the silence and took control.

'Put it through to this office lad, I'll speak with her.'

Mount returned to his desk and picked up the receiver.

'Hello, Sarge, I'm putting you through to

Commander Dawes.'

Lucy had been looking out of her lounge window, watching a couple walking hand-in-hand in the park, wondering whether she'd made the right decision in phoning. She had been considering ending the call when Mount returned.

'Great, thank you for your help. I hope I didn't appear too rude.'

'Not at all, Sarge. Putting you through now.'

The phone ringing in Briscow's office was picked up by Dawes.

'Commander Dawes speaking, who is this please?'

'It's Sergeant Handel sir. I was a member of PolSA Team 2, deployed on the first floor of Downing Street.'

Dawes, prepared to take down notes if necessary, waited with pen in hand.

'Okay Sarge, fire away. What's so important that you need a senior officer?'

'Sir, I was assigned by Inspector Waters to search the master bedroom in the Prime Minister's private apartment.'

'Your Inspector, is that Stephen Waters?'

Lucy was taken aback. 'Yes, it is, do you know him?'

'Let's just say I've heard of him.' He smiled to himself remembering his friend from many years ago.

Lucy was pleased with Dawes reply, mistakenly assuming that Waters had rubbed him up the wrong way sometime in the past.

'Good, I'm pleased you know him. Perhaps it will help you understand my problem.'

Dawes didn't respond, but patiently listened for Lucy to continue. Realising he was waiting; she drew in a deep breath.

'During my search, I discovered an area of carpet concealed behind a settee in the Prime Minister's bedroom that had quite obviously been lifted recently. I reported it to Inspector Waters who came, took a look, but didn't seem concerned.'

Suddenly attentive, Dawes asked, 'Why wouldn't he be interested in something like that?'

Lucy was feeling more confident.

'Because Inspector Waters has always had problems with me taking the initiative or challenging his decisions. Sir, I genuinely believe it would have been worth pulling up the carpet and lifting the floorboards. It would have been the perfect place to conceal a device.'

Drumming his fingers on the table, Dawes' expression changed from intrigued to alarmed; he needed more details.

'Explain exactly what your concerns were with the carpet.'

Lucy was relieved that Dawes was taking her seriously.

'Firstly, the disturbance couldn't be seen until I'd pulled the settee away from the corner; secondly, the carpet throughout the room had been beautifully finished at the edges, apart from in this corner, where it had obviously been recently lifted; thirdly, pulling up a carpet and concealing an explosive device under floorboards would be a perfect hiding place. I was shocked that Inspector Waters couldn't see that.'

'Was the area swept with the wand?'

'Yes, Sir.'

'And the wand found nothing?'

'No, but the wand's not infallible. Nothing can replace a thorough search.'

For a few moments, Dawes was silent then uttered the words Lucy was hoping to hear.

'Thank you, Sergeant, I will deal with this matter personally. And don't worry about Inspector Waters, there will be no comeback against you.'

Lucy tilted her head back and blew out hard; the nerves and uncertainty which had been troubling her were starting to dissipate. She'd been worried about repercussions for going over Waters' head but had now been reassured nothing would happen.

'Thank you, Sir. I wouldn't have called if I weren't genuinely worried. I couldn't forgive myself if there was an explosion in an area I'm supposed to have searched and had given the all-clear.'

'Okay, thank you again Sergeant. You did the right thing and I'm going to look into this right away.'

'Thank you, Sir. Goodbye.'

She ended the call then settled into her favourite armchair and switched off the recording facility on her mobile phone. She was taking no chances.

Dawes replaced the receiver then passed on details of the conversation to Morris and Briscow. Following a brief discussion, they decided that Dawes should contact Waters immediately, using their friendship to oil the wheels.

60

Later that same day, Stephen Waters was trudging down the aisle in Tesco's with his wife when his mobile phone rang; his screen showed the caller was Mark Dawes. He hadn't heard from his old friend for a couple of years and was delighted, if somewhat surprised, to receive the call.

'Markey, good to hear from you. What's up?'

Dawes had put the call onto speakerphone, allowing Morris and Briscow to listen in.

'Hello, Steve, sorry to bother you. I've got Superintendent Morris and DCI Briscow here with me and you're on speakerphone. Are you free to talk? It's a rather serious matter.'

Dawes' words and the seriousness of his tone stopped Steve in his tracks, literally. He came to a halt with the shopping trolley, allowing his wife to walk off along the aisle ahead of him, unaware that her husband was no longer following. When she did finally look around, he was twenty metres behind her, talking on his mobile phone. She walked back to him and he explained he had to take an urgent call from work. She rolled her eyes, snatched the trolley, and stormed off.

'Give me a couple of minutes, Mark. I'll find somewhere quiet to talk.'

'No problem, Steve, we'll wait.'

Once outside, he walked to a quiet area of the car park.

'Right, I can talk now. What is it?'

Dawes told him of the call from Lucy and her concerns about the area of carpet that appeared to have been lifted.

'She feels that her concerns were not taken seriously. She's worried your response was somewhat personal. What's your side of the story?'

Waters could barely believe what he was hearing and was initially furious but then gradually found himself smiling, a smile that became a grin and then a laugh.

Listening in Briscow's office, the three senior officers looked baffled at his apparent amusement. After ten seconds Morris had had enough.

'What on earth can you find in this situation to laugh at?'

Bringing himself under control, Steve apologised then explained why he'd not gone along with Lucy's worries, including his comments to her to her about fitting carpets.

'Look, she's been challenging my authority ever since she joined the team. If you speak with any of the PC's on my unit, they'll tell you what she's like, so I'm not surprised she's done this.'

'Okay, thanks for that, Steve. Please don't contact Sergeant Handel about this and don't discuss this matter with anyone else, especially not members of your team.'

Waters laughed. 'Don't worry. I've no intention of seeing that bitch ever again. I retire next week so I'll be emptying my locker, handing in my appointments, and clearing my emails. After that, there's just my retirement bash and she's already made it plain she won't be there. Apparently she's 'busy'.'

Dawes shared knowing looks with Briscow and

Morris.

'Understood, Steve. We're going to need a little time to digest this. If we decide to lift the carpet and floorboards, please don't think it reflects badly on you.'

Waters grunted. 'I won't. To be honest, I'm so close to leaving, it really wouldn't bother me.'

Dawes ended the call and looked at his fellow officers.

'Right, whatever else you're doing, drop it. We need to make a decision on this right now, in fact, in the next few minutes. No one leaves this office until we've come to a consensus. There's nobody to give advice so it's down to the three of us and the buck will stop here.'

Morris looked at Dawes.

'I know that you're friends with Waters, Mark, but I don't know either him or Sergeant Handel and I'm happy to give you my decision right now.'

Dawes pursed his lips and nodded, 'Okay, shoot.'

Morris leaned forward; his hands clasped together.

'We don't really have a choice. I know it's a one-in-a-million possibility that someone could plant a device in the PM's bedroom, but can we afford to take that chance? We'd be strung up if there was an explosion. It does sound like Waters has a problem with this officer which might be affecting his judgement.'

Scratching his head above his right ear, Dawes looked perturbed. Briscow could see that he was struggling with something.

'What's on your mind, Guv?'

Standing up, Dawes rubbed his face vigorously with both hands.

'Steve Waters is a strict guvnor, and he often puts the backs up of people under his command.' He looked at Briscow, then Morris. 'Lucy Handel isn't unique in disliking his methods, she's just the most recent victim of his particular style of supervision. Believe me, there have been many others who've struggled with it before her. On the other hand, he is the most professional officer I've ever worked with. If he genuinely thought for one second there was the slightest chance of somebody having lifted that carpet, I'm confident he would have called it in immediately.'

'The Sergeant seemed pretty convinced he was wrong,' said Morris.

'Yes, but she would say that, wouldn't she? He's clearly pissed her off over several months and this has given her the perfect opportunity to fight back.'

'So, you think we should leave well alone?' asked Morris.

'I'm not convinced we should do anything. Can you imagine how it would look if, after having given the all-clear, we shut down Number 10 again, reinstate the cordons, lockdown the area and say, 'sorry, there might be a bomb in the PM's apartment after all.' It would create chaos and we'd get absolutely slaughtered, and rightly so!'

Morris sighed. 'So we're fucked whichever decision we come to.'

The room fell silent, as all three absorbed what had been said. Briscow had made his decision.

'I'm with the boss on this. Like you said, Karl, the chances are one-in-a-million that someone could plant a device in there. I'm happy with those odds. I vote we do nothing.'

Turning to Morris, Dawes said, 'Well, Karl, are you sticking with your opinion?'

'Looks like I'm outvoted doesn't it? Can't say I agree, but like you say, Barney, the chances of anything being there are infinitesimal.'

Briscow nodded. 'I can't see any way it could

happen.'

Dawes and Briscow both looked at Karl Morris, awaiting his decision.

Morris knew he was outgunned, and capitulated.

'We'd certainly look stupid if we cancelled the all-clear for nothing. Okay, I'll go along with not re-opening the search.' Then he joked, 'But you both owe me a pint if Number 10 gets destroyed and we're all sacked.'

This comment brought an uneasy ripple of laughter. Despite their concerns, the decision had been made and the conversation changed to other matters. They would do nothing.

Lucy Handel had done her best to persuade the bosses about her concerns, so if anything were to happen now, it wouldn't be down to her, and she had the recording of the conversation with Dawes as proof. She could relax... but the bomb remained in place.

61

One Tree House, Pilgrim's Way, Otford, Kent
Wednesday 18th December 2030, 18.00 pm

Louise shouted upstairs, 'Oliver, Alice, come on, the car's here. The driver's waiting for us!'

She was trying to chivvy the children along while she handed the suitcases to the driver at the front door. Six o'clock had arrived all too quickly, leaving Louise anxious and flustered about the return to Downing Street.

The following morning, she intended going shopping for last-minute presents in Covent Garden Market, and for once, she would be happy for a protection officer to accompany her. At nine, the children would be taken by Sandra and two protection officers to Christmas Winter Wonderland in Hyde Park and wouldn't be back until lunchtime.

The children ran downstairs and onto the drive, jumping up and down at the sight of snow flurries floating down through the trees.

'Mummy! It's snowing, it's snowing!' screamed Oliver, 'Can we go sledging?'

Louise laughed. 'I don't think it's going to snow enough for sledging. Now come on, in the car please.'

An hour and twenty minutes later, they were back

inside the private quarters at Number 10. Louise checked carefully around the apartment and was genuinely impressed; there was hardly a trace that anyone had been there. Everything was in its place and very tidy, the apartment looking exactly the same as when they'd left, even down to the pile of Christmas presents around the huge tree. She examined the area around the settee and was relieved to see it looked how she remembered it.

She was preparing supper when Adam arrived home earlier than expected.

'Any chance of making enough for me?'

The children ran to hug him and above their heads Louise leaned forward to kiss him.

'It's spaghetti bolognaise so I reckon I could make it stretch for four.'

Thirty minutes later they sat down together, enjoyed their meal and chatted until the children's bedtime.

Once the children were in their rooms, Adam and Louise watched TV for a while and went over the events of the past few days. Adam was clearly keen to get to bed, but Louise found herself strangely reluctant. Whether it was guilt or fear, she couldn't say, but simply being in the bedroom made her feel almost sick and the thought of making love just metres from where the device sat, primed and ready to detonate, was almost intolerable. However, she knew she had to behave as if nothing was amiss and performed her role with sufficient enthusiasm to satisfy him.

But at four o'clock on Thursday morning, Louise awoke in a cold sweat from a nightmare in which the device had exploded early, badly injuring them all and destroying the apartment. As she wandered through the wreckage of their home, she could see Millie's face again and again, in a cracked mirror, a photo on the floor, crying.

She lay awake, staring into darkness, knowing that she would not get back to sleep. She found herself remembering the happy times with Haasim; at least, she'd thought they were happy, but now realised he had been using her, grooming her to carry out the will of Harb Alsheueb. She thought about the operations she'd been involved in; blowing up her husband's Department; the abduction and murder of Sarah Cairn; having Ismail eliminated after his blackmail attempt; the deaths of six innocent people in the Regent Street bombing and finally, the murder of her best friend.

She'd hurt so many people she'd never even met, and how could she have done such a terrible thing to her darling Millie? The tears began to flow, and she cried silently into her pillow until it was soaked.

When she wasn't thinking about the appalling things she'd done, she reminded herself that she'd at least done one good thing - kept her family safe. She passed the last hour until the alarm sounded at six, lying on her side and staring at Adam. She'd lied to him and deceived him for years, but from now on, she intended to be his faithful, loving and, above all, truthful wife.

62

Private Apartment, 10 Downing Street, London
Thursday 19th December 2030, 6.00am

The persistent beep beep of the alarm clock on Adam's side of the bed grew steadily louder, until he could no longer ignore it and dozily reached over to silence it. Lying back on his pillow, he glanced to his left to see Louise's gaze fixed on him.

He stretched his arms above his head and pushed hard onto the headboard as he stretched before sitting up.

'Hey, you're awake early.'

'I know. Making the most of being back here with you again.'

'Mmm, it's great. And so was last night – thank you!'

He leaned over and planted a kiss on her forehead. Louise pulled herself up to a sitting position and rested her head on his shoulder. She was struggling to cope with the fatigue of spending most of the night awake with her thoughts as well as a rising sense of dread about the day to come. However, she could show none of this to her husband; as far as he was concerned, this must be just another 'ordinary' day.

Morning dawned with light snow falling and when

Louise looked outside, she was surprised to see the rear lawn covered in a blanket of white. She woke the children with news of the snowfall and was unsurprised when they didn't want breakfast; all they wanted was to be outside playing in the snow.

By eight o'clock, Adam had kissed his family goodbye and made his way down to his office, to be briefed on his day's duties by his private secretary and spend some time going through his speech to the TUC. Just before nine, Adam's car pulled up and he was once more whisked away to carry out the daily duties of Prime Minister.

Oliver and Alice had finally been persuaded to eat breakfast then just before nine Louise raised their excitement levels to fever pitch when she told them that Sandra would be taking them to Christmas Winter Wonderland at Hyde Park.

'Come here so I can get you both dressed. Sandra will be here soon.'

She could almost hear the time ticking on the bomb. Ninety minutes to go. She had to make sure both she and the children were as far away as possible by then. She'd notified the protection officers of their movements and been assured that officers would be available throughout the day to accompany them.

Alice was bouncing up and down on the settee and Oliver was shouting, 'Can we throw snowballs at Sandra, Mummy?'

Louise smiled through her fear.

'No, you can't, Sandra wouldn't like that. You can throw them at trees instead. Now come on, I need both of you to get ready.'

At last the doorbell rang and Sandra walked in with a layer of snow on the shoulders of her overcoat.

'Sorry I'm a bit late. The bus was going really slowly

in the snow.'

The children were now beside themselves with excitement.

'Is it snowing hard, Sandra?' asked Oliver.

'Yes, the flakes are getting bigger and bigger. It's lovely, very Christmassy.'

The children were bundled into snowsuits, hats, gloves, two pairs of thick socks, and wellingtons. Louise gave Sandra ten pounds for each of them to spend on rides and food, and they gave their mum a kiss and cuddle.

'Have fun,' said Louise. Turning to Sandra she said, 'Keep them safe.'

Sandra nodded. 'I will. Enjoy Covent Garden!'

Closing the door, Louise could feel tension spreading across her shoulders and her chest felt tight. She grabbed her mobile phone from the bedside table but in the rush and with her nerves in shreds, she forgot to take it off silent and even left the vibrate function switched off.

Putting on her favourite dark green overcoat, fur-lined moonboots, and green and white bobble hat, she checked that everything in the kitchen was switched off, closed the front door to the apartment behind her, walked along the landing, smiling at a passing cleaner, and made her way downstairs. She passed two more people on the stairs; both were young female assistants with their whole lives in front of them and the unwelcome thought forced its way into her head: *please don't let them be harmed*. Deep down, she knew there was a good chance they would be.

Suddenly, she felt an overwhelming urge to tell one of the protection officers what was going to happen at 10.30. She knew she would be arrested and imprisoned for the rest of her life, but at least those young women wouldn't be harmed, nor that cleaner, nor the members of the Cabinet. Her conscience would be clear, or at least not quite as damaged as it already was, and perhaps she could look herself in the mirror without suffering the terrible self-loathing she'd experienced thirty minutes ago.

Unsurprisingly though, Louise couldn't bring herself to tell anyone. Her memory of what Sulayman had said about Harb Alsheueb's threats against her children should she fail to complete the task were ringing loud and clear in her mind. She realised that she would sacrifice any number of lives to save those of the people she loved. Even if she could persuade the police to enhance security for the children, she knew that one day they would eventually get to Oliver and Alice. The organisation would know that once a few months had passed without an attempt on the children's lives, the level of protection would be reduced and downgraded and that's when Harb Alsheueb would strike, and she simply couldn't allow that to happen. The bomb would have to explode and she would have to cope with the aftermath and the sense of guilt that followed.

In the hallway, she was greeted by police protection officer Sameer Hassan, one of many officers who alternated on a shift system, to ensure members of the family had protection at all times. He was an unremarkable looking man, about thirty-five, of medium height, slightly chubby with a round face, no chin, and a receding hairline.

Louise had heard him make the 'Assalamu Alaikum' greeting to a woman employee at Number 10 wearing a Hijab previously. She felt somehow comforted that she would be protected by a fellow believer at this difficult moment in her life.

'Good morning, Ma'am, my name's Sameer. Where

would you like to go today? I have a car ready and waiting outside.'

'No car necessary thank you. I fancy walking to Covent Garden to buy a few Christmas presents in the market.'

Sameer looked crestfallen; his highly polished black brogues weren't the most suitable footwear for walking in the snow. Added to that, he was only wearing a short overcoat, which wasn't very thick and didn't look waterproof. Nevertheless, he was the consummate police professional, and through his obvious disappointment he managed a smile.

'Certainly, Ma'am. I'll be happy to accompany you.'

Once he'd radioed through to cancel the car, they left Number 10 on foot via the back door, walking through the garden and out of the rear gates, where they turned right onto Horse Guards Road.

Leaving through the rear entrance meant they could they avoid the crowds hoping for a glimpse of someone important leaving Downing Street through the large metal gates at the junction with Whitehall. The snow was now falling heavily and Sameer's feet were soon covered in soft snow and slush, making them cold and very wet. Louise walked along quickly without explaining why she was hurrying; all she could think of was the need be as far away as possible when the detonation occurred.

They turned onto the Mall then cut through Trafalgar Square and the back streets to Covent Garden. With every step, Louise was feeling an increased sense of relief that everything had gone well; the whole family were safe, that's what mattered most. She began to chat with Sameer, asking questions about his career in the police, how he felt about carrying a gun, and whether he thought he could kill someone if necessary. It was a way of deflecting her thoughts away from the carnage she was about to cause and she tried hard to concentrate on his answers.

She completely avoided mentioning his religion, that would only complicate matters for her.

They arrived at Covent Garden at ten and Louise began browsing the market stalls. A couple of small purchases later, she glanced at her watch and saw with shock it was 10:18, only twelve minutes to go. For the next couple of minutes she found it difficult to keep up the pretence of casually shopping. Intending to take her mind off the device, she called Sandra on her mobile to see how the children were getting on.

'Hi Sandra, everything okay?'

'Hi. Yes thanks, but I've been trying to get hold of you. Your phone kept going to voicemail.'

For a moment Sandra's words made no sense before Louise remembered she had left her mobile on silent. Then a worried frown spread across her features.

'Why were you calling me?'

Sameer looked puzzled. He could hear the concern in Louise's voice and realised she had a problem, but couldn't fathom what was going on.

'Sorry, Louise, I didn't mean to interrupt your day, but Adam called to say that a British Tanker had been attacked and sunk in the Straits of Hormuz, so he'd had to interrupt his speech halfway through and return to Downing Street. He's going to chair the Cabinet meeting; they're treating it as an act of war.'

Louise froze with fear. Her husband was supposed to be safe at Congress House, not at the heart of the danger; the device would explode in ten minutes and she had to contact him but knew he wouldn't answer his phone so close to the start of a cabinet meeting.

Then, another awful thought came to her.

'Why would you call to tell me that? Where are you...

where are the children?'

Her final words were almost screamed into the phone, causing several people wandering through the market to stop and take notice. Sandra could tell from Louise's voice that she was deeply upset.

'I'm sorry. I know you wanted them to have a day out but when we got to the Winter Wonderland, we found they had closed it following an accident on one of the rides, so we came home. They're playing in the lounge.'

'WHAT?' Louise's scream was almost hysterical.

'They're here in the lounge with me. Don't worry, they're quite happy. Adam told me to stay here until he'd finished the Cabinet meeting. He's been trying to get hold of you, too.'

Sandra waited for the reaction from Louise, a reaction which never came.

'Hello, Louise, are you still there? Hello... Louise?'

There was no reply; Louise was incapable of speech. She staggered into Sameer and dropped her mobile onto the shiny flag-stoned floor of the market, where the screen shattered and died. Sameer caught her as she fell. Her legs were no longer capable of supporting her weight; she was howling with despair, tears streaming down her face.

Confused and hearing the phone go dead, Sandra tried calling back but there was no response so she shrugged her shoulders, ended the call, and returned to helping Oliver with his Peppa Pig jigsaw puzzle.

63

Although she could barely stand or think, Louise knew one thing: it was either take the chance on Adam, Oliver and Alice dying and keep her freedom, or confess to the one person who could save them, and face a lifetime in prison. She had seven minutes to keep her family alive.

'Sameer,' she looked at him with eyes full of tears. 'Listen to me. There's a bomb under the floorboards in the master bedroom of our apartment in Number 10 and it's timed to detonate in a few minutes. For God's sake warn everyone and get my family out of there!'

Sameer looked dumbfounded. He could see the desperation in her eyes but was struggling to believe what he was hearing.

'But... how do you know?'

'I know because I've been working for Harb Alsheueb for years. I'm a sleeper.'

She could still see doubt on his face and shouted, 'For fuck's sake Sameer, I'm the person who blew up the Department of Trade. I'm the Clothes Bazaar bomber. Get on the fucking radio! The bomb's set to detonate at 10.30, you've haven't got long!'

Louise dropped to her knees, crying and howling hysterically and suddenly Sameer knew she was telling the truth. Lifting his radio from a coat pocket, he made the call.

'Downing Street units from Sierra Oscar two-seven, Downing Street units from Sierra Oscar two-seven, evacuate Number 10 immediately, repeat, evacuate Number 10 immediately. There is an explosive device under the floorboards in the Prime Minister's apartment, due to detonate in five minutes. Sierra Oscar two-seven over.'

Sameer's earpiece exploded with voices and for a few seconds chaos ensued over the airwaves, until the control room silenced all transmissions except for the Gold Commander. Suddenly only one voice could be heard, that of Chief Superintendent Alf Charrington.

'Sierra Oscar two-seven from Gold, please confirm your last.'

Sameer confirmed the message, stating that he had the Prime Minister's wife in custody, and that she'd admitted being the perpetrator. He pulled Louise to her feet, turned her roughly around, placed her in handcuffs and radioed for a van unit to collect them.

'Louise Greenacre, I'm arresting you for causing an explosion and murder. You do not have to say anything, but it may harm your defence if you fail to mention when questioned, something which you later rely on in court. Anything you do say may be given in evidence. Do you understand?'

Louise was beyond making any response beyond a nod. She looked and behaved as if in a trance, silently allowing herself to be manhandled by Sameer.

Two uniformed officers on foot patrol in Covent Garden witnessed the arrest and joined him while he was on the radio to Charrington. They didn't know what was happening or why he was making the arrest as their personal radios were on a separate channel, so they hadn't heard the transmissions. Indeed, until they reached him, they weren't even aware that the woman in handcuffs was the Prime Minister's wife. Sameer briefly explained what had happened and that he had radioed for a local van unit to attend.

Chief Superintendent Charrington sent out an urgent message.

'All units, on my authority commence Operation House with all haste. We have less than five minutes!'

The words had barely left his lips when there was a deep 'thwoomp' and a distant rumbling like thunder, followed by an immediate message into Sameer's earpiece: 'Major explosion at 10 Downing Street! Commence Westminster lockdown!'

Although she hadn't heard the message, Louise knew instantly what that noise meant and screamed at the top of her voice, 'NOOOOOO!'

Her legs would no longer support her and she once more dropped to her knees on the floor of the market. Sameer was unable to hold her upright and released his grip on her arm, allowing her to flop down on her right side, her hands handcuffed behind her, her face on the ground.

Hearing the device detonating, Louise understood that her life as she knew it was over, along with the lives of many innocent people inside Number 10. The future lives of many more would no doubt be cruelly altered due to their horrendous injuries; people with lives and families just like her. Her training had taught her that violence was sometimes necessary and acceptable but she had been shown in the cruellest way imaginable that such beliefs were wholly untrue.

The position she was in on the ground, coupled with the paralysing misery she was experiencing made breathing difficult and the intense pain in her chest made her think she may be having a heart attack. One question dominated her thoughts: she had to know whether her family were okay. Raising herself painfully and with difficulty to a sitting position, she shouted at Sameer, who was busy alternating between speaking on his radio and mobile phone.

'Sameer, I know I have no right to ask, but please find out if my family are all right!'

Sameer looked down at her with contempt and, without thinking what he was saying, shouted back, 'You mean whether they're dead?' He leaned menacingly over her. 'You've just put back the cause of Islam being accepted by the people of this country by 20 years, you make me sick!'

His words hit her like a hammer-blow and Louise howled like a wolf, banging her head as hard as she could again and again on the leg of a market stall.

'Stop her doing that and fucking pick her up!'

Sameer sounded at the end of his tether as he shouted at the uniformed officers then nodded towards Southampton Street, at the lower end of the market.

'The van's coming up the hill. Let's get her out of here, the crowd are getting ugly.'

By now, members of the public had gathered and heard enough of the conversation to work out what had happened, many screamed threats at Louise. Sameer and the two officers had to force their way out through the baying crowd, pushing Louise into the van's cage through the rear doors. The level of abuse from the crowd was rising fast; a beer can, followed by a bottle, bounced off the roof of the van before it swiftly sped away with blue lights flashing and sirens blaring, to travel the four hundred yards to Charing Cross Police Station.

Louise stared through the side of the Perspex cage at the three officers sitting in the back of the van. Sameer and the uniformed officers were talking animatedly in the back seats, seemingly bemused by the morning's events and unable to take it all in. She rocked backward and forward on the tiny bench, moaning with anguish until, two minutes after leaving Covent Garden Market, they drove through a low arch into the rear yard of Charing Cross Police Station.

64

Sameer swung open the van's side door, allowing himself and the uniformed officers to step down from the vehicle. Seconds later he opened the rear doors and took hold of Louise's left arm.

'Mind your head and mind the step,' he said gruffly as he helped her from the van.

They walked a few short paces to enter a cage attached to the side of a building, which acted as a prisoner holding area outside the custody suite.

Once there, he said, 'I am further arresting you for membership of a proscribed organisation and conspiracy to murder. You do not have to say anything, but it may harm your defence if you fail to mention when questioned something which you later rely on in court. Anything you do say may be given in evidence. Do you understand?'

She weakly replied, 'Yes.'

Louise had stopped crying when the van doors opened. She felt light headed and dizzy, her thoughts confused, and she was struggling to comprehend what was happening to her. The few steps from the van to the cage had felt like wading through quicksand.

Word about the arrest had clearly been passed on by the uniformed officers to the control room and from there to the custody suite because the door was opened almost as soon as they'd entered the cage. They were directed by a uniformed officer up two long ramps to a booking-in area on the first floor, which had swiftly been cleared of other prisoners.

Colin Serrell, the Custody Officer, was a crusty old-sweat Sergeant who'd seen it all during his service, and he wasn't about to be overawed by this. He eyed Louise slowly up and down over the top of his spectacles then looked at Sameer and the two uniformed officers.

'Who is the arresting officer?'

'I am, Sarge,' said Sameer.

'Circumstances of arrest please.'

'Sergeant, this is Louise Greenacre, wife of the Prime Minister. She has admitted planting an explosive device under the floorboards of the master bedroom in the Prime Minister's private apartment inside Number 10 Downing Street. This device has now detonated. She has also admitted carrying out bombings at the Department for International Trade, and Clothes Bazaar in Regent Street. She was originally arrested for causing an explosion likely to endanger life or property and murder. Since then, she's been further arrested at 10.32 for being a member of a proscribed organisation and conspiracy to murder. I have been informed by mobile phone that there are several fatalities at Downing Street.'

Serrell heard a gasp from Louise but continued to type the circumstances onto the custody record, then once again looked over the top of his spectacles at her.

'Mrs Greenacre, do you understand why you've been arrested?'

Louise was going into shock; she felt cold, couldn't stop shivering, and needed to be supported but she managed to whisper, 'Yes,'

Serrell redirected his gaze to Sameer. 'Time of the

original arrest?'

'10.25 Sarge.'

'Arresting officer's name?'

'DC Sameer Hassan, attached to Parliamentary and Diplomatic Protection.'

Serrell turned back to Louise.

'Mrs Greenacre, I'm satisfied there is credible evidence that you have committed an offence. Therefore, I'm authorising your detention to secure and preserve evidence, and for the purpose of interview. Do you understand?'

Louise was now close to collapse, but understood the question and murmured, 'Yes Sergeant.'

'Take off your coat please, then empty your pockets, your handbag, and remove all jewellery.'

Louise falteringly complied with his request, placing everything onto the counter in front of her. When she'd finished, she said, 'That's it.'

Serrell continued, 'The circumstances of your arrest give me cause to suspect that you may be concealing something on your person that could harm yourself or another person, or aid your escape. Therefore, I am authorising that you be taken to a non-CCTV room and strip-searched by female officers. Do you understand?'

'But I've nothing else on me.'

He ignored her, turning to a female detention officer. 'Jill, please go with Amy and search Mrs Greenacre.'

Fifteen minutes later, Louise's search was complete. Back in the booking-in area, her property was thoroughly checked, logged on the custody record, and placed into property bags.

Serrell asked, 'Do you wish to speak to a solicitor? If you don't have a solicitor of your own, you can speak to the duty solicitor.'

She knew nobody could help her but was desperate to see a familiar face.

'I'd like our family solicitor please, Howard Hunty, of Davies, Smith and Hunty, in Richmond.'

A detention officer said, 'I'm on it Sarge,' and began searching for the solicitor's phone number.

'Thanks, Alfie.'

Serrell removed his spectacles and leaned forward on his elbows.

'Mrs Greenacre, I am authorising that you have your fingerprints, photograph, and DNA taken. Please don't feel that you are being singled out, this is required of every person arrested for a criminal offence who is brought into a police station.'

She silently nodded her understanding.

A female detention officer gently took hold of her right arm and walked her through to a side room, where all the equipment she needed was on hand. Sitting down, Louise meekly complied with the request to open her mouth and allowed scrapes of DNA to be taken from the inside of each cheek. Next, she was made to stand up to have her fingerprints taken. Louise understood that any freedom in her life had effectively ended. From this moment on, everything she did would be tightly controlled, just as it was now.

The process of completing Louise's booking-in was finally concluded and she was escorted down a short corridor with cell doors on either side by two detention officers. She was shown into Cell 38, the door slammed shut and the wicket closed, leaving her standing alone in the cell. She couldn't even see out into the corridor.

The feelings of isolation and terror were overwhelming. She walked two or three steps to the blue plastic mattress and pillow on the raised side bench which now doubled up as her seating area and bed. Lying down, she could feel the chill of the mattress down her back so she wrapped the single light blue blanket around herself, curled into a foetal position and broke down, crying and howling until her throat hurt and her eyes stung with tears, for the husband and children she had probably killed.

65

Cell 38, Charing Cross Police Station, London
Thursday 19th December 2030, 3.40pm

Three hours later, the female detention officer lowered the wicket on the cell door and peered in, as she had done every fifteen minutes since Louise had been placed in the cell. A meal had been offered at 1.30, but Louise hadn't felt like eating.

This time it was different and the officer spoke through the opening.

'There's a solicitor waiting for you in the Consultation Room.'

Louise heard a key turning in the lock and the cell door swung open. She stood up unsteadily and was escorted by two officers to a room with a sign saying 'Consultation Room 1' above the door. Walking proved difficult; every part of her body was hurting, but worst of all was the pain in her head.

She'd been told nothing more about the aftermath of the explosion and was desperate to know whether her family were all right.

As Louise stepped inside, she saw Howard Hunty sitting at the table, busily writing down notes. On hearing the door open, he stood up and looked at Louise. She'd known him for a long time but he looked as if he had aged ten years and his expression was just like he was seeing a stranger for the first time, a stranger accused of a terrible crime.

Louise had hoped for some kind of human contact from Howard, at least a handshake; it was something she shouldn't really be craving as a true Muslim woman, but at that moment, it was something she desperately needed. Howard simply indicated the chair on the opposite side of the table. Again, Louise was confronted with the reality that from now on, she would be universally despised, even by old friends and possibly even her own family. She sank into the chair with her head bowed. The detention officer left the room and closed the door, leaving them alone together.

After a few moments Howard started to speak, but almost immediately the door opened again and Louise turned to see a man enter the room. Howard said, 'This is Detective Superintendent Morris from the Metropolitan Police's Counter-Terrorism Command. He has information for you about your family.'

Morris remained standing, staring grimly at Louise.

'Mrs Greenacre, I'm terribly sorry but I have bad news for you.'

Louise clenched her hands together and sucked in deep gulps of air. Without speaking, she looked up imploringly at him.

'Your husband is dead. He was taken alive from the Cabinet Room and lived for an hour. The doctors tried everything possible to save him, but he has since died from catastrophic injuries.'

Louise began to tremble and slowly shook her head from side to side as if she could somehow deny his words, tears trickling down her cheeks. Then she looked up at him again, the desperation etched on her face.

'What about... my children?'

Morris gulped; he could no longer look her in the eye and stared at a spot on the wall somewhere above her head. He delivered his message in a flat tone.

'Alice was killed by a wall collapsing in the lounge. Oliver survived but his left leg was blown off just below the knee and he has lost the sight in his right eye.'

'No...'

The word was almost inaudible. Louise closed her eyes tight and suddenly stopped crying, unable to weep anymore; Morris's message had caused trauma so severe that she couldn't fully take in what she was hearing. Sitting upright, she swept her hair from her face.

'Oh... thank you for telling me.'

'I'm truly sorry for your loss,' said Morris and he moved towards the door. Then he stopped and turned to Louise.

'... but perhaps it's what you deserve. What the fuck else did you expect?'

He banged open the door and walked swiftly from the room.

Hunty didn't know what to say. He knew that her silence and apparent indifference wouldn't last long. He recognised delayed shock, so pressed the assistance buzzer and was relieved to see a female detention officer quickly enter the room.

'Could you remain here for a while? Mrs Greenacre has just been given some terrible news.'

The officer nodded at Howard, pulled up one of two spare chairs, and positioned it close to the door.

Louise said quietly, 'There's no need for anyone else, Howard. I've accepted my fate and what I've done to my family.'

But Howard had seen that vacant expression once

before, when he was dealing with a father who'd killed his two young children after learning his wife was leaving him. The man had made the decision that if she didn't want him, then she would lose her children as well. After an hour remaining relatively calm, the grief and misery had kicked in, and he had cried solidly for six hours, becoming suicidal in the process.

To break the silence, he asked Louise the questions he personally needed the answer to.

'Why did you do it? What were you thinking of? What on earth possessed you?'

All he'd done was ask the obvious questions, but that did the trick and the floodgates opened. Louise threw her head back and screamed out like a wounded animal then started ripping and tearing at her head, pulling her hair out in small clumps to hurt and punish herself.

'Allah, please help me, please!' she screamed. 'My family, my beautiful family!'

Suddenly, she banged her head on the table several times so hard that the officer quickly intervened to stop her, but not before Louise had managed to split her forehead open. The officer hit the panic button on the wall and, standing behind Louise, forcibly pulled her upright and cradled her wounded head in her hands. The door burst open and two more uniformed police officers ran in to assist.

On seeing them, Louise began struggling and fighting hysterically. She was moved with difficulty by the officers to the Medical Room, screaming and struggling all the way. Her words were unintelligible, her breathing erratic and laboured; dribble and foam formed in each corner of her mouth and she appeared to be having some kind of fit. Fortunately, the experienced Dr Green was at the station attending to an injured officer and it was he who ordered that she be held down on the treatment table, and who injected her with a sedative which calmed her down within five minutes, reducing her to an almost catatonic state.

The doctor then carried out a full examination, saw to the wound on her head and prescribed further medication to be given every four hours for the next two days. He also recommended that she be seen by whichever doctor was on duty each morning and evening throughout the remainder of her time in custody.

Louise was returned to her cell, where the Custody Officer directed that she be placed on constant supervision; her cell door would remain open with a female officer sitting on a chair just outside the door so that she could be visually monitored at all times.

Three hours later, the effects of the sedative began to wear off and Louise gradually returned to consciousness, bringing with it the full force of misery, bereavement, self-loathing, and fear for her future. Swinging her legs off the bed took all her strength; she didn't know if she was weak through grief or as a result of the sedative the doctor had administered. Her head started pounding as soon as she sat upright, so she lay back down on the mattress and drifted into a fractured sleep, haunted by dreams of her family, calling to her.

66

As Louise came to next morning, she looked around at the plain walls in confusion. Then she recalled where she was – and why. She refused all food but accepted occasional glasses of water. It was now 8.50 and a young female PC was doing one hour on and one hour off on constant watch, alternating with an older female PC, who glared at her with genuine hatred in her eyes.

It was the younger officer's shift and Louise decided to ask her the question which was now tormenting her.

'Please, Officer... can you please tell me how many people were hurt in the explosion?'

'Don't answer her, Constable.'

The words came from a deep male voice somewhere outside in the corridor. The young PC looked over her shoulder and saw a man in a navy-blue suit; he nodded at her, showed his warrant card and walked into the cell, accompanied by a woman wearing a black skirt and jacket with a white blouse, who also produced a warrant card.

The male officer said, 'Take a break for five minutes please, Officer, we need to speak with Mrs Greenacre alone.'

Once she had left, he walked calmly over to the bed, indicated the mattress and said, 'May I?'

Louise shrugged, so he sat down next to her; the

female officer remained standing by the door. He regarded Louise with an expression she found difficult to interpret.

'Hello, Louise.'

Her eyes were dreadfully sore and felt like they were had been rubbed with sandpaper, but she managed to return his gaze.

'Who are you?'

'I'm Commander Mark Dawes.'

Louise immediately recognised the name, which she'd heard Adam use several times before. He indicated the female officer.

'And this is Detective Sergeant Alice Bowers.'

Hearing the name 'Alice' started Louise's tears flowing; the pain was almost unbearable. She lifted herself from the bench and collected tissues from the toilet alcove, wiping her eyes and blowing her nose. Composing herself, she sat back down.

Dawes continued, 'I am the senior officer assigned to this incident from Counter Terrorism Command. A Sergeant told me yesterday afternoon that she suspected there might be a bomb under the floorboards in the Prime Minister's apartment, but I didn't listen to her. She has passed on details of her phone call with me to my bosses, and I might well lose my job because of you.'

He pursed his lips and fixed her with an icy stare, but Louise didn't flinch, and didn't comment.

'However, that is of minor consequence. I wanted to pass on details of the casualties you've caused. I know you're already aware of the deaths of your husband and daughter, together with the life-changing injuries to Oliver.' He let the impact of his words take effect, seeming to enjoy reminding her of the devastating damage her actions had done to own family.

Louise remained silent. The man's cruel words were

like blows to her heart but she would accept them as part of her fate.

'Nine other people died,' he continued. 'Six cabinet ministers, including the Chancellor of the Exchequer, the Foreign Secretary and the Leader of the House of Commons.' He paused.

'They were obviously your targets, so perhaps their deaths could be anticipated.' He stopped for a couple of seconds, controlling his anger before continuing, 'But sadly, your callous actions also killed two young female assistants, and your nanny, Sandra Cuthbert.'

He looked away for a few seconds, exchanging glances with Bowers.

Louise could feel herself shaking. It quickly became so severe it must have been noticed by Dawes, but she was determined not to break down and remained silent.

'In addition to eleven fatalities, thirty-two people have been injured. Many of these victims have lost limbs and a couple have lost their sight; several of them are critically injured, so it's highly likely that the number of fatalities will rise. The consequences for those that survived, not to mention their friends and families, will last for the rest of their lives.'

He leaned towards her and said through gritted teeth, 'That's quite apart from the victims of your previous attacks.'

He leaned away again. 'Still, I'm sure your paymasters in Harb Alsheueb will be over the moon.'

He didn't speak for a while, and they sat in silence. Louise remained with her head bowed.

'Of course, your bosses are probably relaxing in their homes or planning their next attack from a fucking cave somewhere in the mountains of Afghanistan or Pakistan. They're still free to carry on with their lives, but you're here Louise, having destroyed your family and with nothing to look forward to other than the rest of your life in prison.'

He stood up and paced around the cell.

'It's funny how the leaders of terrorist groups claim to believe so vehemently in their causes, but never take direct action themselves. Strange that, isn't it?'

Louise knew he was absolutely right, but still she said nothing.

Dawes leaned against wall.

'I will be making an application for an extension to your custody time tomorrow morning. Due to the personal trauma you're going through, in the doctor's opinion you are not fit for interview at the moment, so going ahead now wouldn't be fair on you... or the officers carrying out the interview.'

He looked to be controlling his anger.

'But be assured, Mrs Greenacre, you will be interviewed tomorrow morning, whether you like it or not. There's nowhere to hide anymore, it's time for you to pay for the choices you've made.'

He exchanged a glance with DS Bowers, and she returned his look with a nod. As he walked out after her, Dawes said, 'Goodbye, Mrs Greenacre.' He didn't bother turning back to look at her.

The young PC returned to the cell as Dawes and Bowers left and retook her seat near the door. She said nothing, probably acting under instructions not to communicate with the prisoner, but a brief flicker of sympathy showed on her face and, for Louise, any show of human kindness, however small, was welcome. She lay back on her bed and stared at the ceiling, dreading the day and night that stretched ahead of her, and the morning, when she would have to re-live and account for her actions.

67

Cell 38, Charing Cross Police Station, London
Saturday 21st December 2030, 8.20am

Following a night during which she'd hardly slept at all, Louise forced herself to eat one slice of toast and butter for breakfast. She didn't feel in the slightest bit hungry but knew that being detained in a cell was to be her life from this day forward, and that she needed to eat to survive.

Despite all that had happened, including the terrible loss of her family, she realised that she wanted to carry on living. Allah had bestowed her with the blessing of life and she would not reject that blessing, no matter how painful her existence would be from now on.

At 8.30 she was taken from her cell to a consultation room, where Howard Hunty was waiting for her. This time, he rose to his feet and extended his hand. The sensation of receiving human contact from another person after the terrible suffering she'd caused to others was almost overwhelming and Louise accepted it gratefully.

Howard gently prised his hand from hers and pointed to the chair at the table.

'Please, sit down. We need to go through what you intend to say in interview.'

Louise sat, placing her right hand on top of her left on the table. With an expressionless face she shook her head.

'There's nothing to discuss. I've been a fool and caused untold suffering to dozens of innocent people,' her eyes filled with tears, 'including my own family.'

'So, you want to confess everything. Is that what you're saying?'

'Yes, it's time for me to suffer the consequences of my actions. I want to tell the detectives everything. I want the whole appalling mess out in the open... you can tell them I'll help their investigation in any way I can.'

Howard was busily scribbling down notes.

'I think you're doing the right thing, Louise.'

'I know I'm doing the right thing. Harb Alsheueb can't hurt me now and I couldn't care less if they kill me in prison.'

Howard raised his eyebrows. With an almost imperceptible nod of his head he said, 'You've confessed to an officer and the bomb exploded at the time and place you indicated, so there's nothing to be gained by silence.'

He began doodling in his notebook, using his pen to draw a circle with a square inside it, then a triangle inside the square.

Watching him, Louise could see that he was troubled by something, 'What's on your mind?'

'It's only fair to explain something to you Louise.' He lifted his eyes to meet hers. 'Nothing you can say will lower your term of imprisonment. You will undoubtedly go to prison for the remainder of your life and there will be no possibility of parole. You do understand that?'

Louise noticed Howard was distinctly uncomfortable

passing on this information and felt genuinely sorry for him. Leaning across the table she placed a hand on his.

'I'd worked that out for myself. I'm not stupid, Howard. I've killed twenty people and injured over a hundred and I don't expect or deserve any sympathy or consideration from anyone. That's not the point here.'

Over the next two hours, Louise told her story in detail, starting with her sympathy for Mohammed at school, her experiences in Afghanistan, and her relationship with Haasim. She described the training camps where she was indoctrinated then the astonishing story of her return to the UK as a sleeper; her meetings with Sulayman; the abductions and murders of Ismael Ahmed and Sarah Cairn; planting bombs in the Department for International Trade and the Clothes Bazaar. At this point, she almost couldn't continue, but forced herself to tell him how she had cut the throat of her best friend Millie and finally, planted the bomb inside their bedroom at Number 10.

She explained how it wasn't until she overcame the brainwashing that she understood that what she was doing was wrong. Up until that point, she had been convinced it was right; she even admitted that she actually got satisfaction from her activities.

Howard was busy scribbling down notes as she spoke. He remained silent.

Louise began to cry as she repeated how they had forced her to comply with their wishes by threatening the lives of Oliver and Alice. Finally, she repeated how she bitterly regretted everything she'd done and accepted that she could never hope for any understanding or forgiveness from others.

At 10.40 Howard Hunty was satisfied that Louise was ready to tell all. He pressed the call button and a WPC opened the door.

'We're ready for interview,' he said.

Five minutes later the door was opened by a very tall man in his late 50's, with a dark tanned face and a physique which suggested he still attended the gym regularly.

'Good morning, Mrs Greenacre. My name is Barney Briscow, I'm a Detective Chief Inspector in SO15 Counter Terrorism Command and I'll be interviewing you along with DC Susan Fensome. Will you both please follow me?'

He led them along the corridor to a room with a sign saying 'Interview Room 3' above the door. Here, Howard and Louise were greeted by an attractive woman with dramatic crew-cut black hair, who directed them to the chairs on the far side of the table and introduced herself as DC Fensome. DCI Briscow closed the door which sealed with the soft sucking of a soundproofed room and settled onto the chair alongside Fensome.

Louise looked around the room; the sense of history being made suddenly hit her. She saw three cameras positioned in corners of the room for CCTV recording of the interview; a panel with a small screen was built into the top of the desk, where the interviewing officer could type in the custody number; small voice recording microphones were attached to both the wall and the side of the table and there was a small open-sided cabinet next to DC Fensome which contained various paper forms. The walls were bare and, despite the drama that was about to occur within those walls, the room was spartan and bland.

'Right,' said Briscow, as he tidied the bundle of papers in his hands, 'are we ready to start?'

Howard glanced at Louise, who was grim-faced. Looking haggard and as if about to burst into tears, she lowered her head in a silent bow to indicate she was ready. Howard squeezed her hand then turned to Briscow.

'My client wishes to assist in every way possible with the police investigation, including details of where she received training and the names of everyone involved. She deeply regrets her actions and although she understands she can never make amends, wishes to help the police and security services dismantle Harb Alsheueb, which she now regards as an evil organisation.'

Briscow raised his eyebrows and exchanged a glance with Fensome.

'Thank you for that. Your co-operation will be greatly appreciated.'

Fensome said, 'Ready when you are, Sir.'

'Okay, let's get started,' said Briscow.

Fensome pressed the red button to commence the interview, which made a long buzzing sound. When the buzzing stopped the four people in the room introduced themselves, then Briscow reminded Louise that she was still under caution and commenced questioning.

Louise's interview was so lengthy, extensive, and detailed, that the police were granted two further custody time extensions from a judge, to allow them to continue. Throughout the rest of Saturday, all of Sunday and up until late Monday afternoon, Louise told them everything. She gave as many details as she could about Haasim, Sulayman, Kareema, the Asian woman who'd delivered the devices, the black couple in Green Park, and the black taxi driver who'd dropped her off in Regent Street.

The interview was conducted in two-hour stints, with regular pauses for meals, drinks, and toilet breaks. There were times when Louise broke down in tears and was unable to continue and she had to undergo physical and mental health checks by doctors. There were also further private consultations with Hunty, and she was allowed time to pray. She thought how ironic it was that it took incarceration for her to be able to pray the required five times a day. The police even supplied her with a hijab when she requested one, meaning she finally felt like the Muslim woman she'd wanted to be for so many years.

She left nothing out, repeating everything she had told Howard, from her gradual attraction and conversion to Islam to the awful climax in Downing Street.

At 10.35 on the morning of Monday 23rd December, Louise was charged with numerous offences: twenty-one murders (one of those critically injured in the Downing Street explosion had subsequently passed away), being an active member of a proscribed organisation, attendance at a place for terrorist training, receiving instruction for terrorism, possession of articles for terrorist purposes and, conspiracy to murder using explosives. The Custody Officer finished reading out the charges and cautioned her:

'You do not have to say anything, but it may harm your defence if you fail to mention now, something which you later rely on in court. Anything you do say may be given in evidence.'

Tears rolled freely down Louise's cheeks as she gave her simple reply.

'I am so, so sorry.'

68

Number 1 Court, Old Bailey, London
Monday 7th July 2031, 10.20am

The Clerk of the Court rose to his feet and looked across to where barristers and solicitors for the prosecution and defence were gathered. He was directing his words towards the woman wearing a black Hijab sitting in the dock.

'Stand up, please.'

Louise felt as if she had somehow strayed into a TV crime drama, her mind finding it difficult to comprehend that this was real life, this was really happening. She was a mass-murder defendant appearing at Number 1 Court in the Old Bailey, the most famous courtroom in the world. The press and public galleries were overflowing with families of the victims and ordinary members of the public, including a distraught Debbie, Derek and Evie, who were accompanied by Millie's parents and two brothers. Her legs shook as she lifted herself to her feet and she could see that every pair of eyes in the courtroom were fixed on her and could read the hatred in every one of them.

The clerk held up a sheet of paper which he solemnly read from.

'Are you Louise Greenacre, formerly of Number 10 Downing Street, London, SW1?'

'Yes.'

'And is your date of birth, 17th January 2002?'

'Yes.'

The clerk then read out charge after charge to Louise, something which caused a ripple of excitement around the packed courtroom. The number of charges reached over forty; it took more than half-an-hour to read them all and ask Louise how she pleaded to each charge. She replied, 'Guilty,' to each one.

The Clerk of the Court sat down.

Judge George Barnes-Vokes said, 'Thank you, Mrs Greenacre, please sit down.' He turned to address Louise's defence barrister, Madeline Cornwell QC.

'Miss Cornwell, your client has pleaded guilty before this court to all charges. Have you anything to say in mitigation?'

Madeline Cornwell was a petite woman, with thick, wavy red hair. But when she rose to speak, she had huge presence, everyone in the courtroom became quiet, everyone listened.

'Thank you, My Lord. Yes, I do have something to say on my client's behalf.'

She looked over at the press gallery then turned her head dramatically to face the public gallery before returning her gaze to the judge.

'My client has pleaded with me not to speak on her behalf for too long because she doesn't believe she deserves to have anybody speaking up for her.'

Cornwell removed her spectacles and slowly turned to point a finger at Louise, who seemed as spellbound by her performance as the rest of the room.

'This woman has perpetrated the most hideous, brutal, and evil crimes, crimes against wholly innocent victims.' She turned back to face the judge. 'But she too, is a victim, My Lord.'

Her words brought loud gasps and shakes of the head from members of the victims' families in the public gallery.

'She was brainwashed when still a young woman, into becoming a member of a vile terrorist group, a group that placed her under a huge amount of duress, including threatening the lives of her children to ensure she carried out her final attack on Number 10 Downing Street. She doesn't want or expect sympathy, and she fully understands that she will, quite rightly, be severely punished.'

'String her up!' shouted a man from the public gallery, which heralded a chorus of shouting, fist shaking and jeering from families of her victims. It took the judge several calls of 'Silence in court!' and banging of his gavel before people retook their seats and he could regain order.

Once quiet was restored, the judge said, 'Any further disturbances, and I will have the public gallery cleared! Miss Cornwell, please continue.'

'Thank you, My Lord.' Madeline leaned back against the rail behind her seat and turned her head towards the public gallery. 'Louise Greenacre was a young, naive woman when she travelled to Afghanistan, a country where she volunteered as an aid worker, a place where she intended to help others. She had only good intentions when she arrived there and wanted to be part of continuing efforts to rebuild society in that country. The last thing on her mind was treachery and bloodshed.'

She looked behind her at the dock.

'Louise Greenacre was seduced by a man who she wrongly believed cared for her, but this man introduced her to so-called 'meetings,' which were actually terrorist training camps. It was at these camps, over a period of several months, where she was gradually indoctrinated in the ideals of Harb Alsheueb.' She slowly returned her gaze to the public gallery, 'This young woman was completely and utterly brainwashed, until she didn't know what she was doing.' Madeline Cornwell fell silent.

After several seconds, Judge George Barnes-Vokes said, 'Have you finished, Miss Cornwell?'

'Almost, My Lord. I won't delay the court much longer.'

The judge nodded. 'Please, continue.'

'Thank you, My Lord.'

She glanced at the notes resting on the lectern in front of her.

'As I said, this defendant was brainwashed. For many years she truly believed that what she was doing was for a greater good, she truly believed that it was both acceptable and necessary to use violence to achieve her group's evil aims, and she truly believed that attacking western government targets was a legitimate tactic for followers of Islam.

'More recently, it took the murder of her best friend, Melissa Calvert, to break through the brainwashing and finally bring her to her senses. She clashed with her bosses in Harb Alsheueb and initially refused to carry out the final attack, to plant a device in Number 10 Downing Street. However, the vicious threats of Harb Alsheueb towards her children persuaded her to comply with their wishes. She found herself in an impossible position.

'On the day of the attack she had arranged for her husband, children, and nanny to be clear of any danger, but things didn't go to plan.' She looked solemnly down at the floor. 'As everyone in this court knows, she lost her husband, daughter, and nanny, and her son was horribly crippled and blinded in one eye.'

Louise audibly burst into tears, causing dozens of eyes to look at her, albeit without any real sympathy.

Cornwell finished her mitigation with a plea for understanding of a woman who had been duped. She knew it would have been unwise, not to mention impossible, to defend the indefensible, but she intended to do her very best for Louise.

'My client fully realises the consequences of her actions. She feels shame and total remorse, quite apart from heartfelt condolences she passes to her victims and their families.' She finished by pointing at the dock. 'Louise Greenacre knows she can never repair the enormous damage she has done but intends to spend the remainder of her life making amends in any way she can.'

The barrister turned to look at Louise, offered her a nod, and sat down. The courtroom fell silent.

Judge Barnes-Vokes said, 'Thank you, Miss Cornwell.' then trained his gaze on Louise. 'Stand up, please.'

Louise looked a broken woman as she heaved herself to her feet. She wore very little make-up; her hair was tied back in an untidy ponytail and she was painfully thin. She dreaded hearing the Judge's words, although she already knew what fate awaited her.

'It now falls upon me to pass sentence. In the normal run of circumstances during a serious case such as this, I would send for both psychiatric and welfare reports before sentencing. However, due to your confessions, and the unusual circumstances surrounding this case, these were completed while you were on remand.' He sat forward in his chair, 'This leaves me in the unusual position of being able to pass sentence upon you today.'

Tension inside the courtroom was palpable. Victims and their families were leaning forward and holding hands, tears welling in many eyes. Journalists in the press gallery were furiously taking notes and the silence was almost deafening.

'Louise Greenacre, you have committed the most grievous of offences. You have killed twenty-three innocent people; you have caused life-changing injuries to dozens of others; you followed the teachings and ideals of a proscribed organisation and you planted am explosive device intended to murder and maim those lawfully elected to represent this nation.'

He turned the page of his notes in a dramatic fashion, briefly allowing his gaze to fall upon the jury as he did so. It was obvious that the judge enjoyed playing to the gallery.

'You caused the death of your husband, who was the Prime Minister of our country, and the death of your daughter, Alice. Added to that, you have horribly maimed your son, Oliver. All of this was done in the name of a terrorist group who have now finished with you. They have happily cast you aside, along with those that have gone before you, while their leaders remain untroubled and untouched.'

His eyes locked onto hers then he perused his notes before continuing.

'You have wickedly betrayed this country, the country which raised you, fed you, and protected you for your entire life.' He paused for a moment.

'I have taken into account the fact that you were undoubtedly indoctrinated and brainwashed in Afghanistan, but in my opinion your own personal leanings and preferences allowed that to happen in the first place. I therefore have no hesitation in sentencing you to a whole life tariff.'

He shifted in his chair, before confirming what that phrase actually meant: 'You will never be released, you will live the remainder of your life in prison and you will, in all likelihood, die in prison. Do you understand?'

The public gallery burst into spontaneous applause, supplemented by cheers and whistles. Judge Barnes-Vokes banged his gavel and called for silence, which he eventually received.

Louise pinned her shoulders back and said firmly, 'Yes, I understand.' Then she looked across to Millie's parents.

'I am so sorry.'

The judge addressed the two female gaolers standing on either side of Louise.

'Take her down.'

69

Bronzefield Women's Prison, Ashford, Kent
Monday 26th June 2034, 9.00am

The small classroom in the prison education block slowly filled with female inmates. Fourteen were booked in for the session and as the last one took her seat, the facilitator, a female professor of criminology named Alison Troon from nearby Canterbury University, rose to her feet and addressed them.

'Today's session will be conducted by someone many of you already know, someone who fully understands what each of you has been through.'

She looked to one side of the room, nodded her head towards the doorway, and through it walked an attractive, slightly overweight woman.

'Ladies, this is Louise Greenacre, once married to the Prime Minister, but more importantly for this session, once an active member of Harb Alsheueb.'

She turned to Louise. 'Mrs Greenacre, the floor is yours.'

Walking calmly into the room, Louise smiled at the women seated in front of her. Every one of them wore a hijab, just as she did, and three of them were of white European appearance, just like her. They were mainly in their twenties, although two looked like they were probably in their mid-thirties and one was almost certainly older. This would be the first time in her life that Louise would be running a group session like this, but she fully intended it would not be her last.

She smiled, placed her right hand on the centre of her chest then bowed her head slightly.

'Assalamu Alaikum.'

The inmates responded with various greetings, the majority saying, 'Wa Alaikum Assalam.'

'Good morning. Well, you all know my name and what crimes I've been imprisoned for, and I know that you are all here for committing terrorism offences, the same as me.'

She swept her gaze over the faces of the women; some stared straight back at her, others avoided her gaze, a couple looked completely uninterested. Louise stood still.

'We are all followers of Allah and his teachings. The only difference between us is that we have assimilated those teachings in different ways, and now have widely divergent versions of the same belief.'

She adjusted her hijab and continued, 'I'd like to go around the room and learn how each of you was recruited. I'd like to hear what offences you're convicted of and most importantly, I'd like to learn what your feelings are now towards the group that trained you.'

It took half an hour for all fourteen inmates to tell their stories. Their offences ranged from simply attending a place where terrorist training happened, through to murder and conspiracy to commit murder using explosives. Two of the women at the session had been convicted of being involved in the 5/5 bombings along with Louise: the Liverpool bomber Rashida Nahir, and the Manchester bomber Taalia Noor. When the last of the group finished telling their story, Louise had one simple question for them all. 'How many of you were instructed that violence against western democracies was acceptable and necessary?'

Every one of the women raised their hands.

She then asked, 'And how many of you still believe that instruction to be true, and would happily carry out your crimes again?'

Eleven hands were raised, so Louise directed her next question to the three women who hadn't responded.

'Why do you no longer believe that violence is acceptable and necessary?'

A woman who had been convicted of being a member of a proscribed organisation and who appeared to be the youngest of the group spoke first.

'I was young, impressionable, and angry with the world. I lived in a horrible area of Blackburn and often received abuse from young white men for covering my head.' She shrugged sadly. 'I was probably an easy target for those who wanted to lure me in and radicalise me, but I've since learned for myself that what I did was wrong.'

'Thank you Qabila. For the record, I agree with you.' She turned to the other two.

'Anyone else?'

One of the women looked very withdrawn and said quietly, 'It's my business. I no longer think like I once did. My mind is now clear, but I don't want to talk about it.'

Louise smiled. 'That's fine, I completely understand.' She turned to the remaining woman; it was Rashida Nahir, the Liverpool bomber.

'What about you Rashida?'

Rashida looked uncomfortable, crossing and uncrossing her legs.

'I believe that Islam is a kind and loving religion. I

no longer believe the bullshit of those who brainwashed me into committing my crimes.'

'How did you come to that decision?'

'By listening to my heart.'

'Can you please explain to the group?'

Rashida looked around awkwardly; several of the group were now scowling at her.

'After completing my training in Somalia, I was prepared to do whatever they asked, but even before my first operation I began to feel uneasy.'

Another inmate shouted, 'For fuck's sake, we all felt like that at times, we've all felt uncomfortable. Get over yourself!'

Louise raised a hand to calm things.

'Please allow Rashida to finish, then we can discuss it further. You will all get your chance to speak.'

Rashida felt uneasy, laying bare her struggle.

'The feelings continued and got stronger. I should never have carried out the attack in Liverpool. I soon realised that the people who trained me are not true Muslims, they're madmen. Islam is a peaceful religion, something I realised far too late and I'm now serving thirty-five years because of them.'

Louise smiled. 'Thank you, very enlightening. Now, can anyone who raised their hands to say they'd do the same again, understand what has happened to myself and Rashida?' Her question was met with silence.

She decided to push them further.

'We all received similar training, although in my view it wasn't training at all, it was indoctrination, brainwashing, call it what you will, but you've all said you would commit your offences again, whereas I believe that violence is no way to achieve Allah's blessings. Why are we so far apart?'

Taalia Noor reacted angrily.

'You call it indoctrination and brainwashing; I call it education. Once we'd been shown the true way, we were prepared to attack the regimes that were keeping us down.'

Several inmates nodded and made comments supporting Taalia.

One said, 'Regimes that were treating us like second-class citizens and attempting to side-line Islam. They deserved to be taught a lesson.'

Louise stepped forward, 'Can I please say something, Taalia?'

Taalia folded her arms angrily and defensively across her chest but nodded and remained silent. A few others were shifting around in their seats.

'Thank you,' said Louise. 'I was exactly the same as you once, absolutely convinced that we should strike hard against what I perceived to be my enemy - the British Government. Harb Alsheueb was my guiding light. I truly believed that by serving them, I was carrying out Allah's wishes.'

One woman shouted, 'And you *were* carrying out his wishes, so what's your problem?'

Louise paused to carefully consider her next words before replying.

'Part of the problem was that Harb Alsheueb were my only guiding light, they meant everything to me, and that meant there were no checks and balances in my life. Just think about it for a moment. Normally you listen to the views of your family, your partner, work colleagues, friends, acquaintances, and many others and you weigh them, one against the other. But once we'd attended the training camps, we *were* brainwashed to believe that after God, our faith in the group we were attached to was paramount, that we should love them over even our partners or family members and we were required to believe unquestioningly in everything they told us.'

She paced across the room.

'You see what I'm saying? There were no checks and balances for our thoughts. Once they'd finished brainwashing us, we'd all become zombies, blindly following a wicked doctrine without realising it.'

All eyes were fixed on Louise. The group had fallen silent, some of them clearly paying more attention than they had been previously.

Realising that her words appeared to be capturing her audience's attention, she fetched a chair from a side wall, and seated herself at the front and centre of the room.

'I was no different to everyone here. At first, I had serious reservations about getting involved with radical Islam, but the more training sessions I attended, the more convinced I became that using violence was not only the right thing to do, but the only thing to do. I fell under their spell, just like all of you, and we're now paying the penalty, while the leaders of whatever organisation you worked for remain free to indoctrinate the next generation.'

The woman who looked older than the rest shouted, 'What a load of crap! I cut the throat of my local MP three years ago because he spoke out against Muslim women keeping their children from a school where lessons about gays were being taught and I know that Allah bestowed his blessings on me because of it. You're speaking shit, and I'm not listening to any more of it!'

Louise turned towards the woman.

'That would have been my belief once, but after I committed a truly horrendous act, the trauma was so severe that it cleared my mind, allowing me to think for myself. I was no longer suffering from the effects of brainwashing and blindly believing what others told me.

Think about what you've just said. Is that what you truly believe in your heart, or what you've simply been trained to think?'

The woman turned her head away, ignoring Louise and the point she was making.

Louise breathed in deeply and blew out hard.

'A group of radical men with hatred in their hearts persuaded people like us to attend their 'meetings'.' She made quotation marks with her fingers.

'But these meetings were merely a front for brainwashing and indoctrination training camps. Once we were fully under their spell, they directed us to carry out their wishes, which they claimed were the wishes of Allah, but were actually nothing of the kind.' She adjusted her hijab. 'They were the wishes of the hierarchies that indoctrinated you and me.'

A woman who had previously remained detached and silent suddenly called out, 'What makes you so certain you're right and we're wrong? How do you know they're not the wishes of Allah? Why wouldn't he want to punish unbelievers?'

'Because Allah is a loving God! The Quran tells us to stand up for the rights of all people, of all religions, not just Muslims. Don't be duped by the hatred fed to you by monsters with no love in their hearts. Read his teachings in the Quran, the word of God, and follow his teachings of love and kindness towards your fellow beings.' She paused for a moment.

'I have killed and injured more victims than all of you put together, yet I have learned that the true way to redemption is through love. The love we feel for Allah, and for each other, whatever religion we follow.'

With outstretched arms she entreated her audience.

'Believe me, it's much easier to face years of incarceration with love in your heart, rather than living with hatred burning inside you. Islam is a loving religion, not one of hatred and violence.'

Three of the eleven women who'd said they would commit their offences again were nodding quietly, but the other eight were becoming increasingly angry, hurling abuse at Louise and shouting, 'Allahu Akbar!' The atmosphere had become confrontational and hostile.

Alison Troon could see that things could turn nasty and swiftly rose to her feet.

'Okay, okay, everyone please calm down.' She had to repeat this request several times before all the inmates had retaken their seats and order was restored. She turned to Louise.

'Thank you, Louise. I think your words have made quite an impression but that will be enough for today. Thank you.'

Louise smiled. 'Thank you all for listening.'

As she walked off, she turned; she had one more question for the inmates.

'If the leaders of these terrorist groups are so convinced that the training camps they run and the actions they order are the wishes of Allah, why do none of them take part in those actions themselves? They should surely be happy to carry out operations to receive his blessings, shouldn't they?' She left through a door into an adjoining room, where a guard escorted her back to her cell.

70

Fifteen minutes later Louise's cell door was opened and Alison Troon walked inside, turned to the guard and said, 'It's fine, I'll knock when I need you.'

The overweight guard shrugged, walked out and closed the door. Alison looked around Louise's cell. It was surprisingly comfortable, if Spartan; there was only one bed, which meant a single cell, a luxury in today's crowded prison system. She had a small wooden desk and chair, a bookshelf with about twenty books, and a wall cupboard. On the desk was a radio and a small device for listening to music.

The two women stood looking at one another for a couple of seconds then Alison said, 'How did you find your first session? By the way, thanks again for agreeing to take part in the programme.'

Louise smiled. 'It was nerve-racking, but I really enjoyed it.'

'I thought you might.'

'After five years of praying for forgiveness and missing my family every day it was wonderful to finally start making *some* kind of reparation, you know, doing something positive.'

'I'm so pleased. With your history and experiences,

you have the potential to reach these people. You certainly seemed to make an impression at the end there on some of those women.'

'Yes, I noticed that. It will take time, but I'm certain I could turn a few of them.'

'I'm glad you enjoyed it. I assume you're happy to continue?'

'Yes, two sessions a week as agreed. I'm really looking forward to it.'

'That's wonderful.'

Alison put a folder on the bed headed 'New De-Radicalisation Programme' and removed some papers.

'Can we go over some ideas for next time?'

The following thirty minutes passed pleasantly for Louise. It was a relief to have another human being genuinely interested in her views and opinions. The fact that she now had a positive direction to follow was satisfying and she was sad when the time came for Alison to leave.

'Thank you, Alison, I honestly think I could make a difference.'

'It's me who should be thanking you,' replied Alison. 'You've got that special something that the programme has needed for the past thirty years. See you at the next session.'

As Alison walked out, the guard closed the door with a loud slam, leaving Louise staring at the stark grey metal. She would hear that door slamming for another forty-five years.

EPILOGUE

As those years passed, Louise continued to present sessions, explaining how her thoughts and beliefs had changed over time. She gradually became more confident and more successful in persuading female terrorist prisoners that they would feel much better showing love to others, rather than being consumed with hatred.

Fellow speakers in the new de-radicalisation programme were urged to sit in on her sessions and were themselves trained in her methods.

Whether her talks were so powerful because those listening knew her history, or whether it was the strength of her personality remains a matter for debate, but over time, her ideas were introduced into programmes in all prisons housing terrorists, regardless of their gender.

Her methods of persuading people away from terrorism became more successful than anything that had gone before. Many hardened terrorist prisoners became convinced over time that Louise's way, the way of peace, made more sense than the way of violence. Similar methods had been tried before, but none so successfully. It meant that fewer and fewer of those who had been imprisoned for terrorist offences and subsequently released, went on to re-offend.

By no means were the majority of prisoners

persuaded, but a decent percentage were. So many in fact, that her methods were shared over the years with other countries, producing similar levels of success. Her methods began to be used in de-radicalisation programmes outside of prisons, which further helped to limit terrorist attacks.

Very gradually, almost imperceptibly, as the years then the decades passed, terrorism of all types, but particularly terrorism against western democracies, began to decline, potentially saving thousands of lives. Experts agreed that Louise Greenacre's methods of de-radicalisation had played a major role in that decline.

Louise's parents, Debbie and Derek, had however been unable to forgive her and rarely visited, occasionally at Christmas and once or twice on her birthday. When they did visit, they struggled to make polite conversation with their daughter and seemed glad to leave.

Oliver had been brought up by Debbie and Derek and hadn't seen his mother since the explosion. He walked so well with his prosthetic leg, that many people had no idea he'd had a leg amputated under the knee, and his ultra-modern glass eye was incredibly lifelike. He had gained a place at Durham University to study Law and, despite his disabilities, he was a handsome man and popular with the girls on campus.

Louise had been in prison for more than fifteen years when one day she received a letter from her son, who was now approaching his twentieth birthday. Gradually over time, Oliver had learned more and more about his mother's efforts to reduce terrorism, and had become interested in the movement she had founded. Further letters and emails followed and eventually the day Louise had longed for arrived... the day he visited her. After initial awkwardness, Louise found herself bursting into tears and hugging Oliver as if she would never let him go.

From that time on, Oliver visited his mother whenever he was home from university. He wanted to know more about her work combating terrorism and in doing so, he came to understand, though never fully forgave, the actions which had caused the deaths of his father and sister. Slowly but surely, they became closer, and despite all that had gone before, mother and son became the best of friends.

Louise's work continues.

ACKNOWLEDGEMENTS

I'm grateful to SRL Publishing for taking a chance on Sleeping. *It's a story I've had in my head for over 20 years and I'm beyond delighted to finally see it in print. The subject matter meant i needed to carry out extensive research and required assistance from many people.*

I'm indebted to Danielle Young, who was raised in England and converted to Islam as a young woman. She is now married to her Muslim husband and has 5 children. Danielle helped me fully understand the hurdles that Louise in the story would have to overcome and pointed me in the right direction regarding methods of greeting and correct etiquette.

I had a huge amount of help from Imam Yasser at Tunbridge Wells Mosque. His efforts during long phone calls and visits by myself to the mosque meant i had to correct large sections of the book, where he put me right on certain matters.

Many people kindly read largely unedited versions of the book and their feedback was always appreciated. I particularly want to thank John Hiles, Joy Young, Jennifer Clark, Danielle Young, and Hazel Butterfield.

My beautiful wife, Virginia, had to put up with me endlessly writing, something she suffers without complaint. Thank you darling, you're the best.

Finally, i want to thank you, the reader. Writing can be a lonely and difficult process, but someone bothering to spend their hard-earned cash to read my work makes my heart soar.

ABOUT THE AUTHOR

Evan was born in Pembury, Kent in 1956 and attended grammar school in Tunbridge wells.

He left the metropolitan police after 30 years' service in 2011, serving as one of the country's first Football Intelligence Officers until 1996, then transferring to West End central, where for 15 years he worked in Soho.

For several years, Evan helped run the Soho unit, specialising in combating drug dealing in the west end. During his career he frequently ran test purchase and buy-bust operations against drug dealers, resulting in the seizure of large amounts of drugs, and the successful prosecution of over 200 dealers, many of whom received lengthy prison sentences.

After retiring from the metropolitan police in July 2011, Evan opened 'sweet expectations' in Rochester, Kent, the UK's first vegetarian sweet shop.

In 2016 he sold the shop business and retired, before taking up writing in January 2019.